D0759045

Where Petals Fall

Also by Shirley Wells

Into the Shadows
A Darker Side

WHERE PETALS FALL

Shirley Wells

Constable • London

Constable & Robinson Ltd
3 The Lanchesters
162 Fulham Palace Road
London W6 9ER
www.constablerobinson.com

First published in the UK by Constable,
an imprint of Constable & Robinson, 2009

First US edition published by SohoConstable,
an imprint of Soho Press, 2009

Soho Press, Inc.
853 Broadway
New York, NY 10003
www.sohopress.com

Copyright © Shirley Wells 2009

The right of Shirley Wells to be identified as the
author of this work has been asserted by her in accordance
with the Copyright, Designs & Patents Act 1988.

All rights reserved. This book is sold subject to the condition
that it shall not, by way of trade or otherwise, be lent, re-sold,
hired out or otherwise circulated in any form of binding or cover
other than that in which it is published and without a similar condition
including this condition being imposed on the subsequent purchaser.

A copy of the British Library Cataloguing in Publication
Data is available from the British Library

UK ISBN: 978-1-84529-744-2

US ISBN: 978-1-56947-572-0
US Library of Congress number: 2008051378

Printed and bound in the EU

1 3 5 7 9 10 8 6 4 2

Mixed Sources
Product group from well-managed
forests and other controlled sources
www.fsc.org Cert no. SA-COC-1565
© 1996 Forest Stewardship Council

To Kate, Joe and Elle

Chapter One

Jake was thoroughly pissed off.

It was getting on for six o'clock and his ear was still smarting from the weight of his dad's hand connecting with it that morning. Dave Walsh, a big, fat, loud-mouthed drunk, wasn't even his dad. A stepdad, Jake decided resentfully, had no right to lift a finger to him.

'Sod him!' Jake muttered to himself for the tenth time that day.

His younger brother, Darren, pedalling speedily ahead of him, shouted over his shoulder, 'Get a move on, Jake. I'm starving!'

Darren was always starving. Jake was hungry, too, but he was in no mood to sit down to fish and chips opposite Fat Dave. It was always fish and chips on Saturdays. Wednesdays, too. On Mondays they had McDonald's and on Tuesdays they had KFC. Sometimes, on Sundays, his mam got off her arse to shove a chicken in the oven and chips in the pan.

Stuff 'em. Jake was happier up here, cycling round the disused quarry. With its sheer rock faces and meandering paths, it was a wild, unpredictable place that suited his mood. He pedalled faster to catch up with his brother, and then Darren stopped so abruptly that he cannoned into his back wheel.

'What you doing?' Jake snapped.

'What's that?' Darren asked, pointing to something white a few yards off the dusty track.

1

'How the hell should I know? An old coat, a bundle of rags – I don't know!'

'Let's have a look,' Darren suggested, already pushing off.

'What for?'

'You never know, do ya?'

Darren was gone and Jake, sighing, followed. Whenever they cycled up here, Darren always found some piece of crap. Last week, it had been a cigarette lighter that he'd wasted hours trying to fix.

Jake's ear was hurting because he'd gone off with his mates last night when he should have been baby-sitting. Jake, fourteen, didn't see that his twelve-year-old brother needed baby-sitting, but that's what he was doing now. Baby-sitting.

For all that, he loved his brother. Fat Dave he hated, and his mother, the woman who willingly spent twenty-five quid on muck for her face and then let Darren go around with holes in his trainers, Jake could take or leave. Darren he loved. It was Darren who kept him at home. If it weren't for him, Jake would have gone. He reckoned he could easily pass for sixteen and get himself a labouring job on a building site in Manchester. He'd prefer London, as he wanted to get as far away as possible from Lancashire, but Manchester would do for starters.

Darren screamed, threw his bike to the ground and ran off. Jake guessed a dead animal was involved. Darren was soppy when it came to animals.

Ignoring Darren for the moment, although he was aware of his brother being sick, he got off his bike and wheeled it over to the rags. Except it wasn't rags.

'Oh, no! No!' he cried, dropping his bike and jumping back.

He could have thrown up too. Instead, he picked up both bikes and wheeled them to where Darren was bent double.

'We've got to get out of here,' he said urgently, the gruesome sight still dancing before his eyes and causing the burger he'd had earlier to gag in his throat.

Darren didn't need telling twice and they were soon

racing down the hill. Even at top speed, the track seemed endless. The rocky path threatened to throw them out of their saddles. A black dog appeared from nowhere and began barking as it chased them. It was gaining on them. If they weren't careful, the stupid animal would have them and their bikes in a tangled heap.

'Sod off!' Jake jammed on his brakes and skidded to a halt that sent up a shower of dust and grit. He picked up a large stone and hurled it at the rowdy dog. His shot was on target. The animal yelped and ran off with its tail curled between its back legs. Jake remounted and careered down the hill.

When they stopped at the gate to leave the quarry area, Darren was sick again.

'We'll have to tell the coppers,' he said, wiping his mouth on his sleeve.

'We don't tell them nothing.'

'We'll have to,' Darren insisted, still breathless. 'We don't have to tell 'em who we are. We'll use the phone box.'

'Forget it,' Jake snapped, closing the gate after them. He knew the police; they'd raided the house looking for stuff they said Fat Dave had nicked. They hadn't found it, but Dave wouldn't thank anyone who brought coppers sniffing round again, and Jake was sick of having his ear belted.

'I'm going to phone 'em,' Darren said firmly. 'We've got to. It – it had its neck slashed.'

'I'm not blind!'

They rode past two phone boxes, but Darren stopped at one in Bacup and went inside.

Jake yanked open the door in time to hear Darren say, 'Is that 999? Only we've found a dead body – wrapped up in a white sheet, it is. And it's almost had its head chopped off.' There was a pause. 'It don't matter who I am. It's up at the quarry. Lee Quarry.'

Jake snatched the phone from his brother's hand and slammed it down.

'Come on,' he hissed. 'Forget we ever saw it!'

Fat chance. Jake knew they would remember the hideous sight for the rest of their days.

3

Chapter Two

Sunday dawned bright and sunny, promising another hot day ahead, and Jill took her breakfast of coffee and fruit juice into the garden. If she'd had a decent night's sleep, she might have fancied something to eat. But she hadn't. And she didn't.

Her garden was a mass of colour, thanks mainly to the sprawling pink rhododendrons, but the grass needed cutting. She might do that later. Battling with the lawnmower might lessen her anger and loosen her tense muscles.

Meanwhile, she sat on the old wooden bench, with her Sunday paper on the table in front of her. She'd finished her juice and had reached the travel supplement when she heard a slightly alarming sound. A car was travelling at speed along the lane. She could hear gravel flying up and hitting the metal.

It came to a stop outside her cottage.

Why, she thought irritably, did she suddenly feel nervous? It was only Max coming to apologize for standing her up last night. Not that he was big on apologies.

A door slammed – viciously.

So he was angry. So what? She was absolutely furious. Last night, after she'd got herself dressed up for a party, she'd finally discovered, from his mother-in-law of all people, that 'something had cropped up'. She'd had no choice but to go to the party alone. When she'd returned home, soon after midnight, she'd tried his mobile and his landline again. He still wasn't answering so she'd let off steam by having a good rant at his answer machine.

What had she said? Oh, yes. 'Just phoning to thank you for a delightful evening. Having had three tyres slashed, I raced back from Liverpool for that bloody party and spent the whole evening inventing excuses for your absence. Don't let it worry you, though. After all, it takes thirty seconds to let someone know that something better's turned up. God forbid the mighty detective should waste thirty seconds of his life to phone us lesser mortals.'

Her heart skipped a beat as she remembered how she'd gone on. 'That's typical of you,' she'd yelled at his machine. 'You drag me into your bed and that's it. Forget I exist. You've always been the same.' With a heartfelt 'Bastard!', she'd cut the connection and taken herself off to bed.

Now, as Max came into view, she was finding it difficult to turn the pages of her newspaper. He marched, hands safely in the pockets of his trousers, across her lawn.

'Hissy fit over, is it?' he demanded, towering above her and blotting out the sun. 'Good God, how old are you?'

'Old enough to have learned some manners,' she snapped back.

'You might have guessed –'

'I shouldn't *have* to guess. You found time to call Kate, you could have called me.'

'I could. You're right and I'm sorry. Evil Max.' He slapped his wrist. 'OK? Forget about it now, can we?'

'That's your answer to everything, isn't it? Forget about it. Well, no –'

'Whoa! Hang on a minute. This blazing row you're determined to have, will it be the ten-minute row or the full half-hour row? If it's the latter, I'll have to take a rain check. I've got things to do.'

'Ah. So the mighty detective's *still* too busy.'

'If you're interested –'

'Not particularly.'

He glared at her for a few moments. 'I'll make my own coffee, shall I?'

He began striding towards the cottage, calling over his shoulder, 'Your manners are slipping, kiddo.'

He was almost at her back door when he suddenly stopped, turned around, and began walking back to her.

Once again, he stood in front of her. 'Just for the record,' he said quietly, 'if my memory serves me correctly, and I'm damn sure it does, *you* dragged *me* into *your* bed.'

Without waiting for her response, not that she was capable of giving him one, he turned on his heel and headed for the cottage.

Jill was thankful for that. She put her hands to cheeks that were burning with embarrassment. Technically, he was right. They'd made love, for the first time since she'd walked out on him, in *her* bed, in *her* cottage. She pushed the memory aside and stared determinedly at her newspaper.

How his mother-in-law put up with him, Jill would never know, but she did. Ever since his wife, Linda, had died, Kate had been there for him and the boys . . .

He was soon crossing her lawn with two mugs of coffee in his hand.

'I've made you a fresh one,' he said. 'It might improve your temper.'

'Don't count on it.'

He sat beside her on the bench and, as ever, she was aware of his slightest movement. Only the sounds of distant traffic, a few nearby birds, and a couple of bees buzzing around one of her foxgloves were a distraction. Then someone along the lane coaxed a lawnmower into life.

'I take it a shag's out of the question then?' Max said at last.

'It's not funny, Max. You should have let me know.'

'You're right, and I'm sorry.'

'And stop humouring me!'

Damn it. She could feel the beginnings of a smile trying to break through.

She lived next door to what was possibly the most gorgeous-looking bloke she had ever laid eyes on. So why didn't Finlay Roberts get her pulse beating that bit quicker? Max was as tall as Finlay, but he was nowhere near as handsome. His nose was too crooked, and there was a tiny scar beneath his right eye. Sometimes, his face had a gentleness to it, but more often than not, it was merely arrogant. His hair was greying, too. It was his eyes perhaps that did it for Jill. They were a deep blue and that piercing gaze of his made people believe he knew their every thought . . .

'So how was the party?' he asked.

'Boring.'

'Told you it would be. And how was your trip to Liverpool? Your mum and dad OK? Prue?'

'They're all fine, thanks.'

'As I'd have more success getting blood from a stone, is it worth asking how you got your tyres slashed? I take it that happened at your folks' place?'

'It did. The little sod,' she fumed. 'I happened to glance out of the window, and there he was. No older than twelve. I gave chase, but he leapt over a wall. You know what River View is like.'

'A rabbit warren,' he said, nodding.

How her parents could live amongst such undesirables, Jill had no idea, but there was no shifting them. 'We've always lived here,' Mum would say in astonishment if ever Jill broached the subject. 'Whatever would we want to move for? It's home.'

Jill was thankful it was no longer *her* home.

Thinking about it, apart from the man sitting next to her, and a hefty bill for three new tyres, all was right in her world. She lived in the Lancashire village of Kelton Bridge, and that had to be one of the most beautiful places on earth, she enjoyed her writing, she was returning to her old job with the police force in a fortnight, her parents and her sister were well and happy –

'Last night,' Max broke into her thoughts, 'I did try to call you, but it all got a bit busy. I was up at Lee Quarry. A body was found up there.'

'Oh?'

She knew the disused quarry well. South of Bacup, the rugged landscape was an ideal place for walking and she

7

often went up there to blow away the cobwebs. The only people one met were dog walkers or cyclists. It was very remote, and she could only remember it being in the news once. That was when a sheep had plunged sixty feet down a sheer drop. Fire crews from Bacup, Rawtenstall, Nelson and Preston had been called out and they'd used an inflatable raft to get the sheep off a ledge and across the water at the bottom of the quarry. After all their efforts, the sheep had broken two legs and needed to be put down anyway.

It was a beautiful, peaceful spot. Not the sort of place to find bodies.

Max took a sip of his coffee. 'A body wrapped in a white sheet.'

'A sheet?' She frowned. 'What sort of sheet?'

'How many sorts are there?' he asked, exasperation creeping into his voice. 'Some might call it a winding sheet. Others a shroud. I call it a soddin' sheet. It was wrapped tightly around the body. Oh, and a length of bright red ribbon had been tied around her waist.'

Jill's heart took a brief pause. Déjà vu wasn't a pleasant experience when it involved bodies wrapped in shrouds with lengths of red ribbon tied around their waists.

'You'll be telling me next that the victim was a woman who'd had her throat cut and whose wedding ring had been fastened to that piece of red ribbon.'

Max took another swig of coffee.

'I will,' he agreed, and Jill stared at him in horror.

'You're not serious, Max.'

'Oh, I'm deadly serious.'

Five years ago, Jill had worked alongside Max as they had hunted a killer who had quickly been dubbed The Undertaker. His four victims had been married, childless career women in their late thirties. They had all had their throats cut and then their bodies had been wrapped in shrouds.

Thanks mainly to Jill's profile, however, they'd found the man responsible. Hadn't they?

8

'Has the body been identified?' she asked.

'Not officially, but the doctor recognized her. It's a Carol Blakely. She was thirty-eight, and ran a successful florist's in Harrington. Correction,' he said drily, 'she ran a successful floral design business, although what the difference is, God alone knows.'

'If you wanted to buy a bunch of flowers, you'd visit a florist. If you wanted a stately home, a cathedral or offices decked out, you'd visit a floral design company.'

Max shrugged. To him, a flower was a flower.

'Was she married?' Jill asked, and he nodded.

'No kids? Career woman?'

He nodded again. 'Her husband's been away on a golfing holiday. His plane lands in an hour or so and he's on his way here to identify her.'

The pages of Jill's newspaper fluttered in a sudden gust of breeze and she leaned over to pick up a nearby stone to weight it down.

She watched in astonishment as Max reached in his pocket, brought out a packet of cigarettes and proceeded to light one.

'I thought you'd given up.'

'I have,' he said, tossing the spent match into her hedge. 'I just felt like buying a packet.'

'Oh. Right.' Ask a silly question. Yet she could understand that last night's discovery would unnerve anyone.

He exhaled, and the smoke went straight into Jill's face. 'Chloe Jennings, Zoe Smith, Anna Freeman and Julie Brookes – it's the same MO, Jill.'

Jill could still remember the victims' names, too. Chloe had been an attractive barrister, dark-haired Zoe had held down a high-powered job in banking, Anna had run a successful recruitment agency and Julie, with her short auburn hair, had owned a thriving health and fitness centre.

'There must be differences,' she insisted.

'Yeah?' Max didn't look convinced.

'Had coins been put on her eyes?'

'Yes.'

9

Despite the heat of the day, Jill felt chilled. If she'd made a mistake and The Undertaker was still alive –

'What else have you got?' she asked.

'Not a lot yet. Someone had thrown up about three yards away from the body,' he told her, 'and we don't think it was the victim. She was dead before she got there.'

'The killer? Surely not.'

'Perhaps he'd eaten a dodgy prawn,' Max replied. 'Although I expect it's more likely to be the person who found her. Not a pretty sight.'

'Who was that?'

'We don't know. Someone made an anonymous call. It sounded like a young kid.' He tossed his cigarette butt into the hedge. A thin spiral of smoke appeared, and Jill wondered if she would have to phone the fire service. Then he emptied his mug and got to his feet. 'I'll have to go.' He reached for her hand and absently stroked her fingers. 'Sorry about last night.'

'It's OK,' she replied, grudgingly.

'I'll call in later this evening, shall I?' he asked.

'If you like.'

He dropped a brief, rare kiss on her forehead – an apology perhaps – and strode off.

He was the other side of her lawn when she called out, 'Eddie Marshall is dead, Max!'

'Is he?' And he was out of sight.

A cloud passed in front of the sun, causing Jill to shiver again. Edward Marshall *was* dead. The fact that his body had never been found had no bearing on that at all. He had to be dead.

Chapter Three

Mowing the lawn was hard work and, when it was done, Jill vowed to keep on top of it. If she kept the grass short, it was much easier. For one thing, she didn't have the job of raking up the clippings and that was more exhausting than cutting the stuff in the first place.

'Coo-ee!'

Jill emerged from her shed to see the owner of that voice, Ella Gardner, walking around the back of her cottage.

'You should keep your doors locked,' Ella greeted her, 'until they've found the lowlife responsible for this spate of burglaries.'

'I should, Ella.' Jill was still breathing hard.

'Mind,' Ella sighed, 'there are few that do in Kelton. We've never had a need to until now.'

Ella took the fact that four houses in Kelton Bridge had been burgled as a personal affront. The unknown burglar or burglars were breaking in during broad daylight – no small achievement given the prying nature of local residents – when the occupants were on holiday. How they came by their information was a mystery. Only one of the victims had booked their holiday online, and two didn't even have an internet connection, so they weren't after a computer hacker.

'You look worn out, girl,' Ella noted belatedly, and Jill laughed.

'I am. I've mown the lawn,' she explained, 'and now I'm going to sit under the lilac tree with a well-deserved glass of something cold. Will you join me, Ella, and make it worthwhile opening a bottle?'

11

'I'm delivering the church magazines,' Ella replied, flicking through the handful she was carrying. 'I'm sure it grieves them to let a cantankerous old atheist like me do it, but as Joan's done her ankle in, they don't have much choice.'

Jill laughed. 'Was that a yes or a no?'

'Go on then. Thanks, Jill. Having the magazines delivered by a drunken cantankerous old atheist could well be a first for the village.'

Ella was a great one for walking, and was often seen striding round the village at a cracking pace. Yet, dressed in cream-coloured linen trousers, and loose sleeveless pink top, she was managing to look cool. Jill, in desperate need of a shower, and wearing an old pair of cut-off jeans, felt like a tramp by comparison.

Jill had been friends with Ella almost from the moment she'd moved to Kelton Bridge. Ella, retired and afforded the title of local historian, had a wicked sense of humour that Jill loved. Going on appearances – the short grey hair, the sensible shoes and clothes – one could be forgiven for assuming Ella to be a biddable old soul but, despite the fact that she'd recently lost her much-loved husband to cancer, nothing, outwardly at least, lessened her sense of fun or her pithy observations of life.

'So what's new?' Ella asked when they were sitting in the shade with a glass of chilled white wine each.

'Not a lot.' Ella was discretion itself, but Jill didn't see much point in telling her about the gruesome discovery at the quarry. There was nothing to discuss until they knew more.

'What about this new neighbour of yours? Olive, old gossip that she is, reckons he's into black magic.'

'The tarot and astronomy,' Jill corrected her. 'He runs an internet business. And charges people a fortune for readings, no doubt.'

'Mumbo-jumbo,' Ella scoffed. 'Still, if people are daft enough to pay him . . .'

'Quite.'

'He's a looker, mind,' Ella added. 'I've only seen him a couple of times, but if I were forty years younger –'

'You'd have to join the queue,' Jill finished for her.

Finlay Roberts must have kissed the Blarney Stone. He wasn't Irish, he'd been born in Scunthorpe, but he was full of charm and flattery. His family were circus people, and he'd travelled the length and breadth of the country as a child. He was still travelling, and was only renting the cottage next door for three months because he remembered the area from his childhood and had always vowed to return. His current job, and Jill gathered there had been many, was running his online tarot business. It meant he could work from anywhere that had internet access.

Around the six feet mark, he had a rangy, lean body, brown curly hair and striking green eyes. Whenever he spoke of his business, those eyes shone with devilment and Jill found it impossible to tell if he believed in the tarot or if he was merely running a scam. It was difficult to see through the charm to the man beneath.

'He's attracting a lot of interest,' she told Ella.

'Strangers always do.'

'Don't I know it.' Jill had lived in the village for almost two years now, and some still thought of her as 'that fancy psychiatrist in Mrs Blackman's old cottage'. For fancy psychiatrist read forensic psychologist. But what was the point? It was all the same to most people.

'Talk of the devil,' she murmured as Finlay peered over the hedge.

From the look of him – old, paint-spattered jeans and ragged T-shirt – one would be forgiven for thinking he'd been doing a spot of decorating or sitting in front of an easel for hours. Jill guessed he'd been doing neither. This, she'd come to realize, was his usual mode of dress. It did nothing to lessen his appeal, though.

'Hi, Finlay,' she called out. 'Will you join us in a glass of wine?'

'Is the Pope a Catholic?' He vanished from view briefly before vaulting the low part of the dividing fence. 'I was going to follow your example and mow the grass,' he said, pulling up a chair and positioning it so the sun wasn't in his eyes, 'but this is a much better idea, darling girl.' He smiled at Ella. 'Mrs Gardner, isn't it?'

'It is, but I suppose that, devil worshipper or not, you may call me Ella.'

'Did you hear that?' he asked, grinning, as Jill rose to fetch another glass. 'I'll have you know, Ella, that I've just read the church magazine from cover to cover.'

'That took a while then,' Ella said drily. 'Still, knowing where the nearest chimney sweep hangs out will come in useful . . .'

Jill left them to it and, when she returned with another glass, they were discussing the burglaries.

'I'll be chief suspect,' Finlay said with a grin. 'I'm a new-comer, I'm a traveller and, to top it all, I'm a devil worshipper. I'll have to shift all those TVs and DVD players before the police come hammering on my door.'

'Why not ask the cards who did it?' Ella suggested with a smile.

'Ah, you mock.'

'Oh, yes, I mock.' Ella laughed. 'Not you, but people daft enough to believe in it and pay you.'

Finlay shrugged. 'You'd be surprised.'

'I'd be surprised if there was anything in it other than profit for some people,' Ella agreed.

'I must do a reading later,' he said. 'Jill would make a good subject.'

'Why would I?' she asked, amused.

'Because, in many ways, you're a typical Leo. And because I already feel as if I know a lot about you.'

'Like what?' Ella asked doubtfully.

Finlay Roberts, roguish face smiling, took a sip of wine, then leaned back in his chair and closed his eyes.

'She's generous and warm-hearted –'

'Pah! I could have told you that,' Ella scoffed.

'She's very organized and tends to organize others if she thinks they need it. In most situations, she feels she knows

14

best, but – and this is where it gets interesting – her self-confidence has been battered over the years. She was once in a strong relationship,' he went on, 'and by strong, I mean the depth of commitment was strong rather than the passion. She was living with someone or perhaps even married to someone she didn't love.'

His tone was level, monotonous even, but it was enough to bring Jill out in goosebumps. She hadn't told him that she had been married. Or widowed. And she could use the fingers of one hand to count up the people who knew that she and Chris had discussed starting divorce proceedings before he was killed.

'I think her work scares her,' he continued. 'She's frightened of making a mistake.'

'What? Oh, that's complete crap. I love my writing and I'm returning to my job on the force in a couple of weeks.'

'And the thought frightens you,' he insisted.

'Rubbish!'

Nevertheless, if she'd made a mistake and The Undertaker was still alive –

Why was she even bothering to think about it? It was complete rubbish. Anyone could invent that mumbo-jumbo!

'Here, let me refresh our glasses.'

The three passed a pleasant couple of hours but, left alone, Jill wondered again about the things Finlay had said.

She knew, deep in her heart, that she was anxious about her return to the force. Despite having excellent qualifications and plenty of experience, she had made a mistake. That mistake, in part, was responsible for Rodney Hill, wrongly accused, hanging himself.

Had she made another mistake? Again, it was thanks in part to her profile that the police had gone to arrest Edward Marshall. He'd resisted arrest and made a run for it in a neighbour's car. Two people had been badly injured during a high-speed chase across Yorkshire before Marshall lost control of the car and plunged over a cliff. Experts, taking into account the tides and weather conditions, had tried to predict where and when his body would be washed ashore but it had never been found.

He had to be dead, though. Witnesses had seen him inside the car as it dived into the sea below and traces of blood had been found inside his car. He couldn't have survived that plunge into the sea. No, Edward Marshall was dead.

But had he been the right man?

'My, someone's looking fed up with life!'

Jill looked up with a start and laughed. 'Just thoughtful – and slightly drunk,' she said, standing to give Louise a hug. 'How are you?'

Louise Craven was another friend that Jill had made on moving to Kelton Bridge. She lived along Main Street, in a beautiful stone-built terraced cottage. Not long after moving to the village, Jill had been out walking and had paused to admire her garden. Louise had invited her to have a proper look, and they'd been friends ever since.

'Oh, you know,' Louise replied, sitting on the bench next to Jill.

'Trouble?' Jill asked. 'No, wait. Let me get another glass and then you can tell me all about it.'

As she strode across the garden to the kitchen, she suspected she could guess the reason behind Louise's shadowed eyes and troubled frown.

Twenty-one years ago, an ill-fated love affair had done two things to Louise. Firstly, it had put her off men and secondly, it had left her pregnant. She'd been just nineteen years old. The man concerned had vanished, never to be heard from again, and Louise's life had revolved around her daughter. She'd worked at a variety of jobs, sometimes juggling three at once, to give little Nikki everything she wanted.

Nikki, spoilt from birth, had grown into a wilful child and then an extremely difficult teenager. At sixteen, she was pregnant. She and the father of her unborn child left for London where she planned to have an abortion. From that moment on, Louise heard nothing. She hadn't known if her daughter was alive or dead.

Until four months ago.

Jill could remember the evening clearly. It had been a dark March night and she and Louise had been to the pub for a quick drink before settling down in Louise's lounge to watch a DVD. What that DVD was, Jill couldn't remember. What she could remember was the shock of seeing a young woman, a stranger to her, walking into the lounge and dropping a grimy backpack on the carpet.

'Nikki!' Louise shrieked.

So this was Nikki. Short, probably not even five feet tall, with long, blonde hair that was badly in need of a good wash or at least a brush, she was wearing filthy black jeans, a tatty black jumper and a long, black coat. Everything about her looked undernourished and unwashed.

'Oh, Nikki, love. You've come home!' Louise had to keep holding Nikki, to keep touching her as if she might vanish again.

'I'm not home,' Nikki corrected her, pulling free from her grasp. 'I just need a place to doss for a few days, OK? I need a bath, too.'

'Yes. Yes, love, of course. You do that. Do you want me to –'

'I don't want you to do anything!'

Nikki took off her coat and slung it across a chair. The shabby jumper followed. Underneath that, she was wearing a red T-shirt that didn't quite manage to conceal the needle marks on her arm.

'Won't you say hello to Jill? Jill's –'

Nikki rolled her eyes in exasperation. 'Hello, Jill,' she chanted obediently before she flounced out of the room . . .

Now, four months later, Nikki was still using Louise's home as a 'place to doss'. At first, Louise had been thrilled to have her home. It hadn't bothered her that Nikki was only using her as a soft option, or that her home was being treated with no respect whatsoever.

'Right,' Jill said, plonking a glass and another bottle on the table, 'this will make things look better. I take it Nikki's giving you grief?' she added, as she filled a glass and handed it to her friend.

The last few months had put years on poor Louise. Given a carefree life, she would be a very attractive woman, but, with a constant frown marring her features, and with no energy to reach for a lipstick, she looked drab.

'I don't know what to do for the best, Jill.'

Jill could think of a few things, all of which included standing up to Nikki for once, but she held her tongue. 'How's Charlie?' she asked instead.

Charlie had entered Louise's life shortly after Nikki came home and, unless Jill was very much mistaken, the unthinkable had happened and Louise had fallen in love.

'I haven't seen him for a week. We've spoken on the phone, of course, but it's not the same. He says I shouldn't give in to her.'

'He's right,' Jill told her.

'Perhaps he is, but she keeps threatening all sorts of things. She says she'd rather be dead than have him sniffing around as she puts it.'

'She's a drama queen,' Jill said gently. 'I blame all these soaps on TV. You have to make her see that you have a life and friends of your own.'

'She was such a lovely girl once,' Louse said wistfully.

'Deep down, she still is.' Twice, Jill had seen Nikki in a good mood, and had been astonished to discover that beneath the hostile exterior was a bright, quick-witted and fun-loving girl. Not a girl now. Nikki was twenty-one. 'Sadly, she's mixing with –'

'Scum!' Louise finished for her. 'Last night, I got home at about nine thirty to find six strangers in my house. They were lounging in the chairs and across the sofa, drinking from cans and smoking God knows what. I wouldn't mind her bringing her friends round, but these people were aggressive somehow. I felt quite threatened. Frightened to tell the truth. I went to bed shortly after ten o'clock.'

'God, Louise, you should have kicked them out. Make

sure you do next time. And if they refuse to go, call the police.'

'I spend half my time wishing Nikki had stayed in London,' she said flatly. 'Then I feel guilty for wishing such a thing. When I think of her sleeping rough . . .' She shuddered.

'It's her choice, though. It's time she learned a bit of respect for you and your property. She's not a kid any more.'

'I know that.' Louise sighed. 'You wouldn't believe the mess I had to clear up this morning – overflowing ashtrays, cigarette ends tossed anywhere, dozens of beer cans and I even found a used condom on the bathroom floor.'

'You're joking! Oh, for God's sake, Lou. If it were me, I'd have to evict her.'

'No, you wouldn't, Jill. You'd love her because she's your daughter and you'd hope and pray that the next day will be better.'

It never was, though.

'Those people last night were all high on drugs or alcohol,' Louise went on.

'You need Charlie,' Jill suggested. 'You can't deal with this on your own, Lou. If you both talked to her and stood firm –'

'It's no use. When we've tried to talk to her in the past, she's just reminded us both that it's none of Charlie's business. She hates him.'

'Her feelings for Charlie aren't important. He must tell her that, by upsetting you, she's making it his business.'

Jill knew nothing was that simple. She couldn't wave a magic wand and give her friend the happiness she deserved.

'Charlie offered to take us on holiday,' Louise confided. 'He said Paris or even New York. He thought that if we invited her somewhere that would excite her, she couldn't turn us down. He believes that, if we could get her away from these so-called friends of hers, spend some quality time with her . . .' She sighed. 'I don't know what to do.'

'That's an excellent idea. Think about it, Lou. It would be great. You need to show her that her life would be so much better with Charlie in it, not worse.'

'She refuses to come with us. She'd rather go shoplifting or taking drugs with those friends of hers.' Louise took a huge gulp of wine. 'Every time I walk through the door, I'm relieved to see that she hasn't walked out again. Then, within minutes, I'm wishing she had.'

'I can understand that,' Jill sympathized.

'And I've promised to take her to the Trafford Centre on Saturday. That annoys me as well. She won't even make an effort to find a job – says she won't be around long enough – but she expects me to buy her clothes. And, of course, I will, because I'm too embarrassed to see her wandering about like a tramp.'

She expelled her breath on a long sigh.

'Enough. I didn't come here to bore you with my problems,' she said, smiling ruefully. 'As far as I know, my home is still standing and, for the moment, I'm grateful for that small mercy. Tell me about you. How was the party last night?'

'Pah!'

'What?'

'Max got caught up with work stuff so he didn't make it.'

'Oh, no. God, I bet Max was really sorry to have missed it,' Louise said, deadpan, and Jill laughed softly.

'It was legit, but he didn't even call to let me know. I was furious about that. It was one of those things where everyone is part of a couple so I felt the odd one out.'

'Have you kissed and made up?'

'We've made up,' Jill said drily. 'It's just that Max has a habit of forgetting people exist. It's not good enough.'

'It's a gender thing,' Louise said on a sigh. 'It's a well-known fact that men can only concentrate on one thing at a time.'

'Tell you what,' Jill said, her mind still on Louise's problems, 'I'll give Nikki a call if you like and see if she wants to come shopping with me. I'm free on Saturday so I can easily take her to the Trafford Centre. It'll give you and Charlie some space for the day.'

'Oh, Jill, I couldn't.'

'Of course you could. Don't worry, she'll be fine with me.'

And why, Jill wondered, did that sound ominously like famous last words?

Chapter Four

Max stopped his car on Jill's drive at six thirty that evening, and was about to ring her doorbell when she walked around the side of her cottage to meet him.

'I've got a bottle of wine on the go. Do you want some?'

Her voice was still a bit thin and clipped, but he guessed she'd soon get over it.

'I'd love some, but I haven't eaten since yesterday.' He looked towards her cottage, then realized the futility of that. Jill's cupboards were always empty. He hadn't nicknamed her Fast Food's Dream for nothing. 'Do you fancy nipping out for something?'

'Er, yes. Let me change into something more suitable.'

Tight denim shorts and revealing T-shirt seemed more than 'suitable' to Max, but he wasn't going to argue and risk accusations of chauvinism.

She nodded at the cigarette in his hand. 'Are you still on the same pack, or did you just feel like buying another?'

'It's the same one.' And he only had three left.

She gathered up a half-full bottle of wine and glasses from the garden, went off to change into jeans and a clean shirt, grabbed a sweater and locked up her cottage.

'Been having a party?' he asked.

'Louise has been round.'

'Oh? She OK?'

She shrugged by way of reply, and he guessed Louise was still having problems with that daughter of hers. Nikki was fast becoming a lost cause.

'Before that, Ella was here,' she went on, 'and then Finlay Roberts, my new neighbour, joined us.'

'Oh? What's he like?'

'Tall, brown curly hair, green eyes, drop dead gorgeous.'

Max wished he hadn't asked. He unlocked his car and she got in the passenger seat.

'He seems nice enough,' she added as she fastened her seatbelt. 'A bit of a rogue perhaps, but OK.'

'Married?' Max fired the engine and reversed out of her driveway.

'No. Why do you ask?'

Why indeed. 'Just making conversation.'

A satisfied smile appeared on her face. She knew damn well he'd been checking out the opposition.

He touched a button and his window slid down six inches to let out the cigarette smoke.

'For someone who hasn't smoked for – what? five years? – it's good to see you haven't lost the knack,' she said drily.

'I'm only smoking this one packet.' Except he only had two left now.

'Right. So where are we going?'

'The nearest place that serves food,' he told her.

The nearest place was the Deerplay on the Burnley road and, as soon as they walked inside, Max found his appetite. He hadn't really fancied anything, in fact he'd felt too tired to eat, but he'd known he should have something before he keeled over. Now, he found he was ravenous.

'Well?' Jill asked while they waited for their food to be brought to their corner table.

'You tell me. There are three possibilities.' He held out three fingers. 'One, Eddie Marshall wasn't our man. Two, he's alive and well and living in Lancashire. Or three, we have ourselves a copycat.'

'They're all crap.'

That's what he thought. 'When you come up with a fourth,' he said, 'I'll be delighted to hear it.'

All conversation ceased when their roast lamb was put in front of them. It was delicious, and the red wine even better. Max only wished he wasn't driving.

'It's definitely Carol – what was her name?' Jill asked, dabbing at her mouth with a paper napkin.

'Carol Blakely. And yes, her husband's identified her.'

'What's he like?'

'It's difficult to tell.' Max thought back to his brief meeting with Vince Blakely. 'He's either someone who keeps his feelings to himself, or he's a cold-hearted individual. He hadn't seen her for three weeks. He was away on business and then he took off on the spur of the moment to enjoy a golfing holiday with a couple of friends.'

'So it wasn't a close marriage?'

'They weren't inseparable, no.' Max emptied his glass. 'Spouses are always top of the list of suspects but – no, I can't buy it. We have the same MO here. Either Marshall was innocent or he's alive and well.'

'One of the victims' relatives could have talked.'

'True, but even they weren't told about the rings being tied around the waists. Those were simply handed back to the spouses.'

'He can't still be alive, can he, Max?'

'I don't know.'

Max had never been happy about Marshall's end. It should have been a simple arrest. Instead, it had been one of the biggest cock-ups ever. He'd been in North Yorkshire before traffic cops spotted him. After a high-speed chase, they closed in on him near Whitby, almost a hundred miles away, and then watched helplessly as he drove over a cliff.

'But if he's still alive,' he murmured, 'why would he wait so long before killing again? And if he was innocent, if we got the wrong man, why did he run for it?'

'We got the right man,' she said, but she didn't sound as certain as she had before. 'Even if we didn't, why would the real killer wait so long before striking again?'

Max had no idea.

'Will you come in tomorrow?' he asked.

She must have known he would ask, but she hesitated.

'Half a dozen of us are supposed to be having a day at the races,' she explained. 'I've even got a VIP ticket. I suppose I can pass that on to any one of a number of people, though. The others won't miss me. Yes, I'll come in. I might have made a mistake where Rodney Hill was concerned. . . .'

Her voice tailed off. No matter what anyone said, she still blamed herself for Hill's hanging himself. Max had told her over and over that they'd acted on hard evidence, but she believed, correctly he supposed, that they wouldn't have found that evidence if it hadn't been for her profile. He wished she'd get over it.

'I was spot-on with Eddie Marshall,' she went on at last. 'He was our man, Max, I'm sure of it. Sod it, I'm not having some sick bastard trying to prove me wrong. Either Marshall is still alive or we've got a copycat.'

Could Marshall have survived that dive into the sea? On the other hand, if he was alive and well, why wait until now? And how the hell could a copycat know the MO of the previous murders?

'Thanks,' he said.

'What does Meredith have to say about it?' she asked, and he could see amusement in her expression. They both knew that Max's boss would be on the verge of a coronary if he thought they'd got it wrong with Marshall.

'It's difficult to tell. I had to disturb him at a dinner with every local dignitary you can name last night and I updated him this morning just as he and the Chief Constable were teeing off.'

Jill grinned at that. 'You're popular then.'

'No change there.'

Max wasn't popular with his superiors because of his refusal to do the job by the rules, but they had to accept that he got results. Usually.

'I need to make a move,' he said.

As tempting as it was to linger, Max needed to see if his sons still recognized him. Fortunately, they accepted his erratic working hours. They were good kids, the best, and he was lucky to have them. All the same, he needed to spend a little time with them.

'Do you want a lift in tomorrow?' he asked as they walked across the Deerplay's car park.

'No, thanks. I've got a couple of things to do on the way in. I'll be there early, though. I want to know what's going on as much as you do.'

Max knew that. He only wished this hadn't come up now, just when Jill was due to return to work. If by any chance they *had* made a mistake with Marshall, it would rob her of the little self-confidence she'd managed to claw back.

Max had intended to go straight home. Instead, after dropping Jill at her cottage, he was drawn to the disused quarry. He parked his car and walked up the hill. A large area was still a crime scene and he avoided that. If they'd found anything of interest, he would have been told, and he wanted to be alone with his thoughts.

Away from the quarry itself, all that moved in the fading twilight were a few sheep.

He was breathing hard by the time he reached the top. That was due to either lack of sleep or being out of condition – or the fact that his lungs were unaccustomed to cigarettes.

He took the last one from its packet and lit it. It was five years since he'd quit so he could take them or leave them. Inhaling deeply he decided that, right now, he'd rather take them.

Despite feeling more at home in a town, he had to admit that the view over the valley was stunning. Below was a row of terraced houses and a few isolated farms, and, further down still, nestled Bacup and Stacksteads. He could see the church, the fire station, Britannia Mill's old chimney, the new housing estate on the hill and the one between Rochdale Road and New Line. The number of trees in the area surprised him, as did the size of the cemetery.

His gaze fixed on Kelton Manor standing slap-bang in the centre of Kelton Bridge. Even from this distance, he could make out the huge sign that told passers-by that it was offered for sale by auction. Yesterday morning, when life had seemed to be ticking along quietly, he'd made the most of Jill's trip to Liverpool by having a look round it. Jill loved the place, and he could see why. Huge, old and full of character, it managed to maintain a homely atmosphere.

Jill still had a few reservations about him, he knew that, but, apart from a few wobbles, they were getting there. Hopefully, the day she moved back in with him wasn't too far off.

The manor was in a poor state of repair so was expected to fetch a relatively low price at auction. He had no mortgage on his own house so, as long as he quit smoking, drinking and eating, he could just about afford it.

He'd have to think about that tomorrow. Right now, he had a murder investigation on his hands.

How would someone get a body to this spot? It was a hell of a climb and there was no vehicular access to most of the area. And why? What was so significant about the quarry? Probably nothing, he thought with a sigh.

It would be interesting to know how Carol Blakely's husband gained financially from his wife's death. He'd also like to know how quickly another woman was moved into the marital bed. Very quickly, he suspected.

He made a mental note to see if there had been anything about her in the local rag recently. That, they had decided, was how Marshall had chosen his victims.

Marshall, despite a history of mental illness, had held down a job at the castings factory in Harrington until, one day, he'd beaten his wife to within an inch of her life. He'd been physically abusing her for years, insisting that, until she had his children, she wasn't a complete woman. It was when he discovered she was taking the contraceptive pill that he lost it. She ended up in hospital with a broken jaw, shattered cheekbone, cracked ribs and a broken arm. He ended up in court. After spending six months banged up, he came out and went on a killing spree.

Could they have got it wrong? Could Edward Marshall have been innocent?

No. He was getting as paranoid as Jill.

He sat on a huge stone and, while he gazed at the view, he concentrated on Carol Blakely's last movements.

It was all a bit sketchy so far but, according to witnesses, she'd worked until seven on Friday evening in her florist's shop in Harrington and then driven home alone. A neighbour saw her drive into the garage. Her car keys had been left on the table in the kitchen and an empty cup suggested that she'd had a coffee before going upstairs to change. A neighbour who lived opposite had waved to her as she'd left the house just before 8 p.m., but she hadn't spotted him. According to him, she'd been wearing grey leggings and a dark blue T-shirt. He had assumed that she was going out jogging, something she did regularly.

From there, she had vanished into thin air. It seemed that her neighbour was the last person to see her alive. Other than her killer, of course.

Max heard what he thought was a scream and he jumped to his feet. He ran downhill towards the sound and, as he rounded the corner, he saw a woman looking into a deep hollow. She was yelling at the top of her lungs.

She saw Max and screamed at him. 'He's killing it! Killing it!'

Heart in mouth, Max raced to the edge of the hollow. When he could see what was happening, he realized that a dog, one that belonged to the woman if the leash in her hand was anything to go by, was standing over a lifeless lamb. A black mongrel with a lot of labrador in him, he wasn't killing the lamb. He was merely nuzzling it with his nose.

'He wouldn't come when I called him,' the woman wailed hysterically. 'He just kept on chasing it. Now it's dead. What will I do?'

'Wait here!'

Max half ran and half skidded down the slope towards the animals. The dog came bounding up to him, tail wagging. The lamb lay motionless.

'Right, Fido, let's get you out of the way.'

He grabbed the dog's collar and began dragging him up the bank towards his owner. Halfway up, he turned around and was just in time to see the lamb spring to its feet and race off at lightning speed.

'It's alive! Look!' the woman cried.

'Yes,' Max agreed, breathless again. 'It must have been exhausted.' It wasn't the only one.

It was calling for its mother and the ewe was calling for her lamb – and both were heading in opposite directions. Max wished he'd gone straight home.

Ten minutes later, after Max had done a sheepdog impression and sent the lamb in the right direction, the family was reunited. And Max was knackered.

'Thank you,' the woman said tearfully. 'I don't know what I would have done if you hadn't happened along.'

She looked as if she would have settled for a nervous breakdown if he hadn't happened along. She was late forties or early fifties, Max guessed, and her hair kept blowing into her face so that she was continually shaking her head to keep it back. Her hands were shaking, too.

'If I were you,' Max said, 'I'd keep him on a lead up here. There are a lot of sheep around and, if a farmer catches him chasing them, your dog could be shot.'

'Oh, don't! He does chase them,' she admitted. 'In fact, he chases anything. Yesterday, it was two young hooligans racing down here on cycles. One of them stopped and threw a big stone at Benji. It frightened him, and he came racing back to me. Horrid boy, wasn't he, Benji?' she cooed, stroking the dog's ears. 'And they were both going too fast,' she went on.

'Where did this happen?' Max asked. 'Up here?'

She nodded.

'When you say young lads,' he asked, 'what sort of age are we talking?'

'At a guess, I'd say they were around thirteen or fourteen. Why do you ask?'

'Just curious.' Carol Blakely hadn't been murdered by two young teenagers.

'Actually, I think I might have recognized them,' she said thoughtfully. 'They could well have been the Barlow boys. Live on the estate,' she explained tartly, 'on benefits.' Her eyes lit suddenly. 'The police are up at the quarry, aren't they? I couldn't do my usual walk because it's all sealed off. Do you think they did something wrong? They were racing away as if the devil himself was after them.'

Or hurrying to the nearest phone box.

'Could you tell me everything you remember about the boys?' Max showed her his ID. 'Did you see anyone else? Did you spot anything out of the ordinary? Do you think they could have seen something that might have frightened them?'

'Now then,' she said, her face animated and all trials with her dog forgotten. 'Let me think. Oh, my name's Annie, by the way. Annie Burton, number four, The Mews, Kelton Bridge.'

Max smiled, and nodded encouragingly. Why the hell hadn't he gone straight home? Perhaps, after all, he would buy another packet of cigarettes. Just the one.

Chapter Five

Jill sat at the back of the incident room. There used to be comfortable chairs and tables, but they had disappeared and everyone present had to perch on blue, creaking plastic chairs. Perhaps it aided concentration, or would have if the room weren't so stuffy. Max had opened a window, but closed it again ten minutes later, presumably because he didn't feel up to competing with traffic noise.

There were about thirty officers in the room, and Jill recognized very few of them. Staff came and went more quickly these days.

The first job for Max had been to update most of them on The Undertaker. Not Jill. She remembered every detail of that particular case.

On the board were large photographs of the dead girls – Chloe Jennings, Zoe Smith, Anna Freeman, Julie Brookes and, the new addition, Carol Blakely.

'Right,' Max was saying, 'we have the same MO here. Carol Blakely was killed from behind. Her trachea was cut so she couldn't have cried out and her carotid arteries were severed so she would have died quickly. We don't know where she was killed, but we know her body must have been taken to the quarry shortly afterwards. Her body was then wrapped in a . . .'

Max hesitated, Jill noticed. Carol's body had been wrapped in a white sheet. Fact. But did they refer to it as a shroud, a winding sheet, or her burial clothes?

'In a large white sheet,' Max continued. 'Her wedding ring had been removed and threaded on a piece of red ribbon that was tied around her waist. So we work on three possibilities. First, that Eddie Marshall is still alive. We reckoned that Marshall chose his victims after there had been pieces about them in the local rag. A couple of weeks ago, there was an article about Carol Blakely doing the flowers for some celebrity wedding or other.'

'Whose wedding was that?' a female officer piped up.

'Someone I'd never heard of,' Max said with his usual disdain for celebrities. 'So,' he went on, 'if we assume he's still alive, we delve into his past. I want every family member and friend of his questioned. Not that he was well endowed with either. He might contact his ex-wife, though. Check it out. We also need to check out people he worked with, cellmates and the like. Think of any aliases he might use.' He looked around him. 'Jack, Derek and Sarah, I'll leave that to you.'

During the discussion that followed, Jill gazed at the victims' photos. There was something different about Carol Blakely's, but she couldn't say what it was exactly. It might just be that it was a more recent picture.

'Second possibility,' Max said grimly. 'Eddie Marshall wasn't our man.'

Jill scoffed inwardly at that. He was their man, she'd stake her life on it.

As they discussed that possibility, she thought of Edward Marshall and the way he'd enjoyed killing those women. Each murder had been carried out with a grand theatrical flourish, right down to the coins on their eyes and –

Oh, for God's sake! That was it.

'Thirdly,' Max began.

'We've got a copycat!' Jill declared.

'Yes, quite,' he agreed, surprised by the interruption.

'No, I mean we really have.' She got to her feet and walked to the front of the room to stand by the photographs. 'I assumed she had pennies put on her eyes,' she scolded Max. That was her fault, she supposed. She'd merely asked him if coins had been put on the victim's eyes. 'Now look. Spot the difference between the first four and the last photograph.'

A sea of blank faces stared back at her.

'Edward Marshall was possibly suffering from post-traumatic stress disorder,' she said, trying to enlighten them. 'When he discovered his wife was deceiving him by taking the contraceptive pill, he beat her up and landed himself behind bars. From then on, he had a vocation. His victims were chosen carefully and the murders planned to the last detail. He thought he was doing the world a favour.'

Someone sniggered at that.

'It's what he believed,' she said. 'There are many people who think that the country's in a mess and that society has lost its sense of right and wrong. Eddie assumed those people would be grateful to him. He hated the idea of women's lib. Women, he thought, should know their place.'

'Good man,' a young officer said, and a few titters were heard from the males in the room.

'So Eddie was ridding the world of career women,' Jill continued when everyone had quietened down. 'As far as he was concerned, he was doing society a favour. There was no remorse. The bodies were laid out like that, not as a sign of respect, but because that's how things should be done. Eddie,' she added, 'was born a century too late.'

'And your point is?' Max asked impatiently.

'My point is that Eddie Marshall put old pennies on the victims' eyes. Carol Blakely had two-pence pieces put on hers. Old pennies were around in the days when morals were high. Women raised their children and knew their place. Two-pence pieces are a product of today's society where women are supposedly equal. They wouldn't have been good enough for Marshall.'

She could tell she was making no sense. Their faces had glazed with a resigned look of more mumbo-jumbo . . .

'One penny or ten, it's the same MO,' someone insisted.

'No. Marshall enjoyed arranging their bodies, enjoyed making them look perfect for our cameras,' she pressed on. 'Carol Blakely is different. She had to be killed for some reason, but she's been laid out with dignity. This killer didn't share Marshall's sense of enjoyment, his idea of theatre.'

The expressions staring back at her had changed from blank to sceptical.

'Yes,' she murmured, gazing at the photo of Carol Blakely, 'there's definitely respect here. Marshall enjoyed his killings. Our man is a more reluctant killer.'

'Maybe he was disturbed,' someone suggested, 'and didn't have time to play to the cameras.'

'Those pennies,' Jill insisted, 'would have been obtained in readiness.'

'I don't believe a copycat could get the MO right,' Max said. 'So many details weren't released –'

'It's a copycat,' Jill said quietly, but firmly, as she returned to her plastic chair.

'And if it is?' Max asked briskly, looking around expectantly.

'Check out people Marshall might have talked to,' Val suggested. 'Perhaps he bragged about the killings.'

'I don't think so,' Jill said. 'He was far too controlled for that. It's possible, but doubtful.'

'Check out people involved in the first murders,' Fletch put in. 'Victims' family and friends – someone might have talked . . .'

'Right,' Max agreed. 'Oh, and there might be witnesses.' He grimaced at the gasp of interest. 'Someone saw two young lads up at the quarry on the day in question. There's a woman, name of Annie Burton, who walks her dog up by the quarry every day and she saw two lads. She said they were going downhill hell for leather. It's possible they might have seen something. Or it's possible they were responsible for making that phone call. You can go and talk to her, Fletch,' Max suggested, lips twitching slightly. 'And you may be some time,' he warned drily.

The discussions went on until, finally, everyone dispersed, each with their own job to do.

Jill hung back and looked more closely at the photographs.

'I'm going to have another chat with the grieving widower,' Max said when they were alone. 'Coming along?'

'May as well,' Jill agreed.

'There's a lot of money involved here,' he went on. 'I thought it was just a florist's shop in Harrington, but no. She owned, and we're talking outright ownership, three shops. And that was just a small part of her business. We could be talking several million pounds.'

Jill whistled at the sum involved. 'It's definitely worth having a long chat with her husband then. He gets it, does he?'

'We don't know yet, but I assume so.'

'Hm. And it's a copycat, Max. I'm sure of it.'

'You can't be sure,' he insisted. 'Old pennies versus twopence pieces? You can't take that seriously. As Kelly said, he might have been disturbed. If Marshall is alive, he's done a good job of hiding for the last five years. Maybe he no longer has access to old coins.'

He had a point, Jill knew that, but they were after a copycat. She was certain of it.

Vince Blakely had his own architect's practice and, when Max stopped the car on the driveway, Jill guessed he must have designed his own home. It was ultramodern with a grass-topped roof and an upper floor that looked to be wall-to-wall glass.

'Very flash,' she murmured.

'One of these eco-friendly houses,' Max said. 'All solar panels and recycled paper insulation. Apparently, Blakely's big on sustainable building.'

The garden was beautiful, far more attractive than the house in Jill's opinion. The house was too showy whereas the garden looked much loved, a place of tranquillity and the perfect escape from everyday pressures. They walked to the front door and jangled the bell-pull. Presumably, doorbells used too much power for Mr Blakely's liking.

He answered the door, thanked them both for calling, ushered them into a lounge that had one complete wall in glass, and offered them seats on a long, curving leather sofa which, judging by the faint aroma, was almost new.

When they'd offered condolences, Max asked him about his late wife.

'Had she had problems? Did she mention anything unusual that might have happened? Did she seem worried about anything?'

Vince Blakely shook his head. 'No. She was happy. Not a care in the world.'

Lucky woman, Jill thought, and the reminder that she was dead came as a jolt.

A stunning display of scented flowers graced a long glass coffee table and it was difficult to remember that the person responsible – and it had to be Carol's touch – had been brutally murdered.

As Vince Blakely spoke of his wife's happiness, he didn't look like the grieving husband. Was he shocked? He seemed tired, but that was all. He was a good-looking man, and he was aware of it. His clothes, white shirt and black jeans, were not so much worn as displayed. Tall and clean-shaven, with his fair hair cut short, he looked younger than the forty Jill knew him to be.

He was finding it difficult to sit still. Leather creaked as he stood up and, having walked a small circle, sat down again.

'How was Mrs Blakely's business doing?' Max asked.

'Very well,' he answered immediately and Jill thought she detected a hint of bitterness. 'It meant everything to her.'

'It can be difficult to balance business and family life,' Jill put in. 'How did she manage that?'

'We had no family. I mean, she only had me. When we first married, she wanted to get her business established before having children. Then she went off the whole idea of kids. She didn't really have time for people, or for anything outside the business.'

'She had no other family?' Jill asked.

'She had two sisters.' He sighed heavily. 'Their parents died within four years of each other, when the girls were in their twenties. Then, three years ago, there was an accident. Carol's sisters were going on holiday to Ibiza and the taxi taking them to Manchester Airport collided head-on with a lorry. They were killed outright.'

'How awful,' Jill murmured. 'How did Carol cope with that?'

'Badly. She would have been with them, you see, but she had the chance to win a big contract so she pulled out at the last minute.'

So she would have been racked by guilt. The survivor who had no right to survive. The woman who had put her business first.

'It must have been a difficult time for you both,' Jill said.

He was a long time answering.

'Look, I may as well tell you now. Our marriage was as good as over.' He was on his feet again. 'It's hard to admit it now that she's dead, but I was about to ask her for a divorce.'

Which made her death very convenient indeed.

'When we married,' he rushed on, 'I pictured children playing in the garden, a spaniel lying in front of the fire – you know the sort of thing. But Carol changed. She became ambitious and greedy.'

'I see,' Max murmured. 'Was there anyone else involved? Was your wife seeing anyone? Were you?'

'No. There was no one else for either of us,' he said. 'It was just that our marriage wasn't working out.'

'Did she have a wide circle of friends?' Jill asked.

'Not really. As I said, she didn't have time for people. I suppose her closest friend would be the old Greek witch she employed at her shop.' At Jill's expectant expression, he added, 'Name of Ruth Asimacopoulos. She started work at the shop just before the accident that killed Carol's sisters. I can't stand the cow, but I have to admit she was a great help at the time. Carol went to pieces and Asimacopoulos kept the business going. Oh, and there's a young assistant there, too. Cass Jones. I phoned Ruth this morning to tell her the news, and I instructed her to keep the shop open and carry on as normal.'

'We're on our way to the shop to have a chat with them,' Max said, rising to his feet. 'By the way, does the name Edward Marshall mean anything to you?'

Blakely's expression was blank. 'No. Should it?'

'Probably not,' Max said. 'Right, thank you for that. Sorry to ask all these questions at such a difficult time, Mr Blakely, but as I'm sure you can appreciate, we need all the information we can get. We'll be in touch. Meanwhile, if you think of anything, anything at all, call me.'

'I will,' Blakely promised. 'And thank you.'

Jill thought he was relieved to see the back of them.

'Not the most warm-hearted of people,' she remarked as they got back in Max's car. 'Not particularly distraught, either.'

'No.' Max started the car. 'It doesn't sound as if his wife was particularly warm-hearted, either.'

'I wouldn't be if I was married to him.' She fastened her seatbelt. 'Let's go and see how the old Greek witch and her assistant felt about their employer.'

The Blakelys lived on the edge of the town, but the florist's shop, Forget-me-nots, was in the city centre. Late at night, it was a ten-minute drive. This morning, it took over half an hour to negotiate Harrington's fiendish one-way system.

There was a yard for deliveries at the back of a row of six shops and Max parked there. They walked to the front and saw that, despite what Vince Blakely had told them, the door was locked and a large sign told prospective customers that the shop was closed.

'There's a light on in the back.' Max tapped on the glass.

After a few moments, a woman, presumably the old Greek witch, came out and gestured to the *Closed* sign. Max pressed his ID against the glass and she very reluctantly opened the door.

'Mrs Asim – Asim . . .'

'Asimacopoulos,' she helped him out. 'Don't worry, hardly anyone can pronounce it. Believe it or not, it's quite common in Greece. I married a Greek,' she explained. 'Call me Ruth, it'll be easier all round.'

Ah, so she was English. Jill had thought that the only Greek thing about her was an enviable tan that looked as if it was courtesy of a foreign sun rather than a bottle. She was around the forty mark, Jill guessed, with long, curling dark hair. Tall and slim, she was a very striking woman. Not beautiful, but certainly striking, and there was nothing remotely witch-like about her.

Some distance behind her was another girl, presumably Cass Jones, her assistant.

'You can leave the *Closed* sign up,' Max said. 'We're sorry to bother you both, but we need to ask you about your employer, Mrs Blakely.'

'Yes, of course. You'd better come in.' Ruth closed and locked the door behind them. 'Sorry, but neither of us feels up to dealing with customers at the moment. Cass, love, the police want a word with us.'

Cass was in her late teens or early twenties, tall and blonde. She walked towards them, her eyes red and moisture-filled, and a bundle of damp tissues in her hands.

'Shall we all have a coffee?' Jill suggested, eyeing two empty mugs on the counter. 'This must be a very difficult time for you both.'

'It is,' Ruth Asimacopoulos said. 'And yes, coffee. Cass, put the kettle on, love.' To Max and Jill, she added in a whisper, 'She's better if she keeps herself busy.'

Ruth and Cass seemed very distressed considering their employer supposedly had no time for people . . .

They walked into a large back room and the four of them were soon sitting at a small wooden table, one that was usually used for arranging bouquets. Each of them had a coffee in front of them. The slogan on Max's mug, appropriately enough, read *I'm Boss*. Carol's mug presumably. The one on Jill's said *Over the Hill*.

'What can you tell us about Mrs Blakely?' Max began when suitable sympathies had been expressed.

'She was the kindest woman imaginable,' Ruth said quietly. 'Always ready for a laugh, always a generous, thoughtful employer, never forgot my birthday – never.'

This last comment had Ruth blowing her nose loudly.

'I'm sorry,' she whispered, 'but I can't accept that she's gone. She had her whole life in front of her. It was such a shock when Mr Blakely phoned me this morning. I've been in Spain on holiday,' she explained, 'and I didn't get home until gone eleven last night because the plane was almost six hours late. I got up for work as normal this morning and I couldn't believe it when Mr Blakely phoned me with the news. I still can't take it in.'

So the tan was from Spain. Jill hoped she came back from her own holiday in Spain the same colour . . .

'Do you know Mr Blakely well?' Jill asked.

'No.' Ruth grimaced. 'He's been to the shop a few times, but I couldn't say I know him well. I can only go on what Carol told me about him. And even she didn't speak too badly of him. She hated living with him, and had asked him for a divorce, but she didn't badmouth him.'

Jill frowned. 'Carol asked her husband for a divorce? Are you sure?'

'Yes. He wasn't happy about it, I can tell you that. From what Carol let slip, he wanted a good financial settlement. His own business – he's an architect, you know – isn't doing very well. He's into saving the planet, which is all well and good, but it's too expensive for most people. So Carol wasn't happy about his demands. She saw her solicitor about it.'

'Really?'

'Yes. She wanted a divorce but, understandably, she didn't want him living a life of luxury on the strength of her hard work. She changed her will at the same time, I gather. It was out of date. I think there were still bequests to her late sisters in it. I don't know the details though.'

'When was this?' Max asked.

'About a month ago.'

'Interesting,' Max murmured.

'It were on my birthday.' This was the first time Cass had spoken. 'She bought me this –' The girl showed them a silver dolphin hanging from a chain around her neck. 'She bought me this for me birthday and took me and Ruth out for lunch to celebrate. She sent us on ahead – remember, Ruth? – and said she had to see her solicitor to sign her will.'

'Yes, that was it,' Ruth confirmed.

'It's lovely,' Jill said gently, nodding at the silver dolphin. 'And when was your birthday, Cass?'

'Ninth of June. It were a Friday and she let me go home after we'd had lunch. She were like that.' More sniffling followed this statement.

Less than a month after signing that will, Carol was murdered.

'Which firm of solicitors did she use?' Max asked.

'She saw the young girl, name of Susan, at Godfrey's.'

'Ah, yes. I know them. Thanks.'

'Was there anyone else in her life?' Jill took a sip of – well, she hadn't yet decided if it was coffee or tea. It tasted awful, she knew that much. 'You said she and her husband weren't getting along too well. Was she seeing someone else, I wonder?'

'She did have a couple of dates with someone,' Cass told her, 'but it were only in fun. Lovely-looking he were, too. Came from Bacup or somewhere.'

'I can't think of anyone.' Ruth was shaking her head.

'Yes, you know who I mean. It were that fortnight I should have been off, remember? I was supposed to be going on holiday to Majorca,' she explained for Jill and Max's benefit, 'but Sally, the mate I were going with, caught chicken pox so we cancelled at the last minute. We

41

got our money back OK.' She looked at Ruth. 'You must remember that.'

'Well, yes, but I don't remember Carol seeing anyone.'

'You must remember that chap who came in. He was from Bacup or – no, it was Kelton Bridge,' she remembered. 'He'd just moved there. I think he were renting a cottage. I can't remember his name. It were unusual,' she said, chewing on her lip as she tried to remember. 'Lovely-looking he were, though. I don't know how many times she saw him, but he called at the shop twice to take her out. We laughed, don't you remember, Ruth? Carol were always smartly dressed and he turned up in old jeans and a T-shirt that were covered in paint.'

'Oh, him. He didn't mean anything to her,' Ruth scoffed.

'Finlay Roberts?' Jill asked in amazement.

'That's it,' Cass said. 'Finlay Roberts!'

'He's a neighbour of mine,' Jill explained, recovering from the surprise.

'It was nothing,' Ruth said. 'She saw him twice and that was that.'

'Was there anyone else?' Max asked. 'Other friends? Other people she was close to?'

'Not really,' Ruth answered. 'You know about her sisters? Brenda and Angie?'

'Her husband told us about the accident. Tragic,' Jill murmured.

'God, it was,' Ruth said with feeling. 'I'd only been working here for three months. My divorce was going through at the time. Andreas, my husband, didn't take it well and came over to England a couple of times. It was Carol who helped me cope with that. And then the accident happened, and Carol changed totally. She never did get over it. She was always saying she wished she'd died with them.'

It was a warm day but this room, although ideal for keeping flowers fresh, and they were surrounded by buckets filled with every colour and variety of bloom imaginable, was chilly. And damp.

42

The whole place had a sad atmosphere to it.

Carol Blakely, despite claims to the contrary from her husband, had loved this shop and the people in it. In return, she had been loved.

'This shop,' Max said, gesturing at the front room, 'is it doing OK?'

'Oh, yes,' Ruth answered immediately. 'You'll appreciate, though, that this is a very small part of the business. Having said that, most of the actual work is done here. You can see the order book. There are the weddings and funerals, of course, but the main business comes from the contracts with hotels and suchlike.'

They followed her into a small side office where Max looked at the 'order book'. All records were neatly stored on the computer.

'Can you print out details of the jobs done – people placing the orders, that sort of thing – for, say, the last six months?' Max asked.

'Of course.' Ruth was glad to be occupied.

While the printer spewed out pages, Max explained that someone would call later to take the computer away.

'We've got the laptop Mrs Blakely used at home,' he said, 'and we'll need to check this one, too.'

Ruth nodded. 'That's OK. So long as I've got copies of the orders, I'm better with a notebook anyway.'

Until instructed otherwise, Ruth would see that Carol's business ran as efficiently as ever.

'I'm sorry for your loss,' Max told Ruth and Cass again, and Jill knew that he too had been touched by their sadness, 'but I promise you we'll find the person responsible.' He handed Ruth a card. 'If you think of anything else, call me, will you? You may remember someone with an usual request, someone Mrs Blakely was meeting – anything.'

Ruth looked doubtful, but she pocketed his card.

Jill didn't leave headquarters until seven that evening. She left Max there, digging into Vince Blakely's affairs.

On an impulse, instead of going home, she pulled into the Weaver's Retreat's car park. It was a long time since she'd put in a full day and it would be good to relax with a drink. She'd planned to do some writing this evening, but she was too tired.

Once again, she asked herself if she was ready to return to work. Or even if there was a need to. The self-help books she penned provided her with what was just about a sufficient income. Still, it was too late for doubts. The decision had been made and there was no going back. Besides, people were right when they said she was wasting her qualifications. Thanks to her mum's pushing, she'd worked hard as a youngster to escape the Liverpool council estate on which she'd been brought up. And really, she loved the work. A few last-minute doubts were normal.

Yes, she'd made the right decision.

The Weaver's Retreat was busy and she said a quick hello to several locals as she made her way to the bar.

'Had a good day, Jill?' Ian, the landlord, asked as he poured her a glass of lager.

'Sorry? Oh, no. Well, I don't know. Something came up and I had to give the races a miss. I gave my ticket to Bob.' She glanced across at the blank television screen. 'Can I put the telly on, Ian, and check the results?'

'Be my guest.' He handed her the remote control.

As she was going through the results, Barry joined her.

'Mine are still running,' he grumbled.

She grinned at him. 'Still backing the outsiders?'

'Not much point backing the favourites,' he told her. 'I can't see any fun in putting on a pound to win a pound.'

Jill couldn't either, but Barry's bets were bigger than he made out. It was nothing for him to lose five hundred pounds on a horse.

'I had a second, a third and a non-runner.' She scowled at the screen. 'I almost backed The Typhoon, too. He was a good price.'

'He was. Oh, well, I'd better be off. The day I've had, I can't afford Ian's prices. Be seeing you, Jill.'

'See you, Barry. Better luck next time.'

She returned the remote control to Ian. 'A waste of time.'

'What kept you away from the races then?' he asked as he gave change to someone else.

'Oh, something . . .'

'Ah, police work. This murder?'

'Mm,' she agreed.

'Do they have any idea who did it?'

'It's early days, Ian. Is it in tonight's paper?'

He ducked behind the bar for the *Evening Telegraph* and handed it to her. A photo of Carol Blakely dominated the front page and several more had been printed on page two. Jill skimmed the article and handed it back.

'Did you know her, Ian?'

'No. On the rare occasions I need to get flowers for something or someone, I stay local. I don't know the husband either, although he's a member at the golf club and I've seen him up there. That reminds me . . .' He pointed at some raffle tickets. 'Can I sell you a ticket?'

'You usually do,' she replied with amusement. If he hadn't been a publican, Ian would have made a great salesman.

With raffle tickets in her purse, Jill picked up her drink and moved away from the bar. She headed outside to see if anyone was taking advantage of the tables in the small garden at the back of the pub.

Finlay Roberts was sitting at one, staring into an almost full pint of beer. It was rare to see him alone. Usually, he was surrounded by people, carrying on as if he were the life and soul of the party.

'May I join you,' she asked, 'or would you prefer to be alone?'

His face cleared, he rose to his feet and gave her a sweeping bow. 'My darling girl, what a wonderful surprise!'

Stunning-looking he was, but Jill suspected his over-the-top gestures would drive people mad in a short space of time.

'You were looking thoughtful,' she remarked as she sat opposite him. 'Everything all right?'

'Wonderful!' The smile didn't quite reach his eyes. 'How's your day been? You had a day at the races, I hear.'

'Sadly not. I had to cancel. Police work,' she said.

'Ah, yes. The murder. It puts our burglaries into perspective, doesn't it?'

'It does.' Jill took a sip of her drink and waited for him to say more. Nothing was forthcoming, however. 'I gather you knew her,' she said at last.

'Not really.' He pushed his hair back from his face. 'It was like this. I had flowers to order for my ma's birthday so I went into her shop. Three days later, my sister had her baby so I went back. I had to reassure her that I wasn't a stalker.' He smiled at that. 'She was a beautiful woman.'

'So I gather.' He was being surprisingly reticent. 'It's awful when something like this happens, isn't it?' she murmured. 'Especially when you know the person involved.'

'As I said, I didn't really know her. We had a brief chat and a laugh, but that was it.'

It wasn't 'it'. According to Ruth and Cass, he'd taken her out at least twice.

'Hark at us,' he said, smile firmly back in place. 'It's a beautiful evening and I'm sure you don't want to talk work. Let me get you another drink.'

Jill put her hand over her glass. 'Not for me, Finlay. I only called in for a quick one. I've got the car.'

'A soft drink?'

'No, thanks. Really.'

'I don't blame you. Soft drinks are the devil's own brew.'

She smiled, as was expected, but her mind was racing. Why hadn't he said he'd taken her out? Possibly because he thought it was none of her business, she answered her own question. In a way, he was right. She wasn't working with the police officially.

She finished her drink. 'Right, I'm off. Be seeing you, Finlay.'

'See you later, darling girl!'

Chapter Six

Max forced open his eyes and focused on the alarm clock. Five forty-two. The knowledge that he could lie in bed for another hour was bliss. He closed his eyes and rolled over. All was quiet. There was nothing to keep him awake.

Nothing except case notes, witness statements, photographs of murdered women, and memories of the day Edward Marshall drove over that cliff to his death. Possible death . . .

It was Wednesday. Carol Blakely's body had been found on Saturday evening, and they still had nothing concrete to work on.

This morning, he intended to have a chat with Edward Marshall's widow, assuming she *was* a widow. He could remember her well. She had straggling black hair, missing teeth and short skirts that would have looked great on an eighteen-year-old but, on her, were enough to turn the stomach. There was also a mean streak running all the way through her.

He lay down and closed his eyes again, but it was a waste of time. He might as well get up and do something productive.

Ten minutes later, he'd showered, shaved and dressed. All done without waking Harry and Ben, too. Even the dogs hadn't stirred. Holly had crept on to his bed and made herself comfortable, and Fly was no doubt on the foot of Ben's bed dreaming up fresh acts of mayhem.

At least it was another beautiful morning which made being out of bed less painful. He stepped outside

47

to enjoy the peace, and the warmth of the early morning sun . . .

Despite what Ruth Asimacopoulos had believed, Carol Blakely had changed her will to make 'my best friend, Ruth' the main beneficiary eighteen months ago. Until then, there had been generous bequests to her sisters and the rest would have gone to Vince Blakely. Ruth was right in that Carol had amended her will a month ago, but the only change was to add a bequest of ten thousand pounds to the local hospice . . .

Looking around, it struck Max just how tidy his garden was. Full of summer colour, too. Max could take no credit. His mother-in-law must have spent hours filling the borders with bedding plants. They'd obviously been there a while, too. He really should pay more attention.

Sometimes, he thought it would be bliss to retire early and spend his days pottering in the garden. Reality soon kicked in, though, and he knew he would be bored rigid in no time. Today, however, was one of those days when pottering appealed.

Alas.

He went back inside and shouted up the stairs. 'Come on, you two. Move it!'

Ben and Harry were soon up and dressed for school. Once downstairs, they were pushing toast down their throats as if they hadn't eaten for weeks.

'Don't forget it's parents' evening on Friday,' Harry reminded him between mouthfuls.

Ben pulled a face. 'We don't have to go, do we?'

'Are we parents?' Harry scoffed.

'This Friday?' Max asked in astonishment.

'Yes.' Harry wore his resigned expression and nodded at the notice, a bright sheet of A4, pinned to the fridge door.

'I'll be there,' Max promised.

He'd forgotten all about it, but he would be there. It had to be a couple of years since he'd managed the last one, and there was nothing like hearing how academically challenged your kids were. Fortunately, Harry excelled on the sports field. Ben, three years younger than his brother, refused to excel at anything.

'You'd better do some hard graft between now and Friday then,' he added.

The newspaper was pushed through the letterbox.

'Fetch!' Ben said, and Fly, part labrador, part collie, part psychopath, raced off to collect it. When the dog dropped it, unchewed, at Ben's feet, even Max thought he deserved the piece of toast that Ben slipped him.

'Hey, very impressive,' Max said, surprised. He reached for the paper and unfolded it –

'Oh, shit!'

'Dad!'

Two hands shot out. Somehow managing to keep a few more furious expletives to himself, Max dug into his pockets and handed over two fifty-pence pieces for the swear box. Ben and Harry were saving for their holiday in Spain. At this rate, they'd be able to fly all their mates out and put them up in five-star hotels . . .

But shit! Max wondered if his boss's paper was delivered at breakfast time. Phil Meredith would go berserk when he saw it.

Undertaker still alive!

How in hell's name had they got wind of that?

A leak, he answered his own question. Someone on Max's team, someone he trusted, had talked. And if Max got hold of them, they'd be lucky to talk again. Or walk.

Hell and damnation.

Perhaps Edward Marshall *was* still alive and thought it was high time he received some credit for his actions. Or perhaps Marshall was dead and the real killer thought *he* was due some time under the spotlight.

It was no use speculating.

'Come on, you two!' He tossed the newspaper down on the table and grabbed his car keys. More than ever, he wished he could spend the day pottering in the garden.

* * *

49

An hour later, Max was driving, very slowly, through a crowd of reporters gathered outside headquarters. He guessed that if he glanced up at the third floor, he would see his boss's face glaring back at him. He didn't look up.

As he stood no chance of getting into the building un-molested, he parked his car as close to the steps as poss-ible, got out and waved his arms at the crowd to try and silence them. He felt like King Canute trying to stave off the waves.

'We'll issue a statement at 6 p.m.,' he shouted at them. 'Meanwhile, I'm sorry, but I can't answer any questions.'

'Is it The Undertaker?'

'Should we warn women –'

'Sorry,' Max said pleasantly, 'but, as I said, I can't answer your questions at this particular time.'

With that, he lunged for the door and left them outside like a pack of baying wolves.

Frank Busby was behind the main desk. 'They've been here for hours,' he told Max.

'Then get them bloody shifted!' Max snapped.

'Er, will do. Oh, and the boss wants to see you. Pronto.'

'I bet he does.'

Max checked in his office to see if there was a 'we've got him' note waiting for him – there wasn't, of course – and headed for the executive suite occupied by Phil Meredith.

Meredith must have been waiting, poised, because as soon as Max entered, he threw a newspaper on to the desk with as much force as he could muster. It wasn't much. Newspapers are ineffectual when it comes to giving vent to rage. The heavy glass engraved paperweight that had pride of place on his desk would have had more effect.

'Yes, I've seen it and no, I don't know how they got hold of it.' Max thought it was one of those occasions when stating the obvious wouldn't go amiss.

'Someone – someone on your bloody team has been talk-ing to reporters!'

Meredith had just celebrated his fiftieth birthday, and there had been hopes among the staff that it might mellow him a little. It hadn't. His brown hair was thinning, he'd gained a little weight but was merely stocky as opposed to fat, and he'd recently changed his glasses so that now they were rimless, but he still peered over them to try and intimidate people, and he still lived for the job.

'Not necessarily,' Max argued. 'When I can speak to that moron of an editor, we'll know more.'

'Didn't you make it clear?'

'Of course I did. They all know the score.'

'Which makes it even worse. If it were some raw recruit – pah! It would still be no excuse. Find out who talked, Max.'

'I'll do my best, but it wasn't necessarily someone from the force. Now, about the press –'

'Bloody vultures!'

'Indeed,' Max agreed. 'I've promised them a statement at six o'clock.'

'Tell them nothing. Say you can't imagine where such a damn fool notion came from.' He straightened the already straight lapel on his jacket and considered this for a moment. 'I'll tell them, Max,' he decided. 'Leave it to me.'

Max had been hoping that vanity and a love of the small screen would win out. It usually did.

'Great idea. Right, I'll go and see what's what.'

That had been surprisingly easy, Max thought, as he closed the office door behind him. However, the fact remained that someone had been talking to the press.

Later that morning, when the reporters had gone, Max decided he deserved to step outside for a cigarette.

DS Warne was on her way to her car.

'Press gone then, guv?'

'For the time being, Grace, yes.'

'I'm on my way to see your favourite newspaper editor. Any messages for him?'

'I've already told him what I think of him. Bloody moron.'

She grinned at that and was about to carry on to her car when she stopped.

'That's Darren Barlow,' she murmured, frowning.

Max looked across at the young lad sitting astride his cycle just outside the car park.

Grace and Fletch had gone to see the Barlow boys but, despite Annie Burton's claims, the brothers denied being anywhere near the quarry last Saturday.

Just as young Darren looked set to cycle off, Grace called out to him. 'Hi, Darren, everything all right?'

He was clearly undecided. However, he eventually leant his bike against the wall and walked, eyes on tatty trainers, towards them.

'Everything all right?' Grace asked again.

Grace was a good officer, one of the best. Having six brothers of her own, she was good with boys, too.

'No school today?' she asked casually. 'Or have you nipped out because it's lunchtime?'

'Yeah. Yeah, I've done that,' he said, grateful for the ready-made excuse. He scuffed his trainers on the tarmac. 'Up at the quarry,' he said at last, 'it were me and Jake. I phoned you when we found that – body.'

'We thought you probably did,' Grace told him. 'A lady saw you. She said her dog chased you.'

'Oh.'

'It was good that you phoned us,' Max said.

The lad nodded.

'Were you sick?' Max asked him.

'Yeah. It were horrid.'

'It was,' Max agreed.

Darren looked at him. 'Can I go now?'

'Of course you can,' Max said. 'Thanks for dropping by. We appreciate it.'

Darren nodded again. He was a boy of few words. Mainly, Max suspected, because his stepfather, Dave Walsh, had had too many run-ins with the law.

Max handed the lad a ten-pound note. 'You'd better stop

off at McDonald's on your way back to school. Missing meals isn't good for you.'

'Wow! Thanks, mister.'

Darren ran back to his bike and cycled off.

'Very des res,' Jill said.

Irene Marshall had moved to Preston before her husband was released from prison. As Max stopped the car outside her house, he guessed she'd done nothing since. And that included cleaning the windows.

It was a red-brick terraced house with a small, walled front garden that was overgrown with weeds, and dotted with wind-blown carrier bags and beer cans that had been tossed there by passers-by.

'I bet it's a damn sight more attractive than its occupant,' he replied.

'Ha! And she always spoke so highly of you.'

'Mm. So I recall.' He looked at the house and shuddered. 'Come on then, let's get it over with. When I phoned her, she said she had to go out at two.'

The door – dark red flaking paint – swung open as they were negotiating their way up the path.

Irene Marshall had aged a lot, probably because she chain-smoked. Even make-up that looked as if it had been applied with a bricklayer's trowel couldn't hide her deep wrinkles. Her hair, usually black, was mostly grey, the colour having faded, and she was wearing a short, grubby, tight denim skirt and a top that might once have been white. Her teeth had been fixed, though. She now sported a full set of nicotine-stained false teeth. She was stick-thin and Max wouldn't have been surprised to learn she was taking drugs of some description.

'He's alive, isn't he?' she greeted them, the obligatory cigarette glued between nicotine-stained fingers.

'We don't know that,' Max replied. 'Can we come inside and talk?'

'Don't have much choice, do I?'

Nice to see her natural charm was still intact.

They followed her down a narrow hallway where two black sacks of rubbish waited to be taken somewhere. A damp patch on the dingy brown carpet squelched as Max trod on it.

She took them to the filthiest kitchen Max had ever seen. Everything had a thick coating of grease, even the cheap wooden chair that he saw Jill inadvertently touch and then leap back as if she'd been burnt.

It was one of those houses where you wiped your feet on the way out. He wanted to be on the way out.

'You know why we're here,' he said, 'so you know that the murder of Carol Blakely was very similar to the murders we believe were carried out by your husband.'

She leaned back against the greasy cooker. 'He's still alive, isn't he? Christ, what does that make me? One of them fucking bigamists?'

Max frowned. 'You've remarried? I didn't know that.'

'Of course I haven't. Bleeding 'ell, you don't fall for that twice. I've been living with a bloke off and on, though.'

'Then there's nothing to worry about,' Max assured her. 'So can I take it that Eddie hasn't been in touch with you?'

'Course he hasn't. Just as well. If he came back from the bloody grave, I'd bleedin' top myself. And how would he find me? Eh?'

'If he *was* alive,' Max said, 'who might he contact?'

'Dunno.' She thought for a moment. 'He were short on friends. Not bloody surprising when you think of his temper.' She inhaled deeply on her cigarette. 'He can't be alive. I'd have heard about it.'

For all that, she didn't look convinced. She looked terrified that he might walk through the door at any moment.

'We're sure he isn't,' Jill said smoothly, 'but the murder of Carol Blakely was too similar to ignore a connection. We can only imagine that Eddie talked to someone. Perhaps he bragged about the murders.'

She shrugged at that.

'You had lots of fights with him,' Jill went on. 'How did he behave afterwards?'

'As if sweet FA had bleedin' happened,' she replied scathingly. 'He'd say sorry, if I were lucky, and then forget it. A fat lot of help that were to me. I couldn't forget it, could I? Not with a busted jaw.'

She ran a hand across that jaw.

'You couldn't,' Jill agreed, and Max heard her struggling for a sympathetic tone. 'But who was he close to? Who would he have spoken to?'

'I've no idea,' Irene Marshall snapped. 'No one that I can think of.'

'He drank a lot,' Max reminded her. 'Most people talk too much when they're drunk.'

'Not him,' Irene scoffed. 'And he certainly didn't talk to me. He were too busy knocking me about.' She stubbed out her cigarette. 'Look, I had nothing to do with him then. After he put me in hospital, I never saw him again. How the 'ell should I know who he talked to?'

Max supposed she had a point.

'We'll talk to ex-cellmates and fellow inmates,' Jill told her, 'but who else could there be? Where did he drink?'

'The Horse and Jockey in Harrington. Oh, and the Red Lion. He were barred from most of the other places.' She thought for a moment. 'He used to go to Sal's, too. You know the caff on Broad Street?'

Max remembered the place. 'It's been closed down for a couple of years.'

'Oh. That's no good then. There was that Ken Barclay. You know him who has the lorries? He was supposed to have promised Eddie a job as a driver. That was before he ended up doing time, though. And I don't know how true it were.'

'We'll check it out.' Max was grateful for any lead.

She came up with a few more names, but nothing sounded promising and Max was glad when it was time to leave.

'If you hear anything, you'll let us know?' he asked.

'Too right I will. If the bastard's still alive –'

'We're sure he isn't,' Jill said calmly.

Max wished he could sound as confident.

'He'd better not be. I'll want bleeding compensation from you lot if he is.'

'Quite right,' Max agreed as they reached fresh air. Phil Meredith would be delighted to deal with that. The thought made him smile as he got in his car.

'Shall we find somewhere to eat?' he asked as he knocked the car into gear and pulled away.

'Only if it's somewhere clean.' Jill shuddered. 'God, even your car feels pristine after that place!'

The backhanded compliment made him smile.

'So what did you think?' he asked after a while.

'I think she's scared he's still alive. If she knew anything, she'd tell us. She hates him.'

'With good reason.'

'Yes. We've got a copycat on our hands, Max, I'm sure of it, but I can't imagine Eddie Marshall talking to anyone. He was a nasty piece of work with a vicious temper but, as Irene said, he forgot it afterwards. He wasn't the type to talk.'

'So how would anyone know the MO? How would someone –?' He cursed beneath his breath. 'A copper would know. The same copper who possibly leaked this story to the press.'

'Come on, Max, we don't even know that it was a copper.'

No one liked the idea of someone on the force being less than a hundred per cent honest. And worse, much worse, was the idea of a policeman turning to murder. It went against nature.

'Even if it was,' she went on, 'it's not necessarily as bad as it seems. A couple of drinks in the pub, a reporter posing as an innocent member of the public – it happens.'

'Not on my patch, it bloody well doesn't!'

Chapter Seven

Max sat in his new swivel chair with his feet on his new desk and read through Finlay Roberts's statement again. He didn't like it.

He didn't like the chair, either. It looked good, the ultimate in style and design, but it wasn't as comfortable as his old one. He resented it, too. All he heard was budgets and bloody shoestrings when he asked for more manpower, but it seemed there was no shortage of cash for furniture. This desk of his had cost a fortune.

He turned his thoughts back to the statement. Roberts claimed he'd had two evenings out with Carol Blakely. On the first occasion, a Friday, they had visited the Ashoka Indian Restaurant in Burnley. The following Wednesday, they'd been to Mario's Restaurant in Bacup.

Perhaps the fact that, seemingly on a whim, he rented a cottage in Kelton Bridge for three months and then got involved with a woman who was murdered soon afterwards was nothing more than coincidence. Max hated coincidences.

Roberts didn't have an alibi. While Carol Blakely was being butchered, he was at home 'chilling out alone'. He seemed an intelligent individual so one would expect him to make sure he concocted some sort of story if he had anything to hide.

With a sigh, Max swung his feet off the desk, gathered up the papers scattered across his desk to put them into a neat pile, and then went in search of Jill.

Fifteen minutes later, he was driving them to Preston where Tommy (Spider) Young was currently in residence.

'What's he in for?' Jill asked.

'Breaking and entering. Assault.'

'And why Spider?'

'You'll know when you see him.'

Tommy Young was an ex-cellmate of Edward Marshall's. It was six years since they'd shared that cell and Young had been released, banged up, released and banged up again since.

According to the records, though, Edward Marshall had visited Tommy once, soon after his release. Soon after he began his killing spree.

'What's he like?' Jill asked as Max pulled off the motorway.

'A whining, grovelling con. Yes, Mr Trentham, no, Mr Trentham, three bags full, Mr Trentham. He's due out in a couple of months, but I expect they'll have the good sense to keep his bed warm.'

'How old is he?'

'Fifty-two.'

'About the same age as Marshall then,' she calculated.

'He's a couple of months older.'

After passing the Tickled Trout Hotel, Max carried on to the roundabout and on to New Hall Lane. He turned right and saw the prison next to the County Regimental Museum. Fortunately, he was able to park nearby and, surprisingly, formalities at the prison were quickly dealt with.

Before long, a smiling Tommy Young was sitting opposite them.

'Chief Inspector Trentham,' he said. 'A pleasure, I'm sure.'

His tattoo, a huge spider's web covering his neck, was incongruous with the polite smiles.

'If only it were mutual, Tommy.'

The prisoner was looking questioningly at Jill.

'Jill Kennedy,' Max introduced her.

58

'Ah, yes, the psychologist. It's an honour to meet you, my dear. I read about you when poor Eddie met his Maker.' He beamed at Max. 'And that's why you're here, to speak to me about Eddie. You think he's still alive.' Still smiling, he tapped the side of his nose. 'I do read the newspapers, you know.'

But not the big words, Max assumed.

'You shouldn't believe all you read, Tommy,' he said.

'Tell us about Eddie,' Jill suggested. 'You shared a cell, we know that. We also know that he visited you once after his release. You must have grown quite close.'

'Not at all.' Tommy's hands, the fingernails neatly trimmed, rested on the table in front of him. 'It's true what you say, of course, but he was a difficult man to know. A very angry man. Private, too.'

'Angry about what?' Max asked.

'Life in general. He thought the world was against him. He didn't believe he should be locked up for showing his wife who was boss.'

'You were kindred spirits then,' Max said drily.

'No, no.' Young chuckled. 'I'm a reformed character now, Chief Inspector. You'll have no more trouble from me, I can assure you.'

'Are you trying to tell me you'll be sticking to the straight and narrow, Tommy? That takes some believing.'

'It's true.' He leaned back in his chair, his smile gentle and relaxed. 'As soon as I'm free, when I've repaid my debt to society, I'm going to theological college.'

Max groaned. 'Don't tell me you've found God.'

'He found me,' Tommy corrected him. 'I was lost, now I'm found.'

Max groaned again.

'What did you talk about?' Jill asked briskly. 'You and Eddie Marshall,' she put in quickly, 'not you and God.'

'We didn't talk about much at all. He shouted at the injustice of it all and I agreed with everything he said. He had a vile temper so I wasn't going to argue with him.'

'Did he mention his wife?' she asked.

59

'Mention her? He talked about little else. He reckoned it was wrong him being banged up, and he was going to show her that he wasn't a man to be pissed about. I just used to let him hold forth. As I said, I wasn't going to argue with him.'

'Who else did he talk to?' Max asked.

'No one that I can think of. Eddie didn't talk as such. He'd pace the cell and shout and curse. It was more the ravings of a nutter than talk.'

'If there was so little conversation between the two of you,' Jill said, 'how come he visited you after he was released?'

'At the time, I couldn't understand that myself,' Tommy said thoughtfully. 'He was even worse then, too. I thought he was probably on drugs. He had a bright-eyed look. Seemed wilder and more out of control, if you know what I mean. I always said he was mad.' He gave Jill a bold stare. 'He saw enough of you shrinks, but you all reckoned he was sane. I didn't.'

'He must have said something to you,' Jill insisted.

'He said he was going to do for them all, I remember that.'

'Them all?' Jill queried.

'At the time, I'd no idea who he meant by that. Later, I realized he meant those women. Well, he must have, mustn't he?'

'What else did he say?'

'I wanted him to leave. "Calm down, forget revenge and get on with your life," I told him. We had a bit of an argument. As he was only visiting, I felt safer, as if I could say what I liked to him. I told him he wasn't man enough to do half the things he claimed he would, and he went ballistic. "I've done one," he said, "and I'll do the rest of 'em." I told him to stop being so dramatic, but he swore he had proof. Said it was all on film. I tell you, he was mad. I was glad when he left. And no,' he added with a smile, 'before you ask, I never heard from him again, thank God.'

'On film?' Max said. 'Are you sure he said he'd already done one and that it was on film?'

'Oh, yes. He'd bought one of those camcorders. Second-hand, he said it was, but a bargain. Everyone wanted digital, that's why he got it so cheap.'

Bingo. The bastard must have filmed the murders. If Jill was right and they did have a copycat on their hands, that person must have got hold of the film.

'What did he say about it? Think, Tommy! Did he mention the make, say where he'd got it from, anything like that?'

'He probably did, but it didn't mean nothing to me. All I can remember is him saying he'd make a copy of the video and send it to me. As if I was interested in anything that sicko did. Mad he was. Stark, staring mad!'

A video. That had to be it.

'What about letters or phone calls when he was inside?' Max asked. 'Did he write to anyone? Speak to anyone?'

'His brother wrote to him once, I remember. I saw the letter. Not that he showed it to me, but it was hanging around and I couldn't help reading it. It was full of sympathy for Eddie's predicament. Whether his brother had genuine feelings for him, I don't know. Eddie never mentioned it, but he did keep the letter.'

'What about interests?' Jill asked. 'Was he into stamp collecting, coin collecting, antiques – anything like that?'

'Not that I knew of, but it wouldn't surprise me.'

'Oh?'

'He always reckoned life was better in days gone by.' He grinned. 'He blamed most things wrong in our society on giving votes to women. Very old-fashioned in his outlook. He hated women. Oh, except his grandmother. She was a saint, by all accounts. His own mother was one of eleven children, I recall . . .'

Max's thoughts were still on that camcorder, and Tommy couldn't tell them much else.

'I'll see you in court then, Tommy,' Max said as they were leaving.

'You'll see me in church,' Tommy retorted, the smile still in place. 'Meanwhile, I'll pray for you.'

They were soon out of the prison and striding towards Max's car.

'A bloody camcorder,' Jill burst out. 'It makes sense. Eddie Marshall thought he was doing society a favour and he would have wanted society's gratitude. He had to have proof that he was the man responsible. The bodies were laid out for the cameras all right. Our cameras *and* his. The sick bastard was his own audience.'

'It seems like it. Would he film the body, or would he film the murders?'

'Oh, he'd film the lot. Everything would be caught on camera. He was proud of what he was doing. Bastard.'

'So if we can just trace this film –'

'Which will be as easy as tracing this killer . . .'

They were soon out of Preston, but traffic on the M6 was moving slowly.

'Carol Blakely's killer,' Jill mused. 'OK, he probably wasn't filming himself but he was trying to make us think Eddie Marshall was still alive. Fair enough. With the film in his possession, that probably makes sense. After all, if we're busy digging into Eddie Marshall's past, it takes the heat off him. Yet why was Carol Blakely his victim? This isn't someone like Marshall who wants revenge on career women. Carol was chosen for a reason.'

'Indeed. Which has her husband top of my list of suspects.'

'You have a list? Wow. It must be one of hell of a short list.'

It was. Vince Blakely was top and Finlay Roberts, for a reason Max couldn't fathom, was second – or bottom.

'Vince Blakely wanted a divorce,' Max said. 'They both wanted a divorce, but *he* wanted a financial settlement. He didn't know she'd changed her will and left everything to Ruth Asimacopoulos.'

'Who did know?'

'No one. Ruth said Carol never discussed financial matters, that money meant very little to her.'

'So even her best friend didn't know.'

'No.' Max took his gaze from the road briefly and smiled. 'If she had, I'd have three suspects on my list.'

'And if she hadn't been in Costa Wherever at the time,' Jill put in drily.

Max lit a cigarette and wound down the window to release the smoke.

'So, Vince Blakely kills his wife,' Jill said, speaking louder to make herself heard above the traffic noise, 'and expects to live happily ever after on the proceeds?'

'Yes, but there's a flaw there. He was on a golfing holiday when she was killed.'

'Only in Scotland. It's easy enough to drive or fly down from Scotland and then get back.'

It was possible. They needed to check with the hotel again and see if he was unaccounted for on Friday night or Saturday morning.

The traffic was still moving slowly, but Max was in no hurry. He often found that when he was concentrating on his driving, his subconscious was working away on more important issues.

It was another hot, sticky day and, with the air conditioning on, it was more comfortable inside the car than out.

'I need a coffee,' Jill said, breaking a long silence.

'Blackburn Services is about five miles away.'

'And a muffin,' she added.

'Anything else?'

'This whole Undertaker thing –' she said, ignoring that. 'Someone's trying to piss us about. Because we're concentrating on Eddie Marshall, we're missing stuff closer to home.'

'But if we're right,' Max said, 'and there was a video, how the hell would someone get hold of that without knowing Marshall?'

'True.' She sighed. 'I need that coffee. I'll think better then.'

'We'll have a coffee,' Max said, 'and then we'll get Vince Blakely brought in. It's about time we had a long, serious chat with him.'

'He'll want a lawyer there, just to keep everything right and proper. Smug bastard.'

'You're right. Scrap that. We'll have an informal chat with him at his place.'

Chapter Eight

Blakely was sitting in his garden when they arrived, and Jill wondered if it was his relaxed attitude that made her dislike him so much. He might have been working, as he was sitting at a large wooden table with a set of drawings spread out in front of him. There was a bottle of wine in an ice bucket and a half-empty glass by his side, however, which didn't do a lot for that theory. Shorts and a loose red and white shirt were the dress code for the day.

'We were passing,' Max told him pleasantly, 'so thought we'd update you.'

'Good of you. Thank you. Please, have a seat.'

As they sat opposite him, shielding him from the sun, Jill marvelled at how calm he was. He certainly wasn't her idea of the grieving widower.

She cast her mind back to when she, too, had lost a spouse. Like Blakely and his wife, she and Chris had been on the brink of starting divorce proceedings. They, too, had known their marriage was over. The love they'd shared was over and the vows they'd exchanged were meaningless. Nevertheless, on the day Chris was killed, shot by a gang of thugs as he'd worked in the streets of London, she'd been distraught. The sense of loss had been immense. True, there had been no bitterness between them, but even so, the man she had once thought herself in love with, the man she'd woken beside each morning, the man who should have had a long, happy life before him was dead.

Yet Vince Blakely was emotionless.

'How are you coping, Mr Blakely?' she asked curiously, a sympathetic smile pinned in place.

'Life goes on,' he replied. 'It doesn't sink in really. A huge shock, of course. It's very difficult but, as I said, life has to go on, doesn't it?'

'Of course,' Jill agreed.

'So?' He looked from one to the other. 'What progress have you made?'

'We're following several leads,' Max said carefully. 'Trust me, we have every available officer working on this case and we will find your wife's killer.'

Several leads, Jill scoffed inwardly. If only.

Blakely seemed satisfied, and he didn't seem unduly concerned at Max's promise to find his wife's killer. Because he was innocent? Or because he thought they didn't have a hope in hell of catching him?

'Why do you think your late wife changed her will and left everything to Ruth Asimacopoulos?' she asked. 'If, as you say, she had no time for people, it seems an odd gesture.'

'How would I know? As I told you, I didn't even know she'd made a will.'

'You must have discussed the matter at some point,' Jill said. 'Couples do.'

'We didn't.' He thought for a moment. 'In the early days of our marriage, we said we ought to make them – you know, when we saw one of those ads that solicitors put in the paper. That was as far as it went, though. We never got round to it.'

'You haven't made one either?' Jill asked curiously.

'No.'

'So if you'd died last month, your wife would have inherited everything?'

'Yes. And before you ask, no, it wouldn't have bothered me. If I'm dead, I'm hardly likely to worry, am I?'

That was fair enough. Jill knew he wasn't alone, either. Many people died intestate. Most people assume they have plenty of time to put their affairs in order. Others are superstitious. They believe that, as soon as a will is made, their number will be called.

'Look,' he said, 'I wouldn't know why or when she made a will. She didn't discuss money.'

'But why Ruth Asimacopoulos?' Max murmured.

'Because the old witch was her closest friend. Besides, the business was everything to her. She'd want it to carry on.'

'There's no provision for that in the will,' Jill pointed out. 'Everything goes to Ruth – Mrs Asimacopoulos – regardless of whether she keeps the business or sells it.'

'She'll keep it. You mark my words.'

'I suppose,' Jill murmured, tracing a pattern with her finger on the wooden table, 'that she wanted to make sure you didn't benefit from her assets. That was the reason for her refusing a divorce, wasn't it? You couldn't agree on the financial settlement.'

'Oh, you're right in that she wouldn't want me to get anything,' he said bitterly, 'but as I told her on several occasions, I wanted a divorce more than I wanted her money.'

Liar. If that were the case, he'd have been granted that divorce.

'The success of her business,' he went on, ' was due, in the main, to the capital I forked out in the beginning. My own business was doing well at the time so I helped her to get hers going. I only wanted what I felt was rightfully mine.'

'I see,' Jill murmured.

'Do you know a man called Finlay Roberts?' Max asked, changing the subject.

'No. Should I?'

'Mrs Blakely went out with him a couple of times,' he explained.

Blakely shrugged. 'That was her business. I wasn't her keeper.'

'If we knew about anyone she was seeing socially, it would help,' Max pointed out.

'We never discussed such things.'

Another lie. Jill couldn't imagine any married couple, happy or otherwise in their relationship, not discussing, or at least making snide remarks about, anyone the other person was seeing.

'Look, I'd love to help,' he said, 'but her life was exactly that. Her life. She could have been sleeping with half of Lancashire for all I knew.'

He didn't say 'or cared' but it hung in the air between them.

'One other thing,' Max said casually, 'we wondered if we could look at her DVDs, CDs, old records, videos –'

'Whatever for?' Blakely asked in astonishment.

'There were a couple of internet sites she visited,' Max lied. 'We've had one under observation for some time. If we can find something she purchased – they specialize in older stuff, vinyl and videos.'

'You can look.' He stood up and began walking to the house. Jill and Max followed.

The inside was as immaculate as the first time Jill had seen it.

'They'll be in her den,' Blakely threw over his shoulder.

They followed him along a thickly carpeted hallway, down two steps and into the den. It was a large study where Carol Blakely's computer had lived until the police had taken it away. Unlike the rest of the house, this room was cosy and cluttered. In short, it looked lived in.

'You'll have to excuse the mess,' Blakely said. 'Apart from the things your bods moved, it's just as she left it. This is how she lived,' he added, and it wasn't meant as a compliment.

'I like it,' Jill said.

The large wooden desk was covered – apart from the empty space where her computer had sat – with trinkets and framed photographs. For someone who had no time for people, she certainly liked photographs.

'Her sisters?' Jill guessed, pointing at the photos.

'Yes.'

A complete wall was shelved and full of books, floor to ceiling, and a quick glance at the titles told Jill that Carol had collected old books on gardening and flower arranging.

'Your people spent hours in this room,' Blakely reminded Max, 'so I expect they'd have found anything if it was here.'

'Yes, I'm sorry for this further intrusion, but we weren't looking for anything specific at that point. I'm sure that you and your late wife's family want her killer found as quickly as possible. This could give us a useful lead.'

A small unit housed a few music CDs and half a dozen DVDs, all romantic comedies. There were no old videos. Jill hadn't expected to see any.

'Are there more in the house?' Max asked. 'It may be that she bought you a gift –'

'I have loads of old music videos,' Blakely said. 'You're welcome to look, but I don't remember her buying any of them. In any case, most of them are stuff I taped from the television.'

'If you wouldn't mind.'

They were taken to a second study at the other end of the hallway, this one used by Vince Blakely. Prints of classic sports cars adorned the walls and Max admired those while Jill looked at the rest of the room. It was used mostly for work. He had an office in Harrington, but he must work from home a lot. His desk was glass and chrome, with not a speck of dust on it. The cleaner he employed did a good job. A heavy glass ashtray sat on the desk, holding down yet more drawings.

A cabinet with smoked glass doors stood next to the desk and, much to Jill's surprise, Blakely produced a small key from a bunch in his pocket.

'You keep this locked?' she asked.

'Um, yes. Our – my cleaner's a nosy old biddy and I wouldn't want her seeing some of these. Oh, it's only soft porn, the same as everyone has, but she'd feel duty bound to tell everyone she met.'

There was nothing of interest in his video collection or in his study. The soft porn looked to be exactly that, and it was on DVD anyway. The old videos were, as he'd said and as he took them into the lounge to demonstrate, concerts that he had taped from the television.

He hadn't loved his wife, he hadn't even liked her, and he wasn't sorry she was dead. But that didn't make him a killer.

He was neat. A perfectionist in fact. If he'd got hold of those videos and wanted to play copycat, his MO would have been exactly the same as Edward Marshall's. Marshall put old pennies on the victims' eyes and Vince Blakely would have done the same, no matter how difficult it was to obtain old coins.

Chapter Nine

Jill parked at the back of Forget-me-nots and then walked round to the front of the shop. It was almost six o'clock, but the *Open* sign was still showing so she walked inside.

She was having a day at the races tomorrow, and had lots to do this evening, but she'd been driving past and had been surprised to see the shop still open. There were several people looking at the fresh flowers, a couple looking at silk flowers, a woman inspecting a display of vases, and a man trying to choose a greetings card from the stand.

Jill hadn't realized that Carol Blakely's business was so lucrative, or that this shop was such a small part of it. Including Ruth and Cass, Carol had employed a staff of eighteen. Practically every hotel and town hall in Lancashire, it seemed to Jill, boasted contracts for flower arrangements with Carol. When the solicitors had done their bit, Ruth would be a wealthy woman.

Seemingly oblivious to this fact, the woman was wrapping white roses for a young, suit-clad man.

'Can I help?' she asked Jill when the man had left.

'Jill Kennedy,' she reminded her. 'I was hoping for a word about –'

'Ah, of course. Sorry, I didn't recognize you for a minute. Come through to the back.'

'Thanks.' Jill followed her to the back room.

'Can you give me a couple of minutes to help Cass with the rush?'

'Of course.'

71

'Help yourself to tea or coffee,' Ruth added as she headed back out front.

Jill didn't bother with coffee. Instead, she looked around the chilly room. Flowers sat in buckets of water, and despite the fact that the shop would soon be closing for the day, several tied bouquets awaited collection or delivery. The room at the side looked exactly the same apart from the empty space where the computer used to live. The monitor and printer sat forlornly with their cables dangling.

Ruth returned and Jill was pleased to see her looking stronger, more able to cope. She was wearing a long, mauve skirt, a black waistcoat and lots of bracelets and necklaces. On Jill's last visit, Ruth either hadn't applied any make-up or it had been washed away by tears. Today her face was made-up and she looked more striking than ever.

'We've been busy all day,' she told Jill, taking a seat at the desk. 'We're always busy first thing with people on their way to work. It's the same at lunchtimes, and just before hospital visiting times. We usually have a rush about now, with people leaving work to go home, but it's been exceptional today.'

Morbid curiosity, Jill suspected. People would have read about the murder and come for a closer look at Carol's shop. However, she didn't say so. They talked about the business for a couple of minutes until Jill got to the point of her visit.

'I wondered if you'd had more time to think about things? We're really trying to find out if Carol – Mrs Blakely – was romantically involved with anyone.'

'I've already been asked the same thing, and no, I'm sure she wasn't. She would have told me.'

That's what Jill had thought.

'We know she saw Finlay Roberts a couple of times,' Jill went on. 'Did she tell you about that? I know you and Cass saw him when he came to the shop, but did she mention having a couple of evenings out with him?'

'Not that I remember.' Ruth played with a stray thread on her skirt. 'We were close. If there was anything important, she would have told me.'

'Phew!' Cass came through to join them. 'I've locked up,' she said, and Ruth nodded.

'That's it for another day then.'

'Cass,' Jill began, 'do you remember Carol mentioning her dates with Finlay Roberts?'

'Oh, yes. She laughed about it. Don't you remember, Ruth? She said she must be mad because she was going out with a customer just because he was handsome and he made her laugh. She said he could be an axe-murderer for all she –' Cass put a hand to her mouth, horrified at what she'd said. 'Sorry, but that's what she said. Those exact words.'

'And that was all?' Jill asked.

'As far as I can remember, yes.'

'What about when you saw him in the shop?' Jill pressed on. 'What happened then? How did they seem together?'

'It were mad, weren't it, Ruth?' Cass smiled at the memory. 'Carol were a quiet person, not shy, not in the least, but a bit reserved. A private person. He were different again. At one stage, he were dancing around the shop with a red rose between his teeth. Then he put it in Carol's hair and danced her around, didn't he, Ruth?'

'He did, yes. Gosh, I'd forgotten that.'

Unless Jill was mistaken, Cass was another who had fallen for Finlay's roguish charm.

'Then,' Cass rushed on, 'saying that red suited her, he bought a length of red ribbon – you know, the sort we use for the bouquets? – and tied that in her hair.'

'Red ribbon?' Jill could feel her heart hammering against her ribcage.

'Yes.' Cass laughed. 'He bought the whole roll, in fact.'

'Oh? Have you got some here? Can you show me a piece?'

'Of course we have.' Ruth got to her feet. 'Is it important?' she asked, heading for the shop.

73

'Who knows?' Jill said lightly.

The ribbon that had been tied around Carol's waist had been checked at the lab, but they'd found nothing that might help. All they could say was that it was a common ribbon that could be bought almost anywhere. They'd found no fibres, no clues . . .

Ruth returned to the back room with four rolls of red ribbon.

'I can't remember which sort he bought,' she said. 'I have it in my mind it was this one.' She handed the roll of two-inch wide ribbon to Jill. 'Although it may have been this one,' she added, handing over another, slightly narrower roll.

Jill knew that the ribbon tied around Carol's waist had been half an inch wide.

'May I take samples of each of these?' she asked.

'As much as you want.' Ruth reached for the scissors. 'Is this important?'

'I don't know,' Jill said, surprised at how heavy her heart felt.

She liked Finlay Roberts. She enjoyed his sense of fun, his refusal to take life seriously. Added to which, she didn't want to think she might be living next door to a killer.

'It was definitely this colour?' she asked, her throat dry.

'Oh, yes.'

'Do you sell any other sizes?'

'No,' Ruth told her. 'Just these four widths.'

Ruth carefully cut six-inch strips from each of the rolls, put them in a small, white paper bag and handed it over.

'Thanks.' Jill put it in her handbag. 'Finlay Roberts and Carol – did they seem close, do you think? Could it be possible that they'd known each for a long time?'

'No,' Ruth scoffed. 'They hadn't met before. They were like a pair of school kids really. As Cass said, Carol was quiet and reserved normally, but he made her laugh. He was behaving like a clown. They were just having a bit of fun.'

Just having a bit of fun . . .

They were strangers, or so everyone believed. Carol had never met Finlay Roberts until he walked into her shop one day. So what took him there? Was it really that he needed flowers for his mother and his sister? Or did he have a more sinister motive?

Chapter Ten

DC Simpson didn't feel up to the job. It was his first week back at work after a holiday in Rhodes where he and four mates had tried to drink the island dry. It was his first week back in Harrington, too.

It wasn't his first encounter with DCI Trentham, though. In fact, Trentham was one of the reasons he'd requested a transfer to London three years ago. An ex-wife being the other reason.

The Green Man was opposite headquarters, and after a long day Johnny felt in need of a drink and a laugh with his new colleagues. What he wasn't in need of was Trentham's company. Johnny had read the local rag's shocking headline and he knew someone would come in for some stick from Trentham. He guessed he'd be top of Trentham's list, too.

Four years ago, he'd made an innocent enough comment to a reporter and Trentham had been furious . . .

'Sit down,' Trentham said now and, unable to think of a plausible excuse not to, Johnny sat. It didn't do to argue with Trentham.

These days, people said one couldn't wish for a better boss. It was even rumoured that he'd got a thing going with Jill Kennedy, the psychologist, but Johnny struggled to believe that. She was a looker, in a casual sort of way. She had a great bum and good legs. At least, he thought she had. He'd only seen her in jeans. She could have done a lot better for herself than Trentham, though . . .

The Green Man was enjoying a brisk trade, although

there were more standing outside than in. Those outside were smoking. A large television dominated the far corner of the room, but no one was looking at it and the volume was switched off. There was no music. For all that, it was noisy. Drinkers at the bar had to talk loudly to make themselves heard over the door that was constantly banging as smokers either went out for a smoke or returned.

'So, Johnny,' Trentham began, 'how does it feel to be back at Harrington?'

'It's good.' It could be a hell of a lot better, though.

'Tell me, why did you leave?'

Johnny took a swallow of beer. No way was he giving Trentham the satisfaction of thinking the transfer to London had been down to him.

'Divorce, sir,' he replied. 'My ex was giving me grief and I wanted out.'

'Ah. I didn't know that. I'm sorry. And did it work out in the end?'

Blimey, Trentham looked quite concerned.

'It did, sir. Thanks.'

'Good.'

Silence settled on them as Trentham watched a couple of officers flirting at the bar.

'You were suspended from duty for a while, weren't you?' Trentham said, switching his attention back to Johnny. 'Remind me what that was about.'

Like he didn't know.

Johnny decided that the best way to defend himself was to attack. 'I know what you're thinking, sir.'

'Oh? And what am I thinking, Johnny?' Trentham asked.

'You're thinking that someone on the team has been blabbing to the papers, and you're thinking it might have been me.'

'You're right. I'm thinking exactly that.'

'Well, it wasn't. Why the hell would I?'

'Why the hell would anyone?' Trentham countered.

He had a point. Why would someone speak to the press? What was there to be gained?

77

'I'm serious,' Trentham said as he didn't answer. 'Why would someone do that, Johnny?'

'I don't know.' It might be someone on the team who had a grudge against Trentham, he supposed but, as yet, he'd met no one who qualified. Unlike Johnny, everyone thought the sun shone out of Trentham's arse. 'It could be someone wanting to protect the killer. But probably not,' he added quickly, spotting the scoffing expression on Trentham's face. 'Or it could be the killer out for a bit of publicity. You know? Enjoying his moment of glory. If it was the killer, though, that would make you think that The Undertaker was still alive. I mean, if it's a copycat, he wouldn't want to give The Undertaker all the glory, would he?'

'Mm,' Trentham murmured.

'Or money,' Johnny ran on. 'Perhaps the paper offered a good sum for the story.'

Trentham shook his head in despair at that. 'To do that, they'd have to know there *was* a story.'

Trentham's phone rang, and Johnny quickly downed his pint. 'Time I was off, sir,' he said, getting to his feet. 'Unless there's anything else?'

'Yes, there is. Hang on a minute.' He hit the button to answer his phone.

Johnny gestured to his glass to indicate he was getting another, then thought he'd better point at Trentham's too. Bugger it. Now he had to buy the bloke a pint.

'Hiya,' Johnny heard him say. 'You're kidding me . . .'

When Johnny returned to their table with the drinks, Trentham was ending his call.

'Thanks,' he said, taking the drink from Johnny. 'OK, so what I want you to do is find out who talked to the local rag. OK? All that moron of an editor, Bill May, can say is that it was an anonymous phone message left when the offices were closed. Make some inquiries.'

'OK.' Did that mean Trentham believed him? 'Any suggestions, sir?'

Trentham thought for a moment. 'First off, all phone messages to the paper are taped. They're now claiming they can't find the tape. Find the damn thing. Talk to the girl who sorts out the messages. Talk to everyone on the paper's payroll. Check the phone records. Just do whatever it takes. And put plenty of pressure on Bill May. He'd sell his grandmother for a story.'

'Right, sir.'

Johnny was whistling when he finally left the pub. He'd soon get to the bottom of this. It was just what he needed, an opportunity to shine. His promotion was long overdue.

Chapter Eleven

Will Draper wasn't watching the television. He was vaguely aware that it was on, but he wasn't paying attention.

His daughter, Lisa, wasn't either. She was busy applying a bright blue colour to her chewed fingernails.

'Couldn't you find a more disgusting colour?' he asked, pulling a face.

'Oh, Dad.' Shaking her head, Lisa smiled that despairing smile of hers.

'Your dad showing his age again?' he guessed, and, still smiling, she nodded.

She was a good kid. Not so much a kid now, sadly. She was eighteen and had had a boyfriend for almost a year. Will was expecting to hear the sound of wedding bells or the patter of tiny feet any time soon. He hoped it was bells before feet, but you never knew these days.

Jason, her young man, wasn't the sharpest tool in the box, but he was OK.

In any case, Will thought, brightening, Lisa had a mind of her own. She might not even be thinking of settling down. He hoped that was the case. He'd miss her desperately, far more than he would let her know. She was a good daughter and they'd managed well enough since her mother, Eileen, had died. It was ten years since they'd buried Eileen, and Will often wondered where the time had gone. Lisa had been a shy, vulnerable eight-year-old then. Now, she was working in Superdrug and painting her nails blue.

'Dad,' she said, and Will thought he probably knew what was coming.

'Mm?'

'Why don't you go out tonight? Just down the pub or something? The older you get, the more lonely you'll be,' she went on, warming to her well-worn theme now. 'You need a woman in your life, someone special. Or, if not special, someone to go out with. Now, you won't meet women on a building site, will you? And you won't meet any stuck in front of the telly every night. You don't go anywhere,' she ended in despair.

She was right, of course. After Eileen died, he'd stayed at home. With an eight-year-old to look after, he'd had no choice. As Lisa had grown, the habit was ingrained. It was a habit Will was quite happy with too.

'And you think I'll meet someone at the pub?' he scoffed.

'You might.'

He wouldn't. In any case, he didn't want to meet anyone. He was happy as he was.

The news came on and he ambled into the kitchen to make a mug of tea. He liked to watch the news with a cuppa.

'Do you want a brew?' he called out.

'Sorry, Dad. I'll be late if I don't get a move on.'

When Will carried his tea back to the sitting room, Lisa was on tiptoe in front of the mirror, lipstick in hand, pouting at her reflection. She looked stunning, Will thought, somewhat wistfully.

He sat down with his mug of tea just as a woman's face vanished from the screen.

'Who was that?' he asked, his heart thumping against his ribcage. 'What've they been talking about, Lis?'

'The murder,' she told him. 'That woman who was murdered, yeah? Well, they reckon the bloke who did that was the same bloke who killed some others five years ago. That was one of the women he killed back then.'

'That chap Marshall?'

'That's him. Hey, you worked at the place he used to live, didn't you?' She grimaced. 'That was right spooky.' She grabbed her jacket and handbag. 'Must dash, Dad!'

81

A kiss on the cheek, a whiff of heady perfume, and she was gone.

Will's head was in a spin. He flicked through the other TV channels, but there was nothing. He was sweating, and in order to calm down, he took a series of slow, deep breaths.

It wasn't necessarily the woman from the video. If Lisa was right, the woman on the telly had been dead for five years. He'd only found that video a year ago. On the other hand, who was to say the video hadn't been five years old? And who was to say it hadn't belonged to that killer?

He felt sick now.

Even if it did belong to that madman, Will had done nothing wrong. He'd only found a few videos at a site he'd been working on and sold them on. Perhaps he should have gone to the police with them. But why would he have done that? The police wouldn't have been interested in a few porn videos and that's what Will had thought they were.

In truth, he'd been so pleased to get some extra cash for Lisa's driving lessons that he hadn't thought too much about them. They'd been labelled, he remembered. The titles had consisted of just one word – girls' names. One was 'Chloe'. Guessing they were porn videos, he'd taken the video player to the site the next day to check them out. He hadn't risked taking them home in case Lisa saw them.

Six of them had been working on some flats, but Will had had time to himself to view the videos.

The first one had shown a woman – maybe the woman he'd seen on TV, maybe not – being taunted with a knife. She'd been naked, standing with her hands tied behind her and her feet tied at the ankles. Someone wearing a black hood with eye-slits had been holding a knife to her face. First it was held against her lips, then it had been put against her ear. She'd been screaming for mercy. She'd pissed herself, Will remembered. Given the same circumstances, he'd have done the same. Then, the man had walked behind her and cut her throat.

Will hadn't had the stomach for it so he'd switched it off. The second video had been much the same from the few minutes he'd forced himself to watch.

He'd planned to throw them in the skip, but then that bloke had walked in on him. What was his name? Will couldn't remember. Some big shot architect. Whoever he was, he'd reckoned he knew someone who would pay good money for them.

'These aren't porn,' Will had told him, disgusted. 'They're sick!'

'You'd be surprised,' the bloke had said with a knowing wink. 'Leave it to me. Here, you have a couple of hundred quid for your trouble and I'll sell them to my friend. Forget you ever saw them.'

Will had pocketed the money and forgotten about them. Until now.

Now, he could hear the screams for mercy as clearly as if the women were in the room with him.

Chapter Twelve

It was just after two o'clock the following afternoon when DS Fletcher entered Max's study bearing two mugs of tea.

'Anything?' Max asked.

Fletch had been interviewing Roberts for the last two hours.

Fletch shook his head and handed Max a steaming mug. 'You OK, guv?'

'No, I'm not. Someone's making us look like bloody incompetents and, Christ knows, we're more than capable of doing that without outside interference.' He took a swig of tea. 'Thanks,' he added belatedly.

He got out of his chair, the mug cradled in his hands, and stood with his back to the window facing Fletch. 'What a bloody mess!'

God, his patience was being tried today. He'd felt sure they'd had a breakthrough with the ribbon samples Jill had brought in from Forget-me-nots, but no, they didn't match the length tied around Carol Blakely's waist. They weren't even the same shade of red.

'We're a bloody laughing stock,' he fumed.

'We'll get there in the end,' Fletch said.

Not at this rate they wouldn't. He took a swallow of his tea. 'So what about Roberts? Anything new at all?'

'We don't have much to go on, guv.'

'We've got sod all to go on, Fletch.'

'Yeah, but it is suspicious. He meets Carol Blakely twice, then she's dead. He buys red ribbon from her shop –'

'Not *the* red ribbon, though.' Max ran frustrated fingers through his hair. 'God knows.' He drained his cup. 'Let's have another go at him. Oh, and Fletch, don't let me forget parents' evening.'

'Tonight, is it?'

'It is. It'll be a complete waste of my time and theirs, but I promised I'd go.'

'You don't know that, guv. They're good kids. Bright, too.'

'That's what I always think until I see their teachers struggling to come up with something positive to say about them. Thank God Harry can play football . . .'

Roberts didn't look concerned to find himself sitting opposite Max again. Quite the reverse in fact. He was enjoying every minute of this. Jill had said he was a man who liked to be the centre of attention. What had she called him? Drop-dead gorgeous? The scruffy, unshaven look must be in, Max decided grimly. Roberts was wearing the oldest, tattiest pair of jeans imaginable. There were no holes in them, yet, but they were worn paper-thin. His T-shirt had once been red, but was now multicoloured with various stains.

'Right,' Max said, when the preliminaries had been dealt with, 'we're going to start from the beginning and, this time, I'd appreciate the truth. Tell me again about your relationship with Carol Blakely.'

'I've told you, my man, I saw her twice. No, make that four times in total. The first time, I went to her shop to buy flowers for my mother.'

'Who lives where?'

'She travels – the circus, you know – but she's currently in Devon,' Roberts replied easily. 'So I chose the sort of flowers I wanted, with Carol's help, and arranged for the same sort of thing to be delivered to my mother.'

'As far as I was aware,' Fletch put in, 'Carol Blakely didn't serve in her shop.'

'True,' Roberts said, grinning, 'but she walked in while I was dealing with the young girl and I asked for her opinion. It was the girl – young and blonde – who told me she owned the business.'

'Go on,' Max said.

'A week later, I went to the shop again to choose flowers for my sister. She'd just had a baby, which is why my mother was in Devon. She had a beautiful little girl.'

'Why choose that particular shop?' Max asked. 'You live in Kelton Bridge so why bother driving in to Harrington?'

'I didn't. I was already in Harrington, having a look round, when I remembered my dear old mum. The second time, for my sister's flowers, I drove there on purpose. I thought maybe Carol might be there again. She was. It was then that I asked her if she fancied a bite to eat that evening.'

'You work on the internet all day,' Max pointed out. 'Wouldn't it have been easier to click on the Interflora site that first time?'

'Of course it would,' Roberts agreed, legs stretched in front of him and feet crossed nonchalantly at the ankles. 'But as I said, I was already in Harrington when I remembered my mum. If I'd come home, I might have forgotten.'

'Perish the thought,' Max said drily. 'What was so interesting about Carol Blakely? Why did you want to take her out?'

He smiled at that, a slow, knowing smile. 'She was very easy on the eye. I enjoyed making her laugh. I'd rather have company than eat alone.'

'Yes, but why Mrs Blakely?'

'The main reason? I fancied her and wanted to get her into my bed.'

'Why are you staying in Kelton Bridge?' Max asked, changing tack.

'I remember coming to the area as a child and thought I'd come back.'

'From where?'

'Oh, around. I've had a month in the East Midlands, Derby to be precise, and before that, I was in London.' He smiled at Max, and it was a smile Max didn't like. 'I'm sure

86

my lovely neighbour, the gorgeous Jill, has already told you that.'

Smug bastard.

'Why Kelton Bridge? The nightlife in the village doesn't compare to Derby or London.'

Roberts laughed. 'Too true, but I fancied a change of pace. And hey, there aren't too many places to let for a three-month period.'

Max gazed back at him unsmiling.

'What did you buy from Mrs Blakely's shop?' Fletch asked.

Roberts's gaze didn't leave Max's face as he answered. 'Two bouquets of flowers. Correction. Two orders for bouquets to be Interflora'd. That was it.'

'You were dancing around the shop with a red rose between your teeth,' Fletch reminded him. 'Didn't you pay for that?'

'No. I put it back in the container.' He grinned at Max. 'You're not hoping to get me on a shoplifting charge, are you?'

'The red ribbon you tied in Carol Blakely's hair,' Max said, ignoring that. 'Did you pay for that?'

'As a matter of fact, I did.' The grin didn't waver. 'Carol wasn't sure how much it cost – as you say, she wasn't used to serving in the shop – so I bought the whole roll.'

'And threaded it through Mrs Blakely's hair,' Max murmured. 'How much of the roll did you use?'

Roberts spread out his hands to indicate a length of a couple of feet.

'What did you do with the rest of it?' Fletch asked.

'I shoved it in my pocket.' Roberts shrugged. 'I probably threw it away when I got home. To be honest, I really can't remember. It might still be there.'

'Perhaps you'd care to have a look for it,' Max suggested, adding a grim, 'when you get home.'

'I will if you think it will help.'

Max leaned back in his seat. He, too, could look relaxed when he chose. He wasn't relaxed, far from it. Nothing would give him greater pleasure than throttling Roberts with his bare hands.

'What did the two of you talk about on your dates?' he asked.

'Oh, the weather, her work, my work, her husband, my mother, my sister, her sisters, the food, Harrington, Kelton Bridge, the price of lamb, politics, music, films, books –'

'Fascinating,' Max murmured. 'What did she say about her husband?'

'I can't remember.'

'Try,' Max said, and it was an order, not a request.

Roberts let out his breath as if the effort of thinking was proving too great. 'When I asked about boyfriends – yes, I knew she was married, but a good-looking girl like that, well, it stood to reason – she told me her husband had put her off men for life.'

'Really? And why was that?'

'We were in Mario's in Bacup, and she said that she and her husband – Michael?'

'Vince,' Max reminded him.

'Ah, yes. Vince. My memory,' he said, shaking his head. 'She said they'd been there together and he'd caused a scene. He threatened her, I gather.'

'Why?'

'I don't know, but I got the impression he knocked her about a bit.'

'What did she say to give you that impression?'

'I don't remember.'

'Tell me again where you were on Friday the seventh of July and Saturday the eighth,' Max snapped, adding a sarcastic, 'if you can remember.'

Carol Blakely had been murdered, as close as they knew, between the hours of nine and midnight. Her body had then been taken to the quarry in the early hours of Saturday morning.

'I remember it well. I was at home.'

'All the time? Alone?'

'Yes.'

'Can anyone vouch for that?' Max asked.

'Hardly. Unless the Invisible Man dropped in for a drink.'

'Not even your lovely neighbour, the gorgeous Jill?'

'Nope. I did see her briefly when she got back from Liverpool, but before that, no.'

'So no one saw you on Friday night *or* Saturday morning?' Max asked doubtfully.

'I didn't see a living, breathing soul.'

Max needed a cigarette. And some air. He nodded at Fletch and terminated the interview.

'The smug bastard's doing my head in,' he told Fletch as he closed the door behind them. 'He can sit there and be smug on his own for an hour or so. Get us a brew, Fletch, while I nip outside for a smoke.'

'Still smoking then, guv?'

'Not really. I just fancied the odd one.'

While Max was standing in the car park, he watched, bemused, as a man drove a Vauxhall Corsa into the car park, stopped the car, looked at the building and then drove away again. Less than a minute later, he was back. This time, he looked at the building, killed the engine, got out of the car and stood for long moments looking at the main entrance.

There goes a man with a guilty conscience, Max thought, as he watched him mount the steps and enter the building.

Finlay Roberts, on the other hand, didn't appear to have a conscience. He was playing games with them. Max was certain he knew more than he was telling, but he was enjoying the diversion. Damn him.

Thinking of guilty consciences had him reaching into his pocket for a biro and scrawling PE on his hand. His kids probably wouldn't mind if he missed hearing how they were getting on, but a promise was a promise.

He tossed his cigarette butt across the car park and went back inside.

'Ah, this is Chief Inspector Trentham,' Norah, today's receptionist, announced.

Standing in front of her was the man with the guilty conscience.

'Did you want me?' Max asked.

'Mr Draper says he has information about the Carol Blakely murder,' Norah explained.

Max wasn't hopeful, but at least the chap didn't look like the usual crank.

'Come with me,' he said.

He took him to his office where Fletch was waiting with two cups of tea.

'Would you like a tea or a coffee?' Max asked.

The man shook his head. What he wanted, Max suspected, his curiosity aroused, was out of the building in the quickest time possible.

'This is DS Fletcher,' Max said, nodding at Fletch and grabbing his cup of tea. 'He's working on the case. Please, take a seat.'

The man sat on the edge of the seat, a thin line of perspiration on his top lip. He was about forty, Max supposed, with thinning hair.

'You have some information that might help in our investigation, Mr Draper?' Max asked, and he nodded.

'About a year ago,' he began, his voice shaking, 'I was working – oh, I'm a builder, by the way. I was working on this building in Paradise Way. It was half a dozen flats.'

Max's curiosity was definitely aroused now. Edward Marshall had lived in a flat on the imaginatively named Paradise Way.

'The flats were being knocked about and turned into office space. I was knocking an old chimney breast out when I found some video tapes.'

Max tried not to raise his hopes too high, but it was bloody difficult.

'In the chimney?'

Mr Draper nodded. 'They'd been hidden behind bricks. It hadn't been used for years because the flats had gas fires, and when I pulled the bricks away, I found these tapes.'

'What did you do with them?' Max knew, he just knew he wasn't about to receive a simple answer.

Mr Draper cleared his throat and kept his gaze firmly on the laces in his black shoes. 'They had names on the boxes,' he said quietly. 'One was Chloe, I remember. I assumed they were mucky videos. Porn, you know,' he said at last. 'I was curious,' he admitted. 'I've got a daughter, Lisa, so I wasn't going to take them home in case she saw them.'

Max was aware of Fletch fidgeting in his excitement.

'So what did you do with them?' Max asked for the second time.

'I took our telly in with me the next day,' he explained. 'It's one of those cheap, portable all-in-one things. My Lisa used to have it in her bedroom. Of course, it's all DVDs now, isn't it?'

'It is,' Max agreed.

'And anyway, they might not have been porn, might they? It seemed daft to throw them away without even looking at them.'

He was silent for so long that Max had to prompt him.

'Sorry,' he murmured, clearing his throat again. 'I was working on my own so, when I got to the flats, it was easy enough to rig up the telly and put one of the videos in.' His voice trailed away.

'And?' Max prompted again. 'Was it porn?'

'Some might call it that,' Mr Draper replied grimly. 'I could only stomach about two minutes of it. It was awful. I swear that no one with a daughter of their own could watch it. Naturally, I assumed –' He broke off and paused before continuing, 'I assumed the woman was an actress, but now, I'm not so sure.'

'Oh?'

'I couldn't see the person doing it to her because he was wearing a black leather hood, but she was naked, tied up, and someone was holding a knife to her.' He swallowed hard. 'Then it was against her neck. Here.' He drew a line across his neck with a shaking finger. 'Whoever it was cut her throat. I assumed it was all fake – a fake knife, a bit of clever camerawork, tomato sauce for blood – but it made me sick to my stomach. I couldn't eat for the rest of that day.'

'I can understand that.'

'I put another tape in the machine, just to see if it was more of the same,' he went on, 'and it was. It was disgusting. I can't explain it.'

'That's OK,' Max said. 'And what makes you think there's a connection to our murder inquiry?'

'I had the telly on last night,' he explained, 'and up flashed this picture of a woman, the woman from the tape. At least, I'm fairly sure it was her. So I asked Lisa, my daughter, you know, what they were talking about, and she said that the woman on the telly was one murdered by the same chap who did for Carol Blakely.'

'The videos,' Max said. 'What else was on them?'

'Dunno. As I said, I couldn't stomach it.'

Max hardly dared ask for the third time, but he had to. 'So what did you do with the tapes?'

'That's just it,' Mr Draper said. 'I was about to switch off the telly – the second tape was still running – when this bloke came in and asked what I'd got. Laughed, he did. I told him that I'd found them, but that they weren't porn – or not porn like people thought. He reckoned –' His voice dropped to a whisper. 'He reckoned he could sell them. Told me I'd be surprised who'd be interested in stuff like that.'

The room was heavy with silence for a moment. Or it would have been without the scratching of Fletch's pencil as it raced across the page.

'He gave me two hundred quid and told me to forget I'd ever seen them,' Mr Draper said at last. 'I suppose – well, it doesn't matter what I should have done, does it? I thought about the money, knew it would come in handy for my Lisa's driving lessons, and grabbed it.'

'That's OK,' Max said, smiling to help ease the man's conscience. 'So this man – who was he?'

'I don't know his name,' he replied. 'I don't think I ever heard it. I'm a brickie, so I just do as I'm told. He was in charge of the building works. When I say in charge, I mean he'd done all the plans. Some big shot architect chap.'

Oh, thank you, God! Max could have rubbed his hands together in glee.

'Anything else you can tell us?' he asked.

'No. That's about it. Sorry. But you'll be able to find out who he was. They'll have records, I mean. They'll know the architect who was in charge of the project.'

They certainly would.

'Here, this doesn't have to go in the papers, does it?' he asked anxiously. 'The thing is, I wouldn't want Lisa knowing that her dad had looked at – you know.'

'I know,' Max assured him, 'and no, this will be treated in the strictest confidence.' He got to his feet. 'Thank you for coming to see us, Mr Draper. We'll look into it.'

Mr Draper also got to his feet. 'Is that all?'

'For the moment. DS Fletcher will go over everything you've said and then ask you to sign –'

'Nothing I've said will get out, though, will it? I wouldn't want my Lisa seeing anything.'

'Don't worry, she won't.'

While Fletch dealt with Mr Draper, Max sought out Grace and asked her to look into the work done on Edward Marshall's old residence.

'Check that Vince Blakely was the architect involved,' he told her, 'and see how he came to get the job. See if it went out to tender, who was involved, anything. And get back to me pronto, OK?'

To celebrate what was turning into a very good day, Max was outside having a smoke when Fletch found him.

'Looks like we can nail Blakely then, guv,' Fletch said with satisfaction. 'Does that mean Roberts can go?'

Max had forgotten he was still waiting for them.

'No, leave him for a while.'

'Where's Jill today?' Fletch asked.

'At Chester Races, throwing money at old nags.' And Max would like nothing better than to greet her homecoming with news of an arrest . . .

When Grace caught up with them, Max could tell from her expression that this wasn't going to be as straightforward as he'd hoped.

'I can't find any link to Blakely, guv,' she said. 'The job was dealt with by a big firm of architects – Pullman's.'

Max knew of them. They had offices on The Boulevard.

'A chap called Ralph Atkins dealt with it,' she said, 'and there's no mention of Blakely at all.'

'There must be,' Fletch said. 'It's too much of a coincidence. Videos sold to an architect? A year later, an architect's wife ends up dead? Of course there's a connection.'

'There's a connection,' Max said firmly. 'There has to be.'

For the sake of his sanity, there had to be.

Chapter Thirteen

Ralph Atkins was taking a holiday from his architect's practice but, thankfully, he was taking it at home in Harrington.

As Fletch brought the car to a stop outside The Laurels, Max was surprised to see that Atkins's house had a rundown look to it. It was a traditional, stone-built detached house set on a corner plot. No doubt the prime location would add thousands to its value, but it needed work. The paintwork was peeling, several ridge tiles were missing, and the garden was an overgrown mass of neglect.

Perhaps he'd only recently moved in and was intending to use this holiday to have the necessary work done on it.

The occupant, when he finally opened the door, looked even more rundown, however. He was about fifty, and was wearing brown trousers, sandals, grey socks with holes, and a pale green, creased, grubby-looking shirt that was open at the neck to reveal pale skin.

'Ralph Atkins?' Max asked.

'Yes.' He seemed to blanch before them.

'DCI Trentham and DS Fletcher, Harrington CID.' Max showed his warrant. 'Could we ask you a few questions, please?'

'You'd better come in.'

They followed him into a kitchen where, on the table, a half-full bottle of vodka sat next to an almost empty glass. A newspaper was open.

'What's this about?' Atkins asked.

'We're investigating the murder of Mrs Carol Blakely,' Max explained, and he saw Atkins's bloodshot eyes widen at that. 'I'm sure you've heard about it?'

'Yes, but I don't see why you're here.'

'May we sit down?' Max asked.

'Er, yes. Sorry.' The bottle, glass and newspaper were picked up and moved to the top of the cooker. Max and Fletch sat on oak chairs at an oak table. It was the only decent thing in the room.

'Did you know Mrs Blakely?' Max asked.

'Me? Why should I?'

'She worked in Harrington. You work in Harrington. I was just curious if you knew her.'

'No. I know of her husband,' Atkins admitted, 'but not personally. I might, and I say might, recognize him if he walked in here. He's an architect, you know.'

'That's right. And you never met Carol Blakely?'

'No. I've told you. I don't think I ever spoke to her husband, either. If I did, it was only in passing.'

A large tortoiseshell cat ambled into the kitchen, looked at the visitors and ambled out again. Atkins didn't acknowledge it.

'A year ago, you worked on a conversion in Paradise Way, I believe,' Max said.

'Yes,' he answered slowly.

He had something to hide, Max was sure of it. His answers were too long in coming. They were carefully thought out.

'Old flats were being converted to highly sought-after office accommodation,' he added. 'Yes, I remember the job.'

'And do you also remember any of the men working on the project? The builders?'

'No. Why should I?'

'One of them says you bought some video tapes from him,' Max said.

'Um, oh, yes, I remember now.' He took a grubby red handkerchief from his trouser pocket and rubbed it around his nose. 'I wouldn't recognize him if he walked in here, either. Yes, he found some tapes in the back of one of the chimney breasts, I seem to recall.'

'And they were of interest to you?'

'Not really, no.'

Max felt as if he were knitting fog.

'So why did you buy them from the builder?'

Atkins thought for a few moments. 'I drink too much and I gamble heavily,' he said at last. 'Everyone has their vices and those are mine. Sadly, they're expensive vices. I thought I might find a buyer for the videos, that's all. I slipped the brickie a couple of quid –'

'A couple of hundred?' Fletch put in.

'Was it as much as that? I really can't remember. Anyway, when I had a good look at them, I realized they weren't what I thought they were.'

'And what did you think they were?' Max asked.

'The brickie reckoned they were porn. I assumed he was right, and that they were amateur stuff.'

'And were they?'

'It was certainly amateurish. The bit I saw with – with the builder – had a woman, um, urinating. Lots of blokes get turned on by that. But these –' He cleared his throat. 'These were, um, a bit brutal, I seem to recall. As I said, I can't really remember. They certainly weren't anything I could sell. They were – specialist.'

'Specialist? In what way?'

'Well, they showed women being – threatened.'

'So you didn't sell them?'

'No. I realized my mistake, called myself all sorts of a fool, and got rid of them.'

'What I can't understand,' Max said carefully, 'is that you didn't think of the former occupant of the premises. As I recall, the newspapers were very interested in the work going on at the old home of Edward Marshall – The Undertaker.'

'Edward –' He cleared his throat. 'Ah, yes, now you come to mention it, I do remember that. But no, at the time it didn't cross my mind. It was just a job.'

'Really? So how did you dispose of the tapes?'

'I really can't remember. I imagine I either threw them in my bin here or chucked them in the bins at the back of the office. Probably there. The office had a couple of huge bins and they were emptied regularly. These at home are only emptied once a fortnight now.'

Max didn't believe him. 'Can you think back and try to remember?'

The effort required was obviously too great without sustenance. Atkins stood up, topped up his glass, and sat down again. He took a long, deep swallow of neat vodka. Max could do with a drink himself.

'I honestly don't remember,' he said. 'Is it important?'

'It could be, yes.'

'In what way?'

'We believe,' Max said as if he were addressing a halfwit, 'that they belonged to the previous occupant of the flat, Edward Marshall.'

'Oh, I see. I'm sorry, but I didn't think. I didn't make the connection.'

He was lying. Atkins knew damn well that those tapes had shown the murder of Marshall's four victims. Max would stake his life on that.

'Tell me what you remember about the tapes,' he said. 'Anything at all. The content, the people featured, the labels on them – anything.'

'Handwritten labels,' he said. 'I do remember that. It made me think they'd be poor quality copies. I'd seen a few seconds when the brickie was watching them, and they looked OK, but you can never be sure. But no, they were OK. Amateurish, as I said, but not bad.'

'Were they colour or black and white?' Fletch put in.

'Colour,' he answered as if he were speaking to a five-year-old.

The more they questioned him, the more he drank. And the more he drank, the less he could remember. Not that he was admitting to remembering much to start with.

'What a strange bloke,' Fletch said when they were outside and walking back to the car.

'Mm.'

Fletch was fastening his seatbelt. 'Did you believe him then?' he asked, nodding back at Atkins's house.

'Nope. Did you?'

'I didn't. No.'

Max stared back at the house from the passenger seat. The tortoiseshell cat was sitting in the window staring back at him.

'I want to know every move Atkins made during the last year,' Max said. 'He's hiding something, I'm sure of it.'

'Guv?'

'Yes?'

'Have you forgotten something?'

'What?'

Fletch grinned at him. 'Parents' evening.'

'Oh, hell.' Max glanced at the clock on the dash. 'It's OK, there's still time.' Just. 'Drop me off at the school, will you, Fletch?'

Chapter Fourteen

Ralph watched the policemen leave. What were their names? He couldn't remember. He'd been so shocked, so caught on the hop, that he couldn't remember a word he'd said, either. Breathing a short-lived sigh of relief as their car drove away, he returned to the kitchen and his bottle. He took a deep slug from it and slumped down at the table.

'Tomorrow,' he vowed, staring at the near-empty bottle, 'that's it. No more drink! No more. Teetotal, for me. No drinking, no gambling and no trouble.'

Calming down slightly, he remembered that he had nothing to fear from the police. He'd found some videos and passed them on. That was all. That wasn't a crime.

He took another slug from the bottle.

His hands were shaking and, for once, he couldn't attribute it to the alcohol. He might have nothing to fear, but those coppers had scared the shit out of him.

But he hadn't done anything wrong. Nothing wrong. He kept repeating that. Nothing wrong.

The stupid thing was, he'd been expecting them. Ever since he'd seen that headline in the local paper – *Undertaker still alive* – he'd lived in dread of the coppers coming to his door. He'd known that stupid brickie would talk.

The fact that they were working on Paradise Way had made headlines in the local paper at the time. To sell copies, reporters had even suggested that, as it was the last home of the notorious Undertaker, they might find dead bodies under the floorboards.

That brickie must have been the only bloke on the planet who hadn't realized what the videos were. But to be fair, not that Ralph felt in a fair mood, they could have been amateur porn, just as the brickie, and even Ralph at first, had assumed. He'd watched them for as long as five minutes before he'd understood what they'd stumbled across. Ralph had thought he'd found gold.

'Deluded, drunken fool,' he scoffed.

At the time, it had all seemed so easy. He'd known a man who was noted for two things; finding buyers for anything and everything, and not caring a jot for the law. He'd known *of* him, at least. Katherine had spoken of him so often Ralph had felt as if he'd known the man personally.

Katherine hadn't seen him or had contact with him for more than twenty years, but it had been easy enough to track him down.

As Katherine had been so ill at the time, he hadn't wanted to worry her with details. Instead, he'd told her that he'd found an old piece of silver that he wanted him to sell . . .

So he'd arranged a meeting.

Funny, thinking back, that Ralph hadn't taken to him at all. Over the years, Katherine had spoken of the man's exploits with great affection. 'No police record, of course,' she'd assured him. 'He works on the right side of the law.'

Ralph had taken an instant dislike to him.

He hadn't liked handing over those video tapes to someone he now thought of as a stranger, either.

'It'll take a while, but I'll get a good price for you. Forty per cent for me, you said?'

'I said twenty,' Ralph retorted. However, knowing that left to his own devices he wouldn't have had a clue where to even start looking for a buyer, he'd relented. 'OK. Forty per cent. If the price is right.'

'I'll start putting out a few feelers,' he'd said.

That was twelve months ago.

'It's very delicate material,' Ralph had been told.

Of course it was bloody delicate. That's why Ralph had sought him out in the first place.

'I can't put them on eBay, can I?' he'd been told six months ago.

'Have patience,' the month after that.

Then, Ralph had seen the headline in the local paper – *Undertaker still alive* – and he had known.

Ralph opened another bottle of vodka. What the hell?

An hour later, practically incoherent with rage, he tapped out a number on his phone.

'Yes?'

'You idiot,' Ralph slurred. 'I knew it was you. As soon as I saw the headline in the paper – as soon as I knew the coppers thought he was still alive – I knew what you'd done. You stupid fucking idiot!'

'Still drinking then, Ralph?'

'You won't get away with it. The coppers have been to see me today. The brickie who found the videos talked. I knew he would. You won't get away with it!'

'What did you tell them?'

'I didn't tell them anything,' Ralph snapped. 'What do you think I am, stupid?'

'Let's hope not, Ralph, for your sake.'

'I said nothing,' he insisted, 'but they'll be back. You can bet your life on that.'

'I fear you're right, Ralph.'

The connection went dead.

'Fucking stupid idiot,' Ralph fumed, reaching for his glass.

Chapter Fifteen

'You'll never guess what!'

Jill had to smile. The majority of calls from her mother started with those words. Guessing the call would be a long one, she carried the phone outside, hoping the signal would be good enough to allow her to sit and enjoy the late evening sunshine.

'Then I won't even try,' she replied.

'All hell's broken loose,' her mum went on. 'You know the Archers from number eighteen?'

She did. It was so many years since she'd left River View estate that she'd forgotten most of the residents, but the Archers were one of the more memorable families and, over the years, she had heard all about them.

'Both ginger-haired? Five or six kids, all ginger, except a boy called . . .' She racked her brains but couldn't remember the lad's name.

'Lennox,' her mum supplied. 'Lennox, I ask you. What sort of name's that?'

'Quite a popular one.'

'If you say so. Anyway, Lennox was in a car accident at the weekend – only seventeen he is, and drives like a lunatic. He's passed his test, so he's legal, which is more than can be said for most round here, but even so.'

'Is he all right?' Jill asked, swatting at a fly with her hand.

'He's out of danger, apparently. Now, I don't know how it happened, something to do with a blood test, I imagine, but it turns out that Trevor, that's the dad, isn't the lad's real dad at all.'

'That explains the dark hair then,' Jill remarked with amusement.

'It does. Anyway, there was an almighty bust-up. Trevor got drunk and laid into Maria – they were out in the road shouting and throwing things at each other. Jim Courtney dragged Trevor away and took him off down the pub. So while he was there, Maria cut up his clothes and threw them out of the bedroom window. All his fishing stuff was smashed and thrown out. You should have seen their front lawn. It was like a bomb site. Then, when Trevor gets home, he can't get in, can he? She's barricaded herself in. In the end, he smashed a window and got in.'

Jill had spent the first eighteen years of her life on the estate and could picture the scene all too easily.

'But that's not the best of it,' her mum went on, enjoying every moment of this. 'It turns out that Lennox's dad is none other than Fred Appleby. Can you believe that?'

'Who's Fred Appleby?'

'Oh, Jill.' Despair crept into her mother's voice. 'Chap with dark curly hair who used to run the pub.'

'Ah, got him. Permed hair, we used to reckon.'

'That's him. Married four times and a kid from each marriage. Mind, he's worth a few bob now.'

Jill let her run on with the gossip from the estate and tried to be interested. If not exactly interesting, the happenings on River View usually provided good entertainment.

'I'd better go,' her mum said at last. 'I had another go at our Prue's cheesecake recipe this morning and it's a disaster. I want to try and rescue it.'

'Really?' Jill had to smile.

'I've used exactly the same ingredients as Prue, I've even used the same dish – a disaster. Why is it that two people can use exactly the same ingredients, the same utensils, do exactly the same things and end up with completely different results?'

'It's no good asking me, Mum. You know what my culinary skills are like.'

'True. Thank God for Tesco, eh? Right, I'm off – oh, here's your dad. I'll speak to you soon, love.'

'Bye, Mum.' Jill listened as they bickered affectionately between themselves for a minute, and then her father came on the line.

'Well?' he asked. 'How was Chester?'

'Expensive,' she told him, laughing.

'No winners?'

'One, but it was favourite so it didn't help much. Ah, well. Some you win, some you lose.' What did it matter? She wouldn't starve, the sun was shining, and she and her friends had had a few laughs during the day. 'What about the Archers then, Dad?' she asked with a chuckle. 'I bet River View resembles Beirut at the moment.'

'Daft sods,' he said. 'Trevor must be mental to have thought that young Lennox was his in the first place. Not only is he better looking than those ginger buggers, he's a foot taller and he's clever. The lad's got more brains than the rest of the family put together. Mind you, that three-legged cat that comes round here's got more brains than the entire Archer family. Still,' he went on, brightening, 'it all makes for good entertainment. Who needs *Coronation Street* when we've got this lot on our doorstep?'

That was true enough.

'The coppers have been back and forth,' he said, chuckling. 'This place must keep 'em in domestics.'

She smiled at that.

'That reminds me,' he said. 'I saw your Max on the telly last night.'

'Oh?' For once, she forgot to point out that he wasn't *her* Max. 'What was that about? This murder case?'

'Yeah. He didn't say a lot – just that they were following several leads and would anyone with information please come forward. Just the usual.' He paused. 'That killer – you know, the one they called The Undertaker – he's not still alive, is he?'

'No. He's like the proverbial dodo.' At least, she hoped he was. No, she was sure of it.

'That's good then,' her dad said, breathing a sigh of relief. 'I'd hate to think of you getting caught up with someone like that. You are helping out, I hear.'

'I don't start work officially until a week on Monday, but yes, I'm looking into it. Don't worry about Eddie Marshall, though. He's dead.'

She didn't like to point out that this maniac could be just as dangerous. Still, she didn't think so. Carol Blakely was a one-off. Someone had wanted her out of the way. There would be no other murders.

'So how is Max?' her dad asked, brightening.

'He's fine.' That was her stock answer. When they decided to live together again – The thought brought her up short. It was the first time she'd thought 'when' rather than 'if'. Nevertheless, until then, there was no need for her mother to dash out and buy her wedding outfit . . .

An hour after she ended the call with her parents, the man himself called at her cottage.

'Hi,' he said, bending to drop a kiss on her forehead. 'Good day at the races?'

'So-so.' No need to tell him that she'd lost a small fortune. 'How about you? How was your day?' She stood up and headed towards the kitchen. His stopping for coffee was a habit they'd somehow fallen into. She'd been expecting him. Waiting for him even.

'Frustrating,' he answered. 'Finlay Roberts is hiding something, but I'm damned if I know what.'

'Are they sure about the ribbon?'

'Yep. The ribbon you brought from the shop definitely isn't the same as that tied around Carol Blakely's waist. It isn't even the same colour.'

In a way, Jill was pleased. All day, she had expected to arrive home and find that her neighbour had been hauled off to a cell on a murder charge. It had been a relief to see him strolling along the lane when she'd pulled into her drive.

'Then I thought we'd had a breakthrough,' Max went on. 'A builder, chap called Will Draper, came in and told us how he'd found some videos when working on Eddie Marshall's old home. The flats were turned into offices. He told us that someone offered him a couple of hundred quid for the videos – thought they were porn. The bloke who took them off his hands was the architect in charge of the project.'

'Blakely!'

'That's what I thought, but no, we can't find a link. This chap is a Ralph Atkins who claims he threw them in the bins at the back of his office.'

'There has to be a connection with Vince Blakely,' she said, pouring two coffees from the pot. 'It's too much of a coincidence.'

'You'd like to think so,' Max agreed on a sigh.

'There has to be. Inside or out?' she asked, nodding at the coffee.

'Oh, out.' Max was hardly out the door before he was hunting in his pockets for cigarettes and lighter.

'Hey, this must be a serious relapse,' she said lightly. 'You've given up on the matches and bought a lighter.'

'It's not even a relapse,' he said as he lit it. 'I simply felt –'

'Like buying a packet. I know.'

The sun was sinking rapidly and the air took on a chill. Max didn't seem to notice. He smoked three more cigarettes as he updated her.

'This centres round Carol Blakely,' she said, voicing her thoughts aloud as much as talking to Max. 'The killer, whoever he is, must have got hold of those tapes. He's trying to make us think it's the work of The Undertaker, that it's a random killing, the work of a serial killer.'

'If Atkins is telling the truth – and no, I didn't believe a word he said – but if, as he claims, he threw them in the bins, how would anyone know that the videos were the work of The Undertaker?' Max mused.

Jill had no idea.

'The builder, Will Draper,' he went on, 'said he didn't have the stomach to watch them. Ralph Atkins said they were specialist. Assuming he did throw them away, who the hell would find stuff like that and decide it was the work of The Undertaker?'

'Perhaps they didn't. Perhaps the killer found the tapes and thought to mimic the videos. Perhaps he thought they were actresses. Perhaps he thought it was so good he'd do it all for real.'

'Maybe.' Max flicked a cigarette butt into the hedge, making Jill vow to find a heavy ashtray for outside use. 'When we got the ribbon, I thought we could arrest Finlay Roberts. When I heard the videos had been sold to an architect, I thought we could arrest Vince Blakely.' He gave a rueful smile. 'Now I find myself with no one to arrest.' He downed his coffee. 'So that's my day. A complete waste of time.'

Better than Jill's. Hers had been a complete waste of time *and* money.

'Oh, and I called at the school for an enlightening chat with Harry and Ben's teachers,' he added. 'Parents' evening,' he explained, seeing her frown. 'It seems that Ben is content to dream his life away and Harry – let's just say that Harry's sporting achievements outweigh any academic ones.'

'Perhaps he'll be another David Beckham,' Jill grinned. 'And Ben can train animals for the Hollywood block-busters. Sorted. They'll be worth millions.'

'Yeah, yeah. I do need to see them and have a chat,' he said. 'How do you fancy coming back with me? They haven't seen you for ages.'

'Yes, OK. I'll follow you. I want to see Kate anyway. You go ahead, and I'll follow on when I've fed the cats and locked up here.'

'Why not come with me? You can stay the night with us and I'll drive you back in the morning.'

It was tempting, but she didn't want the boys to get used to her being at the house until things were settled, and they certainly wouldn't be settled while Max was investigating Carol Blakely's murder.

'Thanks, but I've got things to do here later. Some other time . . .'

Jill left the cottage twenty minutes after Max did and, as she drove past Kelton Manor, she saw Andy Collins's car parked outside. Andy's firm was selling the manor and she wondered if he was showing people round.

She stopped the car and sat gazing at the outside of the building. It really was beautiful. She'd only been inside it half a dozen times, but she'd fallen in love with it. Just as she put her car into gear, Andy came out of the front door and began locking up. Jill switched off the engine and got out for a chat.

'Hi, Jill.' He nodded back at the manor. 'Are you a prospective purchaser?'

'I wish.'

'You'd be surprised,' he said. 'It needs a hell of a lot doing to it. I'm amazed that Gordon and Mary let it get so bad. It makes you wonder if they were a bit strapped for cash.'

Jill couldn't believe that.

'What does it need doing to it?' she asked curiously.

'New floors, new doors and windows. The central heating looks as if Noah put it in and the whole place needs rewiring. It's a death trap.'

'Really?'

The keys dangled between his fingers. 'Would you like a quick look? And it will have to be quick because I'm due in Haslingden in twenty minutes.'

'I'd love one!'

The first thing Jill noticed as they stepped inside was a damp smell. Whenever she'd been inside before, it had been for parties that Mary had organized. Thinking about it, though, there hadn't been many of those over the last couple of years. Even so, the house had been warm and cosy. Shabby, perhaps, but cosy.

Andy gave her a whirlwind tour and Jill was amazed to see how much work was required. It would, however, be possible to move in and have work done as and when . . .

'How much do you think it will go for, Andy?'

'Who knows? Auctions are unpredictable. There's a reserve of five hundred grand on it, but –'

'Five hundred? Is that all?'

'That's the reserve.' He shrugged. 'Who knows? Auctions are unpredictable.'

If all went according to plan, Jill would be in Spain when the auction was held so she'd miss it. Not that she was seriously considering – no, of course she wasn't. She couldn't afford it.

Andy glanced at his watch.

'You've got to go,' Jill said. 'Thanks, Andy. I appreciate it. It really is a gorgeous place.'

'I do have to dash off. If you want another look round sometime, give me a ring.'

'I might just do that.'

Andy jumped in his car and drove off, but Jill stood gazing at the building for a few minutes. It was sure to do well at auction. A lot of people would see it as an investment, whereas what it really needed was a family. It was a house that needed to be filled with fun and laughter.

Shaking her head at her thoughts, she got in her car and drove off.

Given the delay, she had expected to arrive half an hour after Max but, just as she got out of her car, he pulled up behind her.

'Did you take the scenic route?' she asked him.

'I stopped off for a pint at the Red Lion,' he explained, 'to see if that moron of a newspaper editor, Bill May, was there. Luckily for him, he wasn't.'

They went inside, straight to the sitting room. The two dogs, Holly and Fly, greeted Max as if he'd been absent for a decade instead of a day, and Harry and Ben both had hugs for Jill.

Pandemonium always reigned in Max's house, but this evening, it was more subdued. There was something –

'Who the hell is that?' Max demanded as they both spotted the stranger.

'Muffet,' Ben said quietly.

'Muffet? Who in hell's name calls a dog Muffet?' Max didn't bother to wait for a reply. 'Where's his owner?'

'Well . . .' Ben began.

Max groaned. 'I don't believe this is happening. Harry, get me a drink. A large whisky. A very large whisky.'

Harry looked relieved to have an excuse to escape to the kitchen.

'Right, Ben,' Max said, 'let's hear it. I've heard so much cock and bull today that another five minutes won't matter.'

'After school tonight,' Ben said, 'me and Harry went –'

'Harry and I,' Max said automatically, and then shook his head as if he couldn't believe he was thinking grammar at such a time. 'You went where?'

'We went to the animal sanctuary because I wanted to take them the photos of Fly and tell them how well he was doing in his obedience classes,' Ben explained. 'We had a look round –'

Max groaned again. 'Why? You know perfectly well that the place is full of unwanted dogs.'

'We only wanted a look,' Ben said urgently, and Jill knew a huge desire to hug the lad to death. He was kind, gentle, loving and he would die for the black dog that was currently hanging on his every word.

'And you saw this dog, right?' Max prompted.

'Yes. He'd been there for three months,' Ben explained. 'People didn't want him because he's old. They only want to take the puppies and young dogs.'

Max looked at the dog. Mostly collie, the animal was black except for a splash of white on his chest and a very grey muzzle.

'How old?' Max asked.

'Ten.'

Harry returned with a glass of whisky which, without even glancing at the dog, he handed to Max.

'Thank you.' Max took a sip, clearly found it to his liking, and returned his attention to poor Ben. 'So, knowing that we already have two dogs and couldn't possibly home a third, what did you do next?'

'Well ...' This was obviously the tricky part. Ben scratched his head, just as his father sometimes did. 'I thought that, as we already had two dogs, another wouldn't make much difference. And it had been raining so his paws were all wet.' He looked up at Max, his blue eyes like saucers. 'He's old, Dad, and no one wanted him.'

What else was there to be said? Ben had said enough to bring tears to Jill's eyes. Max, she noticed, had a particularly tender expression on his face, too.

Muffet, deciding that perhaps he was safe for the moment, sidled up to Ben and rested a shaggy head against the lad's knee. Ben absently stroked his ears.

'He's only here on a weekend trial,' he explained, 'so we can take him back on Monday if he doesn't like it, or if Holly and Fly don't get on with him.'

'I see,' Max murmured.

'But he does like it,' Ben put in quickly, in case his father thought taking him back really was an option, 'and they do get on well.'

'Hm.' Max thought of something else. 'Where's Nan, anyway?'

'She's just gone to look for something,' Ben explained. 'She'll be back in a minute. So can Muffet stay with us, Dad?'

Max looked at the dog, then he looked at Ben, then he looked at Jill and the expression on his face had her suppressing a giggle.

'Do I have any say in anything that happens around here?' he demanded at last. 'He can, but you're banned from setting foot in that blasted animal sanctuary ever again. OK?'

'Wow. Yeah.' Ben threw his arms round the dog, then grabbed Fly so that he had a dog in each arm.

'Second thoughts, go back there tomorrow and see if they've got the odd giraffe or zebra kicking around. We could open this place to the public and charge an admission fee.'

'Great idea, Dad,' Ben said, grinning cheekily. 'Can I go and tell Nan?'

'Scram!'

Both boys raced off with Fly and Muffet in pursuit.

'You see what I have to put up with?' Max said, still struggling to believe what had happened.

Jill spluttered with laughter. 'If only the hardened criminals could see you being manipulated by a kid.'

'I wasn't manipulated, I was – well, what could I have said? And I bet he lied about the dog's age.'

'He's adorable.'

'Maybe, but I bet he's younger than ten.'

'I was talking about Ben,' she informed him, 'but yes, the dog's cute, too. Old, unloved, unwanted – aw, it melts your heart, doesn't it? And those wet paws . . .'

'Huh!'

Other than the dogs' toys scattered all over the place, Max's house was just as it had been when she'd lived with him. They sat in the lounge, and it felt like home. This is how it had been, she thought. After a day's work, they would sit in this room, discussing some case or other. This is how it could be again, an inner voice reminded her.

Kate arrived then, with boys and dogs in tow and, for a while, everyone was trying to talk at once. The thought of returning to a cottage with only her cats for company wasn't appealing.

Finally, however, Ben and Harry went to bed. Ben was planning to sleep with Fly *and* Muffet on his bed.

'Rather him than me,' Max said with amusement.

'He's a very well-behaved dog,' Kate pointed out. 'He must have come from a good, loving home. Of course, we don't know his history, only that his owner had to go into rented accommodation.'

'He is good considering it's all strange for him,' Max allowed.

'Now then,' Kate said briskly, 'I haven't mentioned anything to the boys yet, but I've decided to give Spain a miss. I'll stay here and look after the dogs instead. As Muffet's new, I can help him settle in. I can nip over and see your cats, too, Jill. I know Louise is going to feed them, but they might like the extra company.'

Jill stared back at her in amazement and had to silently repeat Kate's words. 'You're not coming?'

'Not this time, no.'

'Why?' Max wanted to know. He frowned at her. 'You're not ill, are you?'

'For heaven's sake, Max,' Kate scoffed, on a burst of laughter. 'Of course I'm not ill. Far from it, I feel exceptionally fit for my age. I've loads to do here and exercising three dogs will take up all my time.'

'But why?' Jill asked.

'Because I've got plenty to do here,' Kate said in a tone that indicated she wasn't prepared to argue. 'Besides, you're both perfectly capable of keeping an eye on two boys. Not that they need much of an eye keeping on them. They're sensible kids. Maybe next year,' she finished, rising to her feet. 'Right, I need to get back. I'll see you soon, Jill. Goodnight, both.'

The door closed quietly behind her.

'I need another drink,' Max said. 'Can I get you anything?'

She hesitated.

'Leave your car here and stay the night,' he suggested.

It was tempting. 'Thanks, but I'd better not.'

When Max returned, he took his house keys from his pocket and jangled them in the air. 'Every time I use these, I feel as if I've entered the twilight zone. There are dogs everywhere, my sons can twist me round their little fingers and now, to cap it all, my mother-in-law's gone mad. What the devil was all that about?'

'I don't know,' Jill said carefully, 'but I think she wants –'

'Ah!' Max clapped a hand against his forehead as understanding dawned. 'Of course. She believes that, without her tagging along playing gooseberry, it'll be easier for me to convince you to marry me so that we can all live happily ever after.'

'That's about it, yes,' Jill agreed, lips twitching.

'The trouble is,' he said slowly, 'that without her there to watch the boys, we won't get time alone.'

'I expect we'll manage.' It had been knowing that Kate was going that had made Jill accept the invitation. Now, strangely, she found she wasn't disappointed in the least.

That's if they got to Spain . . .

'Right,' she said briskly, putting her mind to more important matters. 'Let me get a pen. We need to think of all we know about Vince Blakely.'

Chapter Sixteen

Still half asleep, Max reached out to silence the alarm, but it wasn't the alarm. It was his phone. He managed to focus on the clock and was surprised to see that it read 5.04 a.m. He'd thought it much earlier. He didn't feel as if he'd been asleep more than five minutes.

'Yes?'

'Sorry, did I wake you?'

'Of course you woke me, Fletch. It's the middle of the sodding night.'

'Sorry, guv, but I thought you ought to know. Fire crews were called out to Ralph Atkins's place just after two o'clock this morning.'

Max was awake and stumbling out of bed. 'His house or the office?'

'His house. A neighbour raised the alarm. It's a bad one, too.'

'How bad?'

'Well, if he was inside, there isn't going to be much left of him.'

'Bloody hell!' Max grabbed his jeans from the back of the chair. 'I'm on my way.'

Muttering enough expletives to keep the boys in luxury for months, Max dressed, left a note for Harry and Ben, grabbed his car keys and headed for The Laurels.

As he drove, he phoned Kate. Typically, his mother-in-law was already out of bed and enjoying breakfast.

'Don't worry, love. I'll be there for them,' she told him.

She always was and, yet again, Max thought how lucky they were to have her.

At least it was light so it didn't feel like the middle of the night. It always surprised Max that there was so much traffic about at such an early hour. On a Saturday, too.

Perhaps the fact that Atkins's house caught fire less than twenty-four hours after Max had questioned him was nothing more than a coincidence. Did he smoke? Max couldn't remember seeing any ashtrays or packets of cigarettes about. He drank heavily, though. He could have left something on the cooker perhaps.

Max thought it unlikely. It was too much of a coincidence and Max didn't like coincidences. He'd bet his life they were looking at arson.

When he arrived, Fletch was already there and was talking to a crowd of neighbours who had gathered as close as possible. Fletch spotted him and strode over.

'Well?' Max demanded. 'Was he in there?'

'No one can get in yet, guv.'

Max wasn't surprised. The house was a blackened mess. A couple of windows had gone and the roof didn't look safe.

'Is the fire investigator on his way?' he asked.

'Ms Kemp is on *her* way. Yes.'

Max groaned. He and Sheila Kemp had never seen eye to eye. That she was good at her job, Max didn't doubt, but she followed the book to the letter. With her in charge, it would be days before they were any the wiser.

The woman herself arrived in her car and Max wandered over.

'Max,' she greeted him coolly.

'We're looking at arson,' Max informed her, not bothering with the niceties, 'and I'm in charge of the murder investigation. We need –'

'Chief Inspector,' she cut him off, 'I don't have time to waste on idle speculation. I have a job to do. And as you're aware, I always approach these situations with an open mind. Now, if you'll excuse me, I'd like to get on with that job.'

She reached into the back of her car for hat and jacket, then headed towards the fire crew.

'Bloody woman,' Max cursed beneath his breath.

He stared at what was left of Atkins's house. It would have had gallon upon gallon of water pumped into it, and every one would have destroyed a bit more evidence.

Max found Fletch again. 'Anyone see anything?'

'The chap who phoned the fire service is over there.' He pointed to an elderly man wearing a thick blue anorak. 'Apparently, his cat woke him up and when he glanced out of the window, he saw flames coming from the downstairs window. The lady, the one with the baby in her arms, says that Atkins smoked cigars. She serves in the corner shop and he buys ten cigars a week. He was pissed when we saw him, guv, so if he'd been smoking one of those and fallen asleep or something . . .'

'Mm.' Max wasn't convinced. 'We need to know if he went anywhere after we talked to him, if he had any visitors, if he made any phone calls.'

Max hated arson. Hated it. All evidence was lost before the investigation even started. But that was life, he supposed. The fire fighters had to do all that was necessary to save lives and protect property.

Fire was too easy for the criminals, though. Murder, burglaries – all were a lot easier to get away with when fire was involved.

Looking on the bright side, he knew that enough evidence would still exist. Once they'd found the seat of the fire, and if they could find out what sort of accelerant had been used, they would find their man.

And if they found their man, Max suspected that they would find the killer of Carol Blakely.

He'd known Atkins had been lying about those videos. So what in hell's name had he done with them? Or had he kept them for himself? Was he the person responsible for trying to make them think The Undertaker was still alive? No, surely not.

Of course, it was possible that Atkins had started the fire

with the careless drop of a still-lit cigar. He could, as Fletch had suggested, have simply fallen asleep. That way, he would have been overcome by smoke long before flames were seen from the lounge window.

Had someone heard they'd been to see Atkins? Had Atkins told someone? Had that someone decided to silence him for good?

Looking on the bright side, it was possible that, any minute now, Ralph Atkins would stroll around the corner and see what was left of his home but, somehow, Max doubted it.

Chapter Seventeen

'He's well sexy, isn't he?'

'Oh, well sexy!' Jill agreed with a surprised laugh.

She was hunting for a parking space at the Trafford Centre, ready for a gruelling day round the shops. They'd been discussing Max. At least, Nikki had.

'I wouldn't mind a fortnight in the sun with him myself,' Nikki added.

'And you young enough to be his daughter,' Jill tutted with amusement.

It was hard to equate this young girl with the person who tried her mother's patience to the limit. Young girl? That was the crux of the problem; she was no longer a trying teenager, she was an adult.

Jill felt like pointing out that, as far as her mum was concerned, Charlie was 'well sexy', too. Later, assuming the day went well, she would venture on to the subject of Louise and Charlie. The last thing she wanted was a day with a moody, angry Nikki.

Earlier, when Jill had collected Nikki from her house, Nikki had given her mum a quick kiss, said 'Behave yourself!' with a cheeky laugh, and skipped down the path to Jill's car.

'Jekyll and Hyde,' Jill had said with a shrug, and Louise had smiled weakly.

'Thanks for this, Jill. You wouldn't believe how much I've longed to have the house to myself for the day.'

'It's nothing. Enjoy it. And forget housework. Have a day of unbridled passion with Charlie.'

Louise had laughed at that. 'I'm too worn out for un-bridled passion . . .'

On the journey to Manchester, Nikki hadn't stopped talking. Although wary, Jill was enjoying her company. She was also pleased to know that Louise was having a break. No doubt Nikki wouldn't be so well behaved with her mother there.

'Not that I'd want to go out with a copper,' she was say-ing now. 'Too Goody Two-Shoes for me.'

The last words Jill would have used to describe Max were Goody Two-Shoes, but she didn't argue.

Instead, she wondered if she would actually have those two weeks in the sun with him and the boys. Unless they caught Carol Blakely's killer, it was unlikely. And if, as Max believed, they had Ralph Atkins's murderer to find, she might as well forget it now.

Jill had to agree that the fire at Atkins's home was highly coincidental. Yet the man had been drunk, and he was a smoker. Perhaps, after all, it had been an accident. She'd know more later and, until then, it was pointless to speculate.

'Come on then,' she said, switching off the car's engine. 'Let's shop till we drop.'

It seemed to Jill that every UK resident had had the same idea. The place was heaving, a reminder that she loathed shopping. Nothing could dampen Nikki's enthusiasm, however. She held evening dresses against her short, stick-thin body and, giggling, asked for Jill's opinion. She tried on pairs of jeans that all looked the same and discounted every pair. In Debenham's, she allowed a girl to apply make-up . . .

'Enough,' Jill said. 'If I don't get a coffee within the next five minutes, I'll drop.'

'We'll have a pizza, too. I'm starving!'

'Anything. So long as they serve coffee.'

While Nikki wolfed down a pizza, Jill drank two large coffees. She felt human again.

'So when does the lecture start?' Nikki asked knowingly.

'From me?' Jill asked innocently. 'I don't plan on delivering a lecture. No, if anyone wants some sense knocking into her, it's your mum. Sadly, she won't listen to me.'

'Mum?'

'Yes. Who in their right mind would open their home to a guest who treats the place like a squat? I wouldn't. Any guests who visit me have to abide by the house rules. *My* house rules.'

'I'm not exactly a guest,' Nikki protested.

'Of course you are. You left home at sixteen. Fine, that was your choice. Now, because it's an easier option, you've decided to come back. You're a guest – pure and simple.'

The light faded from Nikki's eyes, and her lips tightened into an angry thin line.

'My rules,' Jill went on, 'include no friends round without asking my permission, cleaning up after friends, doing chores about the house in payment for a bed –'

'Chores?' Nikki groaned. 'Like what?'

'Anything. Cleaning, dusting, cooking, washing up. Anything that helps.' Nikki was about to interrupt, but Jill continued anyway. 'It's hard work getting a home of your own. It's something you haven't managed yet but, believe me, it's hard work and it's damned expensive.'

'But I can't –'

'Let me finish,' Jill said, and Nikki shrugged in a sulky manner.

'I could have been like you, Nikki. At sixteen, it would have been far easier to let my mum wait on me hand and foot, or take myself off with a gang of mates. Instead, I worked hard at school and then went to university.' She didn't miss the heavy sigh from Nikki and Jill had to admit that even she wouldn't have been surprised to hear the sound of violins. However, she was determined to have her say. 'It was no fun at all being broke all the time. While my friends were getting jobs and going out to spend their money, I was studying at uni. I was broke. My parents didn't have any money so it was up to me. I took a job in Burger King – and hated it – but at least it paid for food and books. And why did I put myself through all that? Because I wanted the good things in life. I wanted a nice home, a good car, and the occasional holiday. I wanted to live by my own rules. I didn't want to spend time with my mum and dad and live by their rules.'

'In case you've forgotten,' Nikki said sulkily, 'I didn't get any qualifications.'

'Then get some,' Jill retorted. 'You're not disabled, mentally or physically. You can get qualifications as easily as the next person.'

Nikki shrugged, and Jill suspected it was time she held her tongue. She could feel herself getting angry on Louise's behalf.

'You could at least be more grateful,' she said, putting on a smile to take the sting from her words. 'I hear Charlie's offered to take you both on holiday.'

'Charlie? God, I wouldn't go to the end of our road with him.'

'What's wrong with him?' Jill demanded in exasperation.

'What's right with him? I hate him. And don't argue, because you don't know him.'

That was true enough, Jill supposed. She'd met him twice, very briefly, so she couldn't claim to know him. But what she knew, she liked. Or rather, she liked what he did for Louise.

'What's there to dislike about him?'

Nikki was silent for long moments. 'I want to go in HMV,' she said at last.

So that was it. Conversation over. As the mood had changed dramatically, Jill decided to give in gracefully.

'Come on then.' She grabbed her bag and they hit the shops once more.

Nikki soon spent the money Louise had given her, and even Jill was spending a lot more than she'd planned. As well as The Kaiser Chiefs' latest CD for Harry and a DVD for Ben, she bought a couple of skimpy cotton sundresses, a pair of shorts and four strappy T-shirts for herself.

They were heading back to the car when Nikki spotted the ankle bracelet.

'I wish I'd seen that earlier,' she grumbled. 'It's gorgeous.'

Pretty and inexpensive, the bracelet was more feminine than Nikki's usual choice in jewellery.

'It would suit you,' Jill murmured.

Nikki held up her shopping bags. 'Yeah, but I'm skint, remember?'

Nikki was a walking contradiction. She wore earrings, several heavy chains around her neck, and dozens of bracelets. Yet her fingers were bare except for a well-worn plain gold band on her right hand. It had belonged to her grandmother. Jill knew how close the two had been, and she knew it was Nikki's most treasured possession. To Jill, that ring signified hope. Hope that, deep down inside, a loving, kind, generous young woman still existed.

'I'm not,' Jill replied. 'Thank God for qualifications, eh?' She laughed at Nikki's expression. 'Come on. My treat.'

Five minutes later, the purchase was made.

'Thanks, Jill. You shouldn't have – you really shouldn't – but, well, thanks.' Amazingly, there was a shimmering of moisture in Nikki's eyes.

'No need for thanks. I've had a lovely day – tiring, but lovely – so I should be thanking you.' She hesitated for a brief moment, but decided to say her piece anyway. 'When you wear it, remember the fun we've had today. And give your mum a break, eh?'

Nikki dropped her bags, and hugged her. 'I'll try. It's just that –' She broke off, paused and then went on, 'I'll never accept that man in our lives. Never!'

Jill was surprised at the vehemence in her voice. True, Nikki was a drama queen, but she meant this. She would never accept Charlie.

'If it was anyone else, it would be fine. But not him.' A tear oozed on to her cheek and was quickly brushed away. 'Mum's OK, I suppose. And it's up to her to see who she wants. And I know you're right; I shouldn't treat her house like I do.'

On that optimistic note, they left the shops behind and headed back to the peace of Kelton Bridge.

It was just after six thirty when Jill got back to her cottage, and Max was standing outside, leaning against his car.

'I was about to phone you to see what time you'd be back,' he told her. 'Good day?'

'Better than I dared hope.' She lifted her shopping bags from the back seat and handed them to him. 'We had fun.'

'Nikki OK then?'

'Not bad,' she said, smiling ruefully. 'She's even promised to try and behave nicely for Louise.'

'God, how much did that cost you?'

'An ankle bracelet.' Laughing, Jill let them into her cottage. 'Seriously, it was good.'

She went straight to the coffee machine. Her caffeine levels were dangerously low.

'I know she thrives on melodrama,' she went on thoughtfully, 'and I know she's just a kid really, but she said today that she would never accept Charlie in their lives. I believed her. She really can't take to him for some reason.'

'Perhaps she's just jealous, Jill. I expect she came back from London wanting the fatted calf.'

'She got the fatted calf,' Jill reminded him. 'Charlie wasn't on the scene then. But perhaps you're right. Perhaps it's nothing more than jealousy. Oh, and she thinks you're well sexy,' she added, getting cups from cupboard.

'Well sexy, eh?'

'Yep, and she said she'd quite fancy a couple of weeks in the sun with you.'

'Twenty-one-year-olds. Tsk! They can't keep their hands off me.'

'I expect they're after your pension, Max.'

Jill was aware of him leaning against her cooker, hands in his jeans pockets. As well as pale blue jeans, he was wearing a short-sleeved shirt in the same colour. Well sexy just about summed him up, she thought reluctantly, although she'd been surprised to hear that from one so young. Tall and dark he was; handsome he was not.

'Did Louise have a good day with Charlie?' he asked.

'It looked like it. She told me this morning that she was too worn out for unbridled passion, but she certainly looked a bit flushed and tousled when we got back.'

'And what would it take to make you look a bit flushed and tousled?'

'Hugh Jackman. Brad Pitt if Hugh's busy. Meanwhile,' she said, giving him her sweetest smile, 'I'll settle for feeling human.'

She made them both coffee and handed him a cup. 'So what about this fire at Atkins's place? Anything new?'

'They got a body out but, until we can check dental records, we can only assume it's Atkins.' He took a packet of cigarettes and a lighter from his shirt pocket. 'It was definitely started deliberately, though.'

'Really?'

'I never doubted it.' He sat at the table, coffee in front of him. 'Rags were soaked in petrol and then pushed through the letterbox.'

'And you reckon it's connected?' Jill's feet were aching and it was bliss to sit down.

'Oh, come on, Jill. We talk to him about some videos and the next minute he's bacon? Of course it's connected. Someone made sure he kept his mouth shut.'

'Did anyone see anything?' she asked.

'A woman four doors away saw a gang of kids hanging around at about midnight. She thought they were aged between fifteen and seventeen. Said there ought to be more bobbies on the beat,' he added with a rueful smile. 'Two people saw what they thought was a man walking quickly down the road at about midnight. Other than that, nothing as yet.'

Max had taken a cigarette from the packet. Jill was waiting for him to ask if he could smoke in her cottage, but Max being Max, he simply lit it and looked around for an ashtray.

'We may as well sit outside,' she told him, getting to her feet.

As they crossed the lawn, coffee cups in their hands, Finlay Roberts was walking up his drive. Although they couldn't see him, his cheerful whistle was clearly audible.

'He was tucked up in bed when the fire started,' Max muttered. 'No witnesses, of course.'

'I expect most people were tucked up in bed.'

'Including Vince Blakely.' Max sat on the old wooden bench, put his coffee on the table, and leaned back. 'But he had a witness. The new woman in his life –'

'God, that was quick.'

'Apparently, she's been a great comfort to him.'

'Oh, for –' Jill pulled a face at that.

'Quite. Anyway, the stunning Yvonne can vouch for him.'

'Is she? Stunning?'

Max nodded. 'Dim, but stunning.'

'How long have they been seeing each other?'

'According to Blakely, and I never believe a word that bloke says, she used to work for him and they grew close then. Not close enough to be unfaithful to his wife, you understand, but close. About six months ago, they met up again and . . .' He left the sentence unfinished and looked at her. 'Do you think he's an honest sort of chap?'

'Not really,' Jill admitted, 'but I don't think he's a killer, either. I think he likes to make a good impression. He might have been shagging this Yvonne for years, but it wouldn't suit his image. He lies, but only to keep his image intact.'

'Hm.' He flicked his cigarette butt on to her border. 'So are you all packed and ready to go?'

She laughed at that, mainly to hide the fact that the thought of going on holiday with him – albeit with his two sons to amuse them and a separate room – always made her blush scarlet. Ridiculous!

'There's ages yet. And if this mess is still –'

'It won't be,' he said grimly. 'No one, but no one is keeping me from two weeks in Spain with you. Besides, I'm thinking of buying a beach bar.'

'Ha. I've heard it all before. You'd be bored to death.' Another thought struck her. 'You say Yvonne used to work for Vince Blakely. Where does she work now? If she's working at another architect's practice –'

'She isn't. She's working at a travel agent's.'

Chapter Eighteen

Yvonne Hitchins sat in front of her mirror and brushed at her hair. 'Why can't we go out instead?'

It was a Saturday night and Vince expected her to cook.

'Why can't we –? Oh, for God's sake!' Vince picked up the jacket she'd thrown on the bed, her bed, and hung it over the back of the chair. 'I can hardly go and paint the bloody town red, can I? Hm? My picture's in the paper every bloody day. I'm supposed to be the grieving widower. Remember?'

'There's no need to snap!'

'There's no need to keep whinging, either! Christ, it's hardly difficult to throw a salad or something together, is it?'

'I suppose it's not,' she replied airily. 'Right, while you do that, I'll take a bath.'

With that, she flounced out of the bedroom and into the bathroom.

'Let's see how difficult it is when there's not so much as a lettuce leaf in the fridge,' she muttered to herself as she turned on the bath tap.

The thought made her smile. His house, she knew from the three times she'd visited, was immaculate. Everything was hidden away. Even the evening paper was put in the drawer before anyone read it. Her house was different. She wanted to live in her house, not have it featured in some lifestyle magazine.

Not that there was any chance of that. There wasn't much call in the glossy magazines for new two-bedroomed semi-detached houses on estates.

She lay back in the bath and sank down so that the water lapped around her neck.

She couldn't hear Vince over the sound of the water tank filling up. He was probably making a meal from the few items in the fridge and cupboards, and that would test his improvisation skills to the limit. Of course, he might have stormed off, but she doubted it. Vince wasn't the storming-off type. When she left her bath and went downstairs, he'd carry on as if nothing had happened.

That wasn't Yvonne's way of carrying on. To her mind, a good row might clear the air. She didn't particularly want to argue with him, but she would like to know what she meant to him. Before it happened – and she always thought of the shocking murder of his wife as 'it' – they'd snatched precious hours, sometimes whole days and nights together, and Vince had said that, as soon as Carol agreed to a divorce, they would move in together.

'If you moved in with me now,' Yvonne had pointed out, 'she'd have to divorce you. If she didn't, you could wait and do the two-year separation thing.'

'No. Firstly, I don't want to wait two years. Secondly, and more important, I don't want to antagonize her.'

Of course, it was only a week since Carol had been killed and Yvonne had to admit that the shock was indescribable. For all that, she was convinced that Vince was cooling towards her.

She poked her toe in the tap and tried to put her mind to more cheerful matters. It was impossible. Carol's death had spooked her. The slightest creak of a floorboard had her on edge, and she was constantly panicking that some-one was following her. They weren't, of course, but she couldn't relax. Even lying in the bath, supposedly relaxing, she kept thinking that some crazed killer was about to burst through the bathroom door.

If Vince was right and some madman was out there, everyone had to be on their guard.

The bath was doing nothing to relax her so she climbed out, wrapped a towel around herself and wandered into her bedroom. She opened her wardrobe door and ran a hand over a row of dresses.

Smiling to herself, she chose the black one. Backless, low at the front and boasting a long slit at the side, it was one of Vince's favourites. She completed the look with very high heels and walked down the stairs.

He looked at her briefly, then turned his attention back to the cooker.

'It'll have to be frozen pizza,' was all he said.

So much for seducing him, Yvonne thought, stifling a sigh.

She supposed a bottle of white wine was cooling in the fridge, but he could stuff that, she preferred red. She opened a bottle and poured a glass for herself.

God, he was irritating her. She was thirty years old, for heaven's sake. What thirty-year-old would want to sit in on a Saturday night with a boring pizza and a man who was paying her no attention whatsoever?

'So where am I supposed to be tonight?' she asked sarcastically.

'What the hell's that supposed to mean?'

'I just wondered what I'm supposed to say if the police come knocking on my door again,' she replied airily.

She'd lied for him, and he owed her. At the very least he owed her a bit of attention.

'Say what you like,' Vince snapped back. 'For Christ's sake, Yvonne, I wish I hadn't bloody bothered. My wife has been murdered. Remember? The police are asking questions every five minutes. They wanted to know where I was last night and, as I was at home all night, I thought it might save time if I told them you could back that up. But bloody hell, I wish I hadn't bothered. I was only doing them a favour, saving them time. There's no need for all this grief. Tell them what the hell you like.'

'What I can't understand is why they wanted to know where you were.'

'I've no idea. Now, this pizza is ready.'

She perched on a stool at the counter and, with fork poised, said, 'It was because of the fire at that architect's house.'

Vince had phoned her and told her he'd claimed she was with him, but it had still given her the shock of her life to open the door this afternoon and find two policemen on her doorstep.

'It was,' Vince agreed. 'They wanted to know if I knew the chap. I didn't.'

'Do they think you started the fire?'

'Why in hell's name would they think that?' he demanded.

She shrugged, but she couldn't shake off a growing sense of unease. She didn't know why they might think that, but they must have had a reason. What if they found out that she'd lied? What would happen to her then?

But Vince didn't start that fire. Why should he? It was a ridiculous idea. She took a sip of wine and tried to put the notion from her head. There were far more important things to worry about, like persuading Vince to take her out or making him notice her.

Yet the worry remained.

'What will happen to me when they find out I lied for you?' she asked.

'For God's sake!' His hand hit the side of her face with such suddenness and force, she thought he'd broken her jaw.

'Bastard!' she screamed. 'Get out! Go on, get out now!'

'Yvonne, hey, I'm sorry. Come on, sweetheart –'

'Get out, you bastard!'

Still clutching the side of her face, she ran up the stairs and locked herself in her bathroom. She stayed there, in shock, until long after she heard him leave.

Chapter Nineteen

It was Jill's first day back at work with the force after two years, and she was still wondering if she'd made the right decision.

She'd been given an office that was small but did, at least, boast a good-sized window. Her large desk was new, as was the computer sitting on it, but, so far, she'd spent very little time in there.

Now, she was in Max's office with the day almost over and with no idea how it had passed so quickly and fruitlessly.

'Meredith's right,' Max was saying. 'It's two weeks since Carol Blakely was murdered and we've nothing to go on. We didn't find the weapon used by – or allegedly used by – Eddie Marshall, and we haven't found the weapon used on Carol.'

They'd just come from Phil Meredith's office and, as ever, he was growing impatient at the lack of progress.

'We're getting too wrapped up in Eddie Marshall's cases,' she said. 'It isn't important how the killer came by those tapes. He wanted us to think The Undertaker was involved. Let's forget that for the moment and imagine Eddie Marshall had never existed. Let's pretend that Carol Blakely's murder is like nothing we've ever seen before.'

'OK.' Max tapped his pen against his chin. 'Vince Blakely would be chief suspect. Motive? He wanted rid of her, a divorce at any rate, and he wanted money. His prayers would have been answered if she hadn't changed her will.'

'Opportunity?'

'Now that's where it all falls apart. He was definitely on the east coast of Scotland. We've tried everything and there's no way he could have got down here and back.'

'Someone else must have a motive,' she reasoned.

'Ruth Asimacopoulos,' Max said, 'except she didn't know that Carol's death would make her a rich woman.'

'And she was in Spain at the time. Who else?'

'No one that I can think of. A couple of small florists in town would be happy to see her business closed down, but I doubt they'd go as far as murder.'

Jill was doodling on a notepad and, when the page was filled with dozens of flowers and Christmas trees, she flipped it over.

'Right, Ralph Atkins. What do we know about him?'

'Heavy drinker. Gambler. Wife died of cancer eight months ago. Jaded. Disillusioned. No money, but no huge debts, either. No children. No family at all, in fact.'

'And it was definitely his body they brought out?'

'Yes.'

'So who could have wanted him dead?'

'The person who didn't want him telling anyone what he did with those sodding tapes.'

They were going round in circles.

Before they could continue, Grace burst in.

'Guv – hi, Jill – what do you think of this? Three years ago, a guy smashed a window in Carol Blakely's shop. He also sprayed abuse on the walls outside. Carol didn't press charges, but apparently, this guy, name of Terry Yates, claimed she'd ruined his life.'

'Oh?'

'Yeah, and that's not all –'

Jill had to smile at the excitement on Grace's face.

'He sent her champagne and chocolates on her last birthday.'

'In February?' Jill queried.

'Yes! I'll go and have a word with him, shall I, guv?'

'Where is he?' Max asked and, like a conjuror pulling

a white dove from her pocket, Grace handed him a piece of paper.

'No. You're OK. It's on my way so I may as well see him.' He gave her a beaming smile. 'OK, Grace. Thanks. Good work.'

Grace had been married for a year and, despite the hard exterior and that no-nonsense Geordie accent, was devoted to her husband and was happy to wait on him hand and foot. She was equally devoted to Max though and, as she left the room, she looked like an eager young puppy who'd been highly praised by its adored master.

Max glanced at his watch and then at Jill. 'Are you off home or do you fancy paying Yates a visit?'

She had stacks to do at home, but she was curious. 'I'll come with you.'

Terry Yates lived in a modern terraced house in a quiet cul-de-sac. They tried the door, but there was no one at home and they were about to leave when a blue Ford Mondeo pulled on to the driveway.

The owner, male, got out and looked at them both.

'Mr Yates?' Max asked, and he nodded.

Max showed his ID. 'We'd like a word with you about Carol Blakely, if you wouldn't mind.'

He looked as if he minded a great deal, but he simply said, 'You'd better come inside then.'

He unlocked the front door and a small brown dog bounded up to greet him. The animal took no notice whatsoever of his visitors, and Jill was glad about that. It looked like an ankle biter.

By her reckoning, Yates was a good five or six years younger than Carol Blakely. He was tall, lanky even, with short dark hair, and he wore rimless glasses. The suit he was wearing was creased, as if he'd spent a long day sitting in it.

'Come in,' he said, showing them into a small, but neat lounge that looked out on to the road. 'Sit down.'

They sat and, after he'd let the dog into the back garden, he did, too.

'We believe you knew Mrs Blakely?' Max began.

'Yes.'

'How well?'

'Very well.' He played with an invisible thread on the armchair for a few moments. 'We had an affair,' he said at last.

'When was this?' Jill asked.

'Four years ago.'

'How long did it last?' she asked curiously.

'About a year. Just less than a year.'

'How serious was it?' Jill guessed that, from his point of view, it had been very serious.

'Very,' he said, speaking quietly. 'We were both married, but we were prepared to leave all that behind and move in together. I left Beverley, that's my wife, and Carol was planning to leave her husband.'

'But she changed her mind?' Jill guessed.

'Yes,' he agreed, after giving the suggestion a few moments' thought. 'I suppose you know about her sisters?'

'Yes,' Max said.

'Naturally, as they were so close, their deaths hit her very hard. She thought it was God's way of punishing her for getting involved with me. The stupid thing was –' He shook his head as if, even now, he couldn't believe it. 'She'd never had a religious thought until that happened. She didn't even believe in God. But anyway, that's what she thought and she ended things between us.'

'How did you feel about that?' Jill asked.

'Very angry. Oh, not with Carol, more with circumstances. It was rubbish, you see. God wasn't punishing her. I wanted her to see sense, but she wouldn't. They were killed on a Saturday and by the following Wednesday, everything was over between us. She wasn't thinking straight, that's what I kept telling her.'

'And because she wouldn't listen, you smashed a window at her shop?' Max asked, and Yates coloured.

'Yes.'

'Why?'

'Because I was drunk. Because I was angry with her for being so stupid. Because I'd lost my wife and kids, lost my home – I'd lost everything. I'd given it all up for a life with Carol. I gave it all up for nothing, as it turned out.'

'What happened then?' Jill asked.

'Nothing. Someone called the police but she calmed things down. She didn't want to press charges so she made up some story about it being an accident. Afterwards, she refused to see me or answer my phone calls.'

'Five months ago,' Jill said, 'you sent her champagne and chocolates. Is that right?'

'Yes.'

'Why?' Max asked.

'It was her birthday,' he answered simply. 'There wasn't much point sending her flowers, was there? I always sent her champagne and chocolates on her birthday.'

'Did she acknowledge them?' Jill asked.

'No.'

'Mr Yates,' Max said, 'can you think of anyone who might have wanted Mrs Blakely dead?'

'You mean other than her husband?'

'What makes you say that?' Max asked.

'All that ever interested him was her business and how much money she was raking in,' he muttered. 'He was a total bastard with a vile temper. He had loads of women in his life and he didn't care if Carol knew about them or not. All he wanted from Carol was handouts. Well, now he's got the lot, hasn't he?'

Yates was under the impression, understandably perhaps, that Vince Blakely had inherited everything.

'Did Carol ever mention the contents of her will to you?' Jill asked.

'No. The only time she mentioned money was when her husband was making demands. Otherwise, she never spoke of it. Obviously, she'd got a fair bit. A lot more than

137

me,' he pointed out, nodding at their surroundings, 'as you can guess, but it never seemed to matter to her.'

'Did she have enemies, other than her husband?' Max asked.

'None that I know of.'

Jill looked around the room and counted eight framed photos of two young children.

'Your son and daughter?' she asked him.

'Yes, Adam and Cherie. Twins. I get to see them for a few hours at the weekend,' he added. 'Aren't I the lucky one?'

'When did you last see Mrs Blakely?' Max asked.

'To speak to? About three months ago.' He ran a hand through his hair. 'I tried to talk to her. It was a Friday and she's usually at her shop in Harrington on Friday afternoons. There's a café opposite and I had a couple of coffees there and waited for her to leave. We had a brief chat –'

'About what?' Max asked.

'Oh, I tried to get her to talk to me. To have a coffee with me. Anything. She didn't want to know. She drove home and so did I.'

'Have you seen her since?' Jill asked.

'I've seen her about,' he said flatly, 'but only from a distance.'

'You've followed her? Sought her out?'

'A couple of times,' he admitted, colouring.

It would have been more than a couple, Jill suspected. He would have stalked her at every available opportunity. So not only had he lost his wife, his kids and his home, he would also be putting his job on the line.

'Who did she see?' Jill asked. 'When you were watching her, did she meet people?'

'Not really,' he said. 'Usually, she went straight home. There was a chap she saw a couple of times – scruffy bloke who wore tatty jeans and T-shirts – but that was about all.'

That would have been Finlay Roberts. Yates would have followed them and, if he said she only met Roberts a couple of times, that was probably fact.

'Where were you on Friday and Saturday, the seventh and eighth of July?' Max asked.

'What? Now look here, you don't think I had anything to do with her murder, do you? Why the hell would I?'

'Where were you?' Max asked patiently.

'In Liverpool,' he answered, and he was panicking. 'I sell bathroom suites and we had an exhibition on. Three of us – colleagues – stayed over. You can check it out.'

'If you'd be so kind as to give us the details, we will,' Max assured him.

He was quickly hunting through his briefcase, and soon gave Max literature for the exhibition, the address and number for the hotel, and contact numbers for his boss and colleagues.

'That's where I was. I swear it.'

'Thank you,' Max said.

'I was,' he insisted. 'The first I knew of it was when I heard about it on the local news. I swear.'

'Thank you,' Max said again.

Shortly afterwards, they left him to his dog, his loneliness and his bitterness.

'Could he have wanted her dead?' Max asked Jill as he drove them back to headquarters.

'It's possible. He's very angry, but whether it's enough to send him over the edge, I don't know. He blames Carol for the lonely life he has now. At the time, he would have walked out on home, wife and kids without a second thought for their welfare. All he would have thought about was the life he was to have with Carol. Now, he blames her for the fact that he only sees his kids at weekends.'

'So revenge might be a motive?'

'Could be. Also, with her dead, he might be able to pick up the pieces of his life again. There was no hope of that when he spent every available minute stalking her. But,' she reminded him, 'he was in Liverpool at the time.'

'So what?' Max scoffed. 'A few hundred quid in the right pub would get the deed done for him.'

'A chat with his ex-wife might prove useful,' Jill said thoughtfully.

It was rush hour and traffic in Harrington was almost at a standstill. Fortunately, they were going against the worst of it.

They were almost back at headquarters when Max's phone rang. He hit the button to answer it.

'Guv,' Fletch said, 'the night Atkins's house burned to the ground?'

'Yes?'

'We've got the CCTV from the filling station just down the road from The Laurels. At a little after 11 p.m., Finlay Roberts filled up his car there.'

Max shared a brief, surprised glance with Jill.

'Just the car, Fletch? He didn't have cans or anything with him?'

'No, just the car.'

'And his car's definitely diesel, right?'

'It is, guv, but it's odd, don't you think? He said nothing about going out that night. Quite the reverse. He was adamant that he was at home all evening.'

'It is bloody odd, Fletch.'

Max ended the call and glanced briefly at Jill. 'It keeps coming back to Roberts, doesn't it?'

She had to agree that it did.

Chapter Twenty

Terry Yates's ex-wife lived in a pleasant detached house at the end of a small cul-de-sac. The front garden was colourful and neat and, from the little Jill could see, the back garden was large, mainly set to lawn, and dotted with children's toys.

Jill had Grace with her and, although she was a marvel at interviewing suspects, Jill would have preferred Max's or Fletch's company. The main objective was to coax Beverley Yates to talk freely about her husband and Grace could be a little intimidating.

Jill rang the bell and they heard ferocious barking coming from the other side of the door.

'A good job we're not breaking and entering,' Grace muttered beneath her breath.

They heard a woman telling the animal to be quiet, which had no effect whatsoever, and then, as the door opened, a huge yellow dog hurled itself at Jill.

'I am so sorry. Lily, get down. She's only young and she thinks everyone wants to be her best friend. Are you all right? Lily, get down!'

'Yes, I'm fine, thanks. Really.' As Jill regained her composure, the dog bounded around the three of them all as if it were on springs.

'Mrs Yates? I'm Jill Kennedy. We spoke on the phone earlier.'

'Yes, come in. And I'm so sorry about Lily. I'll put her out in the garden.'

'Don't worry, she's fine.'

But Jill was relieved to see Lily banished to the garden and the patio door firmly closed behind her.

'She's a lovely dog,' Grace said, and Mrs Yates smiled.

'I've called her a lot of things since we got her, but lovely hasn't been one of them. She's chewed the dining table, four pairs of shoes and the phone cable so far.' She gazed through the patio door to where Lily was demolishing a football. 'People promise me she'll grow out of it but there's no sign of it yet. Still, the kids love her.'

That, Jill guessed from the smile on her face, was all that mattered.

The house, or the lounge at any rate, was stylish yet homely. The furniture wasn't expensive, but it was well cared for. Children's toys sat neatly in one corner of the room.

'The twins, Adam and Cherie, are having a couple of days with their grandparents,' Mrs Yates explained, nodding at those toys, 'and I'm having a well-earned rest.'

'I bet you miss them,' Grace said.

'I do,' she admitted softly. 'Sit down,' she went on. 'I'll sit here with my back to the window. That way I won't see what Lily's doing. The garden's secure so she's perfectly safe.'

She was a very attractive young woman, fresh-faced, and casually dressed in white jeans and a red T-shirt. Her smile seemed relaxed and friendly.

'So,' she said, 'I gather you want to talk to me about Carol Blakely. I assume that's because of my ex-husband's affair with her?'

'Yes,' Jill replied, grateful for the opening. 'You knew about the affair then?'

'Not at first,' she replied. 'He'd been seeing her for six months before he told me he was leaving me.'

'We had a chat with him yesterday,' Jill explained, 'and he told us he'd intended to live with Mrs Blakely? Did you know that?'

'Oh, yes. He had it all planned. Five years of marriage down the drain just like that.' She clicked her fingers.

'I'm sorry to ask such personal questions, but –'

'I understand,' Mrs Yates said.

'Had he been unfaithful before?' Jill asked.

'Not to my knowledge,' she answered, 'but I wouldn't guarantee it. When we first married, he was besotted with me. I thought it was love but, looking back, it was more of an obsession.'

'How do you mean?' Grace asked.

'He showered me with gifts and hated every second we were apart. He hated me going anywhere without him. I was quite touched.' She smiled ruefully. 'Six months later, when I was pregnant with the twins, he was constantly picking fault. Everything I did was wrong. If we went out, he'd criticize my appearance, my clothes, my conversation, everything. You don't see it happening, but he really dented my self-confidence.' That smile again. 'For all that, I was distraught when he told me he was leaving me.'

The dog ran up to the patio door and barked hopefully. Realizing she wasn't about to be let in, she raced off and did several circuits of the garden.

'I'm sorry. You didn't come to hear me complaining about him,' Mrs Yates said. 'Exactly what is it that you need to know?'

Jill liked her openness.

'As you know,' she began, 'we're investigating the murder of Carol Blakely. We know your husband had an affair with her, and we've also heard that he followed her regularly and smashed a window at her shop. What we're trying to do is build as big a picture as possible. We need to know as much as possible about Carol's life and anyone she came into contact with.' She paused. 'Did you ever meet Mrs Blakely?'

'Only once,' Beverley Yates replied. 'I was in town with the twins and we bumped into her and Terry. Terry introduced us all. God, it was embarrassing. For her, too, I think. Humiliating as well. She was everything Terry had told me she was.'

'And that was what?' Grace asked.

'Attractive. Intelligent. Friendly. Smart. Sophisticated.' She rattled off the adjectives as if she'd been forced to learn them parrot fashion. 'I felt like the village idiot by comparison.'

'When was this?' Jill asked.

'About a fortnight after he left me,' she explained. 'Shortly after that, I heard she'd walked out on him, too. I can't say I was sorry. She must have seen the light. He was obsessed with her just as he'd been obsessed with me, but it wouldn't have lasted.'

'How's your relationship with him now?' Jill asked, and she blushed.

'Poor,' she admitted. 'He sees the twins for a few hours each weekend and, for their sakes, we're civilized towards one another. Other than that, we rarely speak. Occasionally, usually when he's had a drink, he begs me to take him back.'

That surprised Jill. She had believed he was still in love with Carol. She hadn't thought that it was, as Mrs Yates believed, an obsession that would have passed.

'No way,' Mrs Yates went on vehemently. 'He hurt me badly and he abandoned us. It took me a long time to get over that. Now, I'm happier without him. We're all better off without him.'

Jill thought how sad it was that so much bitterness existed between them. Civilized or not, it couldn't be good for the children.

'How's his relationship with the twins now?' she asked.

'Adam's OK with his father. He takes everything in his stride, but Cherie's very hurt. She sulks and says she doesn't want to see him. He accuses me of turning them against him. I don't. I never utter a bad word about him in front of them. He abandoned them. How does he expect them to feel?'

Jill smiled and nodded sympathetically as an answer. Really there was no answer.

She was having to revise her opinion slightly. Mrs Yates *was* likeable, but there was a hard edge to her. She might not utter a bad word about her ex-husband in front of the children, but Jill presumed they knew all too well how she felt about him.

'But we're OK, me and the twins,' Mrs Yates added. 'We're fine.'

'I'm glad,' Jill said. 'Your husband smashed a window at Mrs Blakely's shop. Does that surprise you?'

'Not really,' she replied at last. 'He put a brick through my kitchen window one night. He'd been phoning me at all hours of the day and night and I said that, if he did it again, I'd call the police. The next thing I knew, he threw a brick through the window and told me to call 999.'

Was that a man making a cry for help? Jill wondered. Had he believed he was out of control?

'And did you?' Grace asked.

'No. I thought they had better things to do with their time and I knew he'd soon sober up. Besides, for the sake of the children, I didn't want him getting into trouble.'

A scratching at the window had them looking to see Lily with a piece of football in her mouth and a pathetic expression on her face.

'I usually take her for a walk about now,' Mrs Yates said. 'Or rather, she takes me for a walk.'

'Then we won't take up any more of your time,' Grace said, getting to her feet.

Jill supposed she'd finished. All the same, she'd like another chat with Terry Yates. Obsession, and his ex-wife had used the word several times, could be a dangerous thing.

Chapter Twenty-One

Later that afternoon, Jill caught up with Max just as he was nipping outside for a smoke.

'Have you got a minute?' she asked him.

'Yes, of course. What's up?'

'Nothing really, but I'd like another chat with Terry Yates.'

'Oh?'

She told him of the chat she and Grace had had with his ex-wife that morning.

'We're talking of damaged lives,' she said thoughtfully. 'Mrs Yates was distraught when he told her he was leaving her. She claims she's over it now and better off without him, but feelings are still running high there. He's as bitter as hell because he's been left with nothing. Their children must be aware of the feelings that exist between the two of them. Life can't be easy for any of them.'

'OK,' he said. 'We can call on Yates when we finish here if you like. His alibi checks out,' he added.

'I know, but as you say –'

'It means nothing,' he agreed.

'He's never been in trouble before?' she asked.

'No. Apart from a telling off when he smashed the window at Carol's shop, he's as clean as a whistle. No unpaid parking fines, no points on his licence, nothing.'

'Did someone talk to Ruth and Cass at the shop?' she asked, and he nodded.

'I did. I was out that way anyway so I thought I'd call in. Cass had never heard of Yates, but that's not surprising as she hasn't been there long. Ruth only started working for Carol a month before the accident that killed her sisters.'

'Mm. And the two wouldn't have been close enough to share confidences then.'

'Exactly. Ruth said she'd had an inkling there had been someone, but Carol hadn't spoken of it, and she hadn't asked. She couldn't remember a window being smashed.'

'Carol felt guilty about her relationship with Yates,' Jill pointed out, 'so she wouldn't have mentioned it. She certainly wouldn't have mentioned it to Ruth when they were relative strangers. Later, when the two became good friends, Carol would have wanted to forget the affair ever happened.'

'We'll have a chat with him,' Max promised. 'I've got a couple of things to sort out and then we'll go. Unannounced?'

'Definitely. We'll just have to hope he's home . . .'

Jill went to her office and found a huge pile of paperwork waiting for her. She had staff assessments to sort out and a dozen other things to deal with. They'd all have to wait.

She returned several phone calls, sent a dozen emails and then headed off to find Max.

As she walked along the corridor, it surprised her to realize that Terry Yates's relationship with his ex-wife interested her just as much as, if not more than, his relationship with Carol.

Max was ready to go and they walked down to the car park.

'I'll follow you,' she told him, 'and then I can go straight home. I'm due at a concert this evening.'

'Oh?'

'One of these fundraising things that the primary school is so fond of doing,' she enlightened him. 'You're welcome to come along and be bored to death.'

'Thanks, but some other time,' he replied, unlocking his car.

147

Jill got in her own car and followed him out of the car park. As she did so, she switched on the radio and tried to find a station that would give her the racing results. Damn it, she'd missed them. She'd have to wait until she got home.

They struck lucky. Terry Yates's car was parked on his drive. Jill didn't expect he had much of a social life, but his work involved a lot of driving.

When he answered their knock, however, Jill was dismayed to see that he had been drinking. A lot. He was swaying on his feet and his speech was slightly slurred.

'Oh. You're back,' he said.

He hadn't shaved today, she noticed.

'Yes. May we come in?' Max asked, already taking a step forward.

'Of course. You'll have to excuse the mess,' he added, 'but I've been working from home today.'

The small brown dog was pushed into the kitchen and Yates staggered around his lounge gathering up papers that had been scattered on every available seat.

An empty wine bottle stood on the hearth and a half-full one was on the coffee table. Cheap red wine, Jill noticed.

'What a nice way to work,' she said lightly. 'With a glass in one hand,' she added with a smile.

He shrugged. 'It's OK.'

Jill wandered over to the window and looked out at the back garden. It was small, but tidy.

'I had a chat with your ex-wife this morning,' she told him.

'Oh?' He was still putting papers in a pile, but he looked worried.

'I hadn't realized you were hoping the two of you could get back together.'

He sat down while he considered his answer. Although he waved a hand in the direction of the now free seats, Max and Jill remained standing.

'I thought it would be better for the twins,' he said at last. 'She's turning them against me. I know I treated her badly,' he allowed. 'I had an affair and left her. But I couldn't help falling in love with someone else, could I?' He looked to them both for an answer, didn't get one, and carried on. 'I thought we could make a go of things, and I thought it would be better for the twins. She didn't want to know. She's happy causing problems between me and the kids. Vindictive bitch.'

Vindictive bitch? Hardly the best foundation for making a marriage work.

'She says you put a brick through her kitchen window,' Jill pointed out.

'I did,' he admitted.

'Drunk again, were you?' Max asked.

'A bit,' he replied. 'But God, she's been driving me mad. She's on the phone constantly telling me that Cherie doesn't want to see me again or that Adam's doing great at school now I'm out of his life. When news of Carol's death hit the headlines, she was on the phone immediately. "Your girlfriend's dead then," she said. "You'll have to find someone else's knickers to jump into." I mean, for God's sake.' He grimaced. 'Evil bitch!'

Jill walked round the room and stopped to gaze at the photos of the twins.

'Why,' she asked, turning to look at him, 'would you want to live with someone you consider evil and vindictive?'

'Who knows? Probably because she's driven me to insanity.' He thought for a moment. 'In my more crazy moments, I think that, if we lived together again, she'd have what she wanted and stop making my life hell. Stop turning my children against me.'

'But Carol was alive and you were still hoping she'd come to her senses,' Jill pointed out.

'Yes, I know. Carol was never going to come back to me though, was she? I knew that. Deep down, I knew it.'

'So you'd rather have your ex-wife than no one?'

'I'd rather my kids didn't grow up hating me,' he corrected her.

'Now that Carol is dead,' Jill said, watching closely for any reaction from him, 'I suppose there's more chance that your ex-wife will agree to get back together?'

'Who knows how her mind works?' he answered flatly.

His phone rang out, but he made no move towards it. 'The machine will get it,' he told them.

After six rings, the machine clicked into action. Yates's voice, dull and flat, assured whoever was calling that he wasn't available right now but, if they would leave their name and number, he would return their call as soon as possible.

'Call me back,' a voice Jill recognized said. 'If I can persuade Cherie to see you, and God knows that'll take some doing, you can take them out for an hour on Sunday. You can pick them up at four but they'll need to be home by five at the latest.'

The machine beeped and all was silent.

'A whole hour,' Yates said bitterly. 'Things must be looking up. I wonder what this weekend's excuses are. Perhaps Cherie's washing her hair again. Oh no, that was last weekend.' He expelled his breath on a sigh. 'Believe me,' he went on quietly, 'if I ever murder anyone, it will be her.'

'Is that a threat?' Max asked.

'No,' he answered sheepishly.

'According to your ex-wife,' Jill said, 'your marriage was in difficulty very soon after you married, when she was pregnant with the twins, in fact.'

'Yes, that's true.'

'Why was that, do you think?'

'Probably because I was shut out,' he said flatly. 'All she cared about was the welfare of her unborn child – or children as it turned out. Her children. Not mine. As she took great pains to point out, she was the one carrying them. She was the one feeling sick every morning, the one walking around like a bloated whale, the one being poked and prodded at the clinic. When they were born, I had no say in anything – names, feeding, putting them to

150

sleep, dressing them. If I offered to do anything, she'd look at me and demand to know who'd carried them into the world.'

Why, Jill wondered, would he want to try and make a go of a marriage with someone he disliked so intensely? And why did he think there was the remotest chance of his ex-wife agreeing to spend any time at all let alone the rest of her life with him? Neither had a good word to say for the other.

'This alibi of yours,' Max put in, 'doesn't really check out.'

Jill looked at him in amazement. He'd told her it did.

'What?' Yates was as shocked as Jill and a lot more nervous. 'It must.'

'Not really,' Max said casually. 'You weren't at breakfast on the Saturday morning.'

'Well, no. I don't eat breakfast. Never have. I have a couple of strong coffees and that's my lot.'

'Your colleagues were all at a table having breakfast,' Max reminded him. 'So why didn't you have your coffee with them?'

'I never do.' Yates was breaking out into a sweat. 'I have it in my room. The last thing I want to do is watch them stuffing their faces with bacon and eggs. You ask them. I *always* have coffee in my room.'

'You went to your room early on the Friday night too,' Max said.

'What? Oh, for God's sake. I mean, I can't remember but it must have been well past eleven.'

'It was about eleven, as far as I can tell,' Max informed him. 'Your colleagues were in the bar until gone one in the morning.'

'They often are.'

Max sat in a chair so that he was directly opposite Yates. 'So you had plenty of time to get from your hotel to –'

'No!' Yates leapt from his chair so quickly that he staggered and had to grab the back of Max's chair to keep himself upright. 'I swear to you, I didn't leave the hotel.'

151

'You like a drink,' Max said, 'and, when you're away, it's all on the company, right? I'm sure you'd hang around for the free drinks.'

'No. Believe me, I'd rather buy my own.' Frightened eyes darted from Max to Jill and back to Max. 'You have to believe me. I was in my room the whole time. I swear it.'

'How do you get on with your colleagues?' Jill asked.

'They're OK. A bit full of themselves, but OK.'

'A bit full of themselves? In what way?'

'Oh, you know.' He was managing to stand unaided now. 'They like to brag about their grand houses, their beautiful wives, their even more beautiful mistresses, their super-intelligent kids, that sort of thing. They're all very competitive. But yes, I get on OK with them. I've known them for years.' He thought for a moment and the panic blazed once more in his eyes. 'Why? What have they been saying about me?'

'That you're a bit quiet,' Max told him. 'Not much of a mixer.'

'Yeah, I suppose that's right. I am quiet. Quieter than them at any rate.' His gaze locked on the half-full bottle of red wine. 'But that means nothing,' he said, turning back to look at Max. 'And I swear to you, I was in my room all night. I left them at about eleven o'clock and I was at the exhibition by nine the next morning. By then, I'd had a shower, drunk a couple of coffees and made some phone calls.'

He seemed to calm himself a little.

'Besides,' he said, 'why the hell would I want Carol dead? Eh? I was the one doing everything in my power to get her to talk to me. She won't talk to me now, will she?'

'She won't,' Max agreed.

Yates's phone rang again and he rolled his eyes for their benefit. Again, they heard his voice asking the caller to leave a message, and again, they heard Beverley Yates's voice, slightly higher pitched this time.

'I know you're there. Where the hell is Terry No Mates Yates going to be, hm? If you don't call me within the next hour, you won't see the kids at all this weekend. Got that?'

The call ended abruptly.

'I'd better give her a ring,' Yates said reluctantly.

'Wise move,' Max agreed. 'You'll need to call at the station to make a statement, too.'

'But –'

'Any time tomorrow will do. Thanks for talking to us.'

Chapter Twenty-Two

Three days later, Jill woke to the sound of rain lashing against her bedroom window. Pulling the curtain aside, she saw that the sky was a menacing grey and the rain was blowing horizontally from west to east. It must have been raining for most of the night if the huge puddles out in the lane were anything to go by.

By the time she'd showered, dressed, had breakfast and fed the cats, it had eased off enough to dash to her car without getting soaked. As she was doing this, she heard Finlay Roberts's raised voice.

She stopped, and they spotted each other at the same moment.

'Jill!' He came striding over to her, seemingly oblivious to the rain. A man was walking behind him.

'Jill, my darling girl,' Finlay greeted her breathlessly, 'is your phone working OK?'

'Yes, it's fine. Why?'

'Mine isn't.' He turned to his companion, presumably a BT engineer judging by the van parked in the lane. 'So if Jill's is working, and you've checked the pole, the fault has to be in my cottage, right?'

'So it would seem,' the engineer agreed.

'I have to go out,' Finlay told Jill. 'What do you think? I suppose it's perfectly all right, but I don't feel good about going out and leaving a stranger in the house. Not with these burglaries in the village.' He addressed the engineer. 'Will you mind having a key and locking up when you've finished?'

'You could leave a key with me,' Jill offered.

'Would you mind?' he asked hopefully.

'Of course not. I'm not going anywhere today.' She felt the weight of her bag on her arm. 'Well, I was nipping up to the shop, but that can wait. I thought I'd take a day off work and give myself a long weekend. I only need some cat food so any time will do for that.'

She was amazed to hear the lies tripping off her tongue so easily, and equally amazed to discover how eager she was to snoop around his home.

'You, my darling girl, are an angel.' Finlay grinned at the engineer. 'I know you're completely trustworthy, but I'll feel happier with Jill on hand, if you don't mind. The village has had a spate of burglaries, you see, and I wouldn't want anything to happen. I rent the cottage, as you know, and the owners wouldn't be too pleased. If you forgot to lock up, it would put the responsibility on you. Are you sure you don't mind, Jill?'

'Positive. It's no bother to me.'

'I very much doubt if I'll be back before six this evening. When he's gone, just pop the key through the letterbox, will you, darling girl?'

'Yes, of course.'

'So does anyone mind if I shoot off now?' Finlay asked.

'It makes no odds to me,' the engineer said.

'Me neither.'

'Excellent.' He beamed at them both, then winked at the engineer. 'Sorry I was a bit rude to you, but, as things have worked out, you'll be glad of it. Jill here might even make you a cup of tea.'

'Yes. Of course,' Jill said, hardly daring to believe her luck.

'The kettle's already boiled, darling girl,' he called, as he strode off. 'I'll get you the spare key, and then I'll be off.'

The engineer followed him back to the cottage while Jill waited outside. Seconds later, she had a front door key in her hand.

'Just pop it through the letterbox,' Finlay said. 'And thank you. I owe you a drink at the very least for this.'

'It's nothing. Really.'

'Ah, but I still want to buy you a drink.' She was treated to that roguish, rather attractive wink of his. 'See you later!'

Jill watched, fascinated, as he jumped in his car, started the engine and, waving, drove off.

While the engineer busied himself unscrewing the phone socket on the kitchen wall, Jill hunted round for a mug to make him a tea, 'white with three sugars'.

She still couldn't quite believe that she was inside Finlay Roberts's home yet, really, what was she hoping to learn? Max had said that everything kept coming back to Finlay, and he was right. But what did they have? He'd taken Carol out on a couple of occasions. There was no crime in that. And he'd lied about being at home when Ralph Atkins's house was burnt to the ground. Or had he? He claimed later that he'd forgotten about nipping out to the filling station to fill up his car and buy a loaf of bread. That was easily done, she supposed. Really, they had nothing.

As Jill made small-talk with the engineer, she thought how absurd her excitement was. Finlay Roberts was a lot of things, but he wasn't stupid. If he *did* have something to hide, he wouldn't leave it in the cottage for any Tom, Dick or Harry to stumble across.

The engineer went into the sitting room to check the phone socket and Jill followed him. She was disappointed to see so few personal possessions, but she wasn't really surprised. The cottage was rented, and the furniture belonged to the owners. Finlay was a traveller and, as such, he wouldn't be a great one for possessions.

In the kitchen, the most basic of utensils and crockery filled the cupboards and drawers. A calendar hung from the wall but nothing had been written on it. An unopened letter from BT was propped against the bread bin. An empty red wine bottle had been rinsed out and was waiting to be put in the recycling bin.

In the sitting room, a couple of books on the tarot sat on the floral-print sofa. That struck Jill as odd. Why, if you were an expert, or expert enough to run your own internet business, would you need books on the subject? Jill had read up on it herself, but she was no wiser.

The remote control sat on top of the TV. A T-shirt, clearly one of Finlay's judging by the way the seams at the arm were hanging together by a thread, was thrown over the back of an armchair. Well-worn flip-flops had been discarded in front of the fireplace. Come to think of it, Jill had only ever seen him in flip-flops. There was a low sideboard with three centre drawers and a door either side of them. As soon as the engineer had gone, she'd look through that.

The phone rang several times, startling her each time, but it was only the engineer testing it and talking to a colleague at the exchange. Finally, he ended one call, and looked at Jill with a satisfied smile on his face.

'As far as I can tell, everything's working perfectly. It's all this rain we've had. Water was getting on the wire where it enters the house. I've changed that, and I've changed the box in here, so that should have cured it.' He gathered up his tools. 'Fingers crossed, eh?'

'Yes.' Jill went to the window and picked up his empty tea mug. 'Is that it then? I'll just wash this mug and then lock up. Thanks very much,' she added.

'See you,' he called as he was leaving.

She heard his van drive down the lane, then, feeling all kinds of a sneak, began opening cupboards and drawers.

Heart in mouth, she switched on Finlay's computer and looked at that. She couldn't download his emails, of course, but there were dozens in his Inbox and the Sent box. None were personal. Every one was connected to his business.

She headed upstairs and saw that his bedroom was as lacking in personal items as the rest of the cottage. Except for a framed photo on the small table by his bed. That was interesting. A small photo, about five by seven inches, it was black and white and showed two young people, girl and boy, hand in hand at the water's edge, with their backs to the camera. It was a beautiful photograph, taken at sunset, Jill suspected, and by an expert photographer. Could the boy be a young Finlay? She carried it to the window to examine it in a better light, but was none the wiser. If it was him, it had probably been taken twenty years ago.

Yet it must mean something to him. He had no personal possessions at all, yet he kept that photo by the side of his bed. Very interesting.

Turning over the frame, she saw that it was easy enough to take the photo from it for a better look. She thought the photographer's name and address or a date might be shown. Instead, on the back of the photo, the initials TMD had been written in pencil.

Who was TMD? Teresa May Davis? Tracy Marie Dickenson? Or perhaps it wasn't who but what. To my darling?

It could be anything. She returned the photo to its frame and went downstairs.

After a quick look in the garage and at the bins, she decided it was time to lock up. There was nothing of interest, and certainly nothing to incriminate her slightly eccentric but basically likeable neighbour.

She had the key in her hand and was doing a last-minute check of the kitchen to make sure she'd left everything as she'd found it when, for no reason she could later understand, she slid her hand in the gap between the top of the fridge and the worktop. And found a red folder.

'Oh, my –'

Inside were several photos of Carol Blakely. The photographer had caught her unawares as she'd been locking or unlocking her shop, walking to her car, or waiting to cross the road. There were also several newspaper cuttings. The uppermost one had the headline *Undertaker still alive*. Older cuttings were photocopies, and told of the crimes committed by Edward Marshall.

It wasn't conclusive, she reminded herself. All the same, a cold shiver ran the length of her spine.

Chapter Twenty-Three

Max glanced up at the clock in the interview room and was surprised to see that they'd only been there an hour. It felt like a lifetime.

A search of Finlay Roberts's cottage had found nothing more than the file Jill had told him about, the file containing photos of Carol Blakely and the newspaper cuttings.

Max had wanted to bring Roberts in on Friday, but he'd decided to wait until the forensic results were in. Roberts possessed very few clothes, but those he did own had been checked out for blood, saliva, anything. So far, and it was approaching midday on Monday, they'd found nothing.

Roberts had been picked up at eight o'clock that morning, and Max and Fletch had been grilling him since ten thirty. They were getting nowhere.

'Interview terminated at 11.37 a.m.' Max hit the button to stop the tapes and nodded at Fletch.

They both stood up and headed for the door.

'We'll be back,' Max informed Roberts.

'He's a tough one,' Fletch remarked as they headed down the corridor. 'For a murder suspect, he's playing it very cool.'

'He's a tosser,' Max grumbled. 'I'm bloody sure he's guilty. It's just a matter of proving it. We need to bring Jill in on it. Perhaps she can rattle him.'

Jill would be reluctant, he knew that. For one thing, she wasn't sure he was guilty and, for another, he was her neighbour. It put her in a difficult situation. But that was tough. They were dealing with a murder investigation not a sodding tea party.

He left a message for Jill to find him a.s.a.p.

'Did you hear about the Kelton Bridge break-in?' Fletch asked.

'Yes, I did.' Some lowlife had broken into a recently opened shop in Kelton Bridge and helped themselves to DVD players, MP3 players, iPods and various other easy-to-shift items. Presumably, it was the same lowlife who'd been house-breaking in the village. 'It seems like someone's getting greedy, Fletch. Still, that's not our problem. Our problem is currently sitting in the interview room.'

'What else can we try on him, guv?'

'God knows. We just keep on at him. We go over the same ground time and time again until he slips up. He has to be lying, so he'll slip up eventually.'

Jill pushed open the double doors. 'You wanted me?' she asked, and he could see the wariness in her eyes.

'Yes. We need you to have a go at Roberts.'

'So you're still getting nowhere with him?' She didn't wait for an answer. 'And what motive is he supposed to have?' she asked instead.

They'd been over this at least a dozen times.

'Who knows?' Max replied impatiently. 'Maybe she'd paid him for tarot readings and was planning to expose him as a fraud. Maybe they weren't strangers. Maybe they had a past. Maybe he bore a grudge. Maybe she was blackmailing him or maybe –'

'She was an alien from a distant planet,' Jill suggested drily.

Max scowled at her. 'When we get him to confess, then we'll have the motive.'

'Max, all you have are a few pictures of Carol, and he told you himself that he fancied his chances with her.'

'We didn't find a camera at his cottage,' Max countered.

She sighed at that. 'So what angle do you want me to take?'

'Do your usual. Flit from one thing to the next and I'll see if I get any ideas. Just do your best to rattle him.'

'Come on, then,' she said reluctantly.

'Do you want me as well, guv?' Fletch asked.

'No. Keep digging into his past. I want his bank accounts checked and double checked. I want *everything* checked and double checked. OK?'

'OK.' Fletch went off, leaving Max and Jill to walk to the interview room.

'Is that all you've got?' Jill asked as they neared the door. 'Just that file?'

'Yes,' Max admitted.

As soon as they stepped into the room, Roberts was on his feet, his face wreathed in smiles. 'Jill, my darling girl. What a welcome surprise.'

'I'd hardly call it welcome, Finlay,' she said quietly, sitting opposite him. 'This is a very serious matter.'

'Indeed,' he agreed, 'but it's far nicer for me to have a pretty face opposite.'

'Thank you. Now, perhaps you'd like to start by telling me about the file that officers found in your cottage. I gather it contained photographs of Carol as well as newspaper articles about her.'

'That's right,' he replied easily. 'I told you, Jill, I knew her. Not well, admittedly, but it brought it all home to me. In the same circumstances, if you'd had a couple of evenings out with someone who was later murdered, wouldn't you be interested?'

'Interested isn't the word that springs to mind, no. Who took the photos?'

'Who? I did, of course.'

'Oh? What sort of camera do you have?'

'Ah!' He laughed at that, and addressed Max. 'You didn't find a camera, did you? No, well, you wouldn't. I bought one of those cheap, disposable efforts, the ones you can take to any high street developer. I'm no photographer. I just point and shoot. As for digital, forget it.'

'Who developed the film for you?' she asked.

'Asda in Rawtenstall. A good job they made of them, too.' He addressed Max. 'I haven't got the receipt, but I'm sure they keep records.'

Max ignored him. Clever sod.

'You surprise me,' Jill said. 'You maintain your own website for your business. Surely you use digital photos on that.'

'Only ones that people have sent to me. Other than that, I don't have a clue.'

'What about past girlfriends?' Jill asked, changing tack and taking Roberts, and Max for that matter, by surprise.

'Jealous, darling girl?'

'Just curious. Have you ever married?'

'No.'

'How old were you when you had your first girlfriend?' she pressed on.

A lot of people accused psychologists of ascribing everything to sex and, now and again, Max was inclined to agree with them. Jill was renowned for it. However, unless he was mistaken, her question had touched on a nerve. The smile was still there, but Roberts had blinked at the question.

Could he be gay? Having an affair with Vince Blakely perhaps? But Blakely wasn't gay, Max was sure of it. Perhaps Roberts *wanted* an affair with him. Perhaps he was in love with him and wanted Carol out of the way so that he could chase Blakely. Could he have been having an affair with Ralph Atkins? Did Carol find out and try to blackmail him?

'I can't honestly remember,' Roberts replied. 'Sixteen, seventeen, I suppose.'

'You can't remember?' Jill scoffed. 'Oh, come on. Everyone remembers their first love.'

'I don't.'

Max was intrigued. Something about this subject was definitely unnerving Roberts.

'How about losing your virginity?' Jill asked. 'Don't tell me you can't remember that.'

'I remember that,' he replied, regaining his composure. 'I was seventeen and we had sex under the pier at Weston-super-Mare. Her name was Maggie Shaw and she was nineteen at the time.'

'How long did your affair with her last?'

'We had sex twice. I soon realized she was the biggest slag on the planet.'

'What did your mother think about that?'

'My mother?' The smile slid back into place. 'I didn't ask her.'

'Are you close, you and your mother?'

'We must be, mustn't we? I wouldn't have sent her flowers otherwise. They were expensive, too.'

He was speaking to Jill, but looking at Max, that smug smile in place. Roberts was playing games with them, Max was sure of it.

He was right about one thing; the flowers for his mother, as well as those for his sister, had been expensive. Max had seen the receipts. They hadn't been extravagantly so, though. Max was forgetful, and lazy, so he often had to make a last-minute call to the florist's for his mother-in-law's birthday or some such event. He knew only too well how much a simple bouquet cost.

'Pleased with them, was she?' Jill asked.

'Very.'

'I suppose she wishes you'd married and had children,' Jill murmured, sounding casual.

'I suppose she does.'

'So tell me again about the first time you saw Carol Blakely. I mean the first time you saw her, not the first time you met her.'

'I've told you time and time again,' he said with an exaggerated sigh. 'I walked into the shop and was looking at flowers, wanting something special to be sent to my mother. Carol walked in, except I didn't know who she was at the time, and because she was a bit of a looker, I tried to get into conversation with her by asking her opinion. She was very knowledgeable about flowers, you know. She had style. She must have talked for a full five minutes on getting the colours right.'

'And you'd never seen her before then?'

'Of course not. My darling girl,' he said patiently, 'you don't really think I killed her, do you?'

'Chief Inspector Trentham thinks you did.'

'Chief Inspector Trentham is damn certain you did,' Max put in. 'What's more, I'll prove it. There are two things you should know about me, Roberts. Firstly, I'm not a great lover of the rule book. Neanderthal, my boss calls me. I get my man by any means open to me. Secondly, and more important, I never give up. Never. Until you're behind bars, I'll be behind you every step of the way!'

Roberts didn't even blink. The smile didn't slip by so much as a millimetre.

It wasn't an idle threat. Max was sure he'd killed Carol, absolutely, one hundred per cent positive, and, if it took him till his dying breath, he'd damn well prove it.

'Did you sleep with her?' Jill asked.

'No.'

'Did you want to?'

'Yes.'

'So why didn't you?'

'Unlike Chief Inspector Trentham here, I'm no Neanderthal man. I don't try and coax a woman into my bed on our first – or second – date. I like the thrill of the chase. And naturally, I thought I had plenty of time.'

'What's your father like?'

'A total bastard. What's yours like?'

'A total bastard? Why's that? Don't you get on with him?'

'I don't see him. I haven't seen him since I was six years old.' He folded his arms and leaned on the table. 'He walked out on us, you see. He forgot he had a wife and two kids, and he just walked out. Moved in with another woman.'

'Was he part of the circus?'

'No.'

164

'Oh?'

'My mother had left her family to marry him. We lived in a semi in Hounslow. It was when he abandoned us that she returned to her family – and the circus.'

'You sound bitter.'

'No.'

'Why would someone put coins on a dead person's eyes?'

Roberts didn't even blink. 'Who knows? I wouldn't.' He smiled in a way that said he was willing to make this easier for her. 'I'd put a silver coin under their tongue. Given such payment, the ferryman, Charon, will take the person safely across the River Styx.'

'Fascinating,' Jill murmured. 'Why do you sound so bitter about your father?'

'I didn't realize I did.'

'How's your business going?'

'Very well, thanks.'

'How long have you been doing it?' Jill asked him.

'Five years now.' He grinned suddenly. 'I do pay my taxes, you know. You won't get me on that one.'

'Only five years? How did you make a living until then? With the circus?'

'Me?' He seemed to find the idea amusing. 'No, not with the circus. When I left school, I trained as a mechanic. Dirty, filthy job. I managed a pub for a few months, worked as a waiter, then as a taxi driver. I've done a bit of farm work. Jack of all trades,' he informed her. 'Then the internet came along and I did a bit of buying and selling. Antiques, that sort of stuff. I got into the tarot, and the rest, as they say, is history.'

'How did you get into the tarot?'

'I read about it.'

'Who would want Carol Blakely dead?'

'That's what I've been wondering,' he replied easily. 'A nice girl like that. Young, pretty, clever – I can't understand it.'

Jill did her usual flitting from one topic to the next for the next two hours and Max decided it was high time they all had a break. They left Roberts awaiting a sandwich and a cup of tea.

'Fancy nipping over the road for a sandwich?' Max asked, and Jill nodded.

He was waiting for her to tell him that he'd got Roberts wrong, but she didn't. She was thoughtful as they walked out of the building and crossed the road to the Coffee Pot. She sat at one of the tables outside while he went inside for food and coffee.

'Well?' Max asked, as he put a tray on the table and sat beside her.

'I think you might be on to something,' she said, taking him by surprise.

Roberts had said nothing new to make her think that way. On the contrary, he'd been his usual, confident self.

'Has anyone spoken to his family – his mother or his sister?' she asked.

'I don't know,' Max admitted. 'We checked that flowers had been delivered to the right addresses, but – I don't know. Why?'

'Behind that smile, his eyes are as cold as ice.' She blew on her coffee and took a sip. 'There's something calculating there. He's not happy talking about his family, either. It could be worth having a chat with them.' She took a bite of her sandwich. 'You need something, though, Max. All you've got is a –'

'A hunch,' he finished for her, knowing only too well that evidence was distinctly lacking. 'A gut feeling. Instinct. You can call it what you like, but I'd stake my life on his being guilty.'

'But why would he want her dead?'

'Beats me.'

She smiled at that, but it was a very brief one.

An elderly woman took up residence at the table next to them, and all conversation ceased.

It was the last day of July, and not a particularly pleasant one. The sky was leaden with cloud and the air was heavy. Max wouldn't be surprised if they didn't have a thunderstorm before the day was over.

He was idly watching people, as was Jill, when he spotted a young lad striding past. The trainers were as worn and scruffy as ever.

'Hello, Darren,' he called out, and the lad stopped, a guilty expression on his face.

'Oh, hello, mister.' He was so surprised to see Max that he just stared at him. 'Cool,' he said at last. 'I didn't know you coppers came to the same places as normal people.'

Jill gave a hoot of laughter at that, saying in a whisper, 'Ssh, he's in disguise. He's pretending to be a normal person for the day.'

'Enjoying the school holidays?' Max asked him, and Darren shrugged.

'There's nothing to do.'

Max supposed there was little difference for Darren between term-time and holidays as he rarely attended school anyway.

'Where's your bike?'

'Scrapped,' he said, his eyes alight. 'I'm having a new one.'

'Really?'

'Yeah, me dad's had a windfall.'

'That's nice then,' Max said, wondering what sort of windfall Dave Walsh had had. One thing was certain, it wouldn't be an honest one.

'Yeah. See you, mister.' And Darren trotted off.

'Come on, then,' Jill said, standing up. 'You'll never pass for a normal person so we may as well have another hour or so with Finlay.'

Chapter Twenty-Four

By the following afternoon, Max was, very reluctantly, having to agree with his boss.

Phil Meredith, dressed for the occasion, had expected to be telling the media that Finlay Roberts had been charged with the murder of Carol Blakely. Instead, he was scowling at everything that moved. Other than heavy rain lashing against the office window, Max was the only thing moving so he was getting the brunt of it.

'You've got to let him go,' Meredith said. 'Bloody hell, Max, you've had –' He broke off to check his watch and do the calculation. 'Thirty-two hours! What have you got? Nothing!'

'We've got the file –'

'Pah! Probably everyone in Rossendale has the same file. You know damn well what it's like. People see murders on the TV news and accept it. As soon as there's a local murder, everything's different. People go into shock. The ghouls come out. Suddenly everyone's interested. Everyone claims to have known the victim and everyone –'

'Not everyone has taken photos of the victim before they're killed,' Max pointed out.

'You can't hang a man for that!'

'True. He went out with Carol twice, though. He bought red ribbon –'

'And every length sold by that shop has been checked,' Meredith snapped. 'The ribbon the shop sells is completely different to that used by the killer.'

Meredith was right, Max knew it. He also knew that Roberts was too clever to buy red ribbon from his victim. Nothing altered his gut feeling, though. Roberts was guilty and, come hell or high water, Max would prove it.

'We're trying to check out his family,' Max told him, 'and that's not easy. His mother and sister, we've found. They've just moved on –'

'Bloody travellers!'

'Quite, but we're having trouble tracing his father.'

'The man he hasn't seen since he was six years old? Oh, great work, Max. Bloody hell, he'll have a lot to tell you, won't he?'

'Jill thinks he's worth talking to.'

'Jill would!' Max wasn't sure what he meant by that, but he didn't ask and Phil didn't elaborate. Instead, he tapped on a folder that was sitting on his desk. 'How many sightings have there been of Eddie Marshall today, hm?'

'A few,' Max admitted, 'but that means nothing. He's dead. I'm sure of it.'

'No, Max. Jill is sure of it. What if she's wrong, hm? She cocked up on Valentine's case, perhaps she's done it again. You need more officers looking into that. If he's still alive, we'll be a bloody laughing stock. Heads will roll, believe me.'

Max believed him.

Meredith nodded at the door. 'Get out. And let Roberts go!'

'Right.'

As Max walked back to his own office, he decided that Roberts could stay exactly where he was for the next couple of hours.

He was at the top of the stairs, about to descend, when Grace came racing round the corner. She stopped when she saw him, and gathered her breath.

'You're *really* not going to like this, Max.'

He never liked it when she called him Max. It always signalled bad news.

'Go on.'

'A woman out walking with her dog has found a body. By the river in Rawtenstall. PC Woods was the first officer on the scene. Fletch is on his way there now, but it seems likely that Carol Blakely's killer has struck again.'

'What? No. No, it can't be.' It couldn't be. Carol Blakely's killer was in this building under lock and key.

If it *was* the work of Carol's killer, that body had been there since before eight o'clock yesterday morning.

'Come on then,' he said, already striding towards the exit and expecting Grace to follow.

The rain was bouncing off the tarmac and they got soaked running the short distance from the building to Max's car. Thunder was rumbling in the distance.

The traffic was evil. The entire town planning department should be shot, Max decided, as he weaved in and out of traffic. Of course, the rain didn't help. People seemed to take great pleasure in driving like morons at the first spot.

They were soon out of Harrington, skirting Burnley and driving down into Rawtenstall. When Max parked the car as close to the river as he could get, the rain was heavier than ever. Any evidence would be washed away in no time. The area had been sealed off and he dodged through the inevitable crowd of onlookers.

Surprisingly, Aiden, the pathologist, or the Grim Reaper as Max preferred to call him, was bending over a body some distance away. Fletch was talking to PC Woods and Max strode over to them. Grace trotted along behind him, trying to avoid the puddles.

'Well?' Max demanded of Fletch.

'I've only just got here myself, guv, but it seems a Mrs Talbot was walking her dog along here – she does that twice every day apparently, morning and afternoon – and her dog found the body. It wasn't particularly well hidden, though. You can see, it's half under the hedge. She called 999.'

'Where is she now?'

'Her husband came and took her home,' PC Woods explained. 'She's in a bit of a state.'

If she walked along here every day, why didn't the dog find it yesterday? It must have been here yesterday. It must. Perhaps she walked along here *most* days . . .

Max grabbed the young constable's notebook and read the ridiculously brief notes he'd taken.

'Did she walk this route yesterday?' Max asked him.

'Yes. Every day without fail, she said.'

'So why isn't that in your notes?' Max thrust the book back at him. 'What else?'

'It's a young woman, body wrapped in a shroud, red ribbon round her waist –'

Sod it!

'Keep the crowd back,' he snapped, taking his frustration out on Fletch.

People – ghouls, Phil Meredith would call them – had seen the cars and were eager for a closer look.

Max strode along the side of the river. Long, wet grass brushed against his trousers and his legs were soon cold and wet.

'Aiden,' he said, 'how come you're here?'

The pathologist straightened up. 'I was almost here, on the doorstep as it were, so I thought I'd come for a look.'

'And?' All Max could see was a sodden sheet wrapped around a body. He peered round Aiden. 'Oh, no!'

Shock had him taking a step back and turning away. He had to steel himself to look again.

Red ribbon had been tied around the waist. A well-worn wedding ring had been threaded through it . . .

'You OK?' Aiden asked curiously.

'Yes, fine.' But he was far from OK.

'Are you sure?'

'Yes.' It was a good few years since Max had passed out at the sight of a dead body, and he wasn't about to do it now. Not even at the sight of this one. 'Yes, I'm fine. So what can you tell me?'

Chapter Twenty-Five

That evening, Jill ordered a takeaway and, while she ate it, she scribbled notes on a pad. She liked to call them spider diagrams, but really, they were lots of 'what if?' scenarios, which might link up. As yet, however, they were making no sense at all.

For instance, what if Finlay Roberts had known Carol Blakely from way back? She didn't think he had, but it was a possibility. What if blackmail was involved? What if Carol had been about to expose him as a fraud? But that was unlikely. Some believed in the tarot, some didn't. It was the same with horoscopes. Jill's mother, for instance, wouldn't leave the house until she'd read her horoscope and prepared herself for the day ahead.

What if Vince Blakely was involved?

She pushed her notepad aside and reminded herself, yet again, that she wasn't a detective. It was her job to deliver a profile. That wasn't easy, though. It never was with a copycat.

What did she know? That, unlike Edward Marshall, this killer didn't have an audience. This killer was more reluctant and treated the dead with more respect. Ironically, they could have been looking for an undertaker. This killer had wanted Carol Blakely dead. It wasn't a random act. Unlike Edward Marshall's victims, this had nothing to do with the fact that she was a childless career woman. No, this killer stood to benefit from her death.

But why, if he'd wanted her dead, did he go to such lengths to make them think it was Edward Marshall's work? To throw them off the scent? To confuse the issue? He had certainly done that.

Sam wandered inside and jumped up on to the table. Jill picked him up and put him on the floor. 'Paws off!'

She'd made the mistake of ordering chicken and it was Sam's favourite. He could smell it from miles away. She realized that he'd come in from outside and was dry. Sure enough, the rain had finally stopped.

With her meal finished, she grabbed her jacket and locked up the cottage. Perhaps some fresh air would clear her mind. A walk round the village always cheered her. She loved the place and the people, and had never felt so at home as she did in Kelton Bridge. It had taken a while, and people still thought of her as the 'newcomer', but they had a warmth and an openness that appealed.

She walked very slowly past the manor. It was ludicrous to even think about buying the place. On the other hand, it probably wouldn't be up for sale again.

And what about Lilac Cottage? She'd had a lot of work done on the cottage since she'd moved in including a loft extension, new roof, new windows and doors and the ground-floor extension which was supposed to be her study but which was currently being used for storage. She didn't really want to sell up.

She saw Olive Prendergast, retired postmistress and local gossip, walking ahead of her, but didn't hurry to catch her up. Olive was the exception to the rule, and the word 'warmth' didn't figure in her vocabulary. Any chat with Olive involved the obligatory character assassination of several Kelton Bridge residents. Jenny had taken over from Olive in the post office, and the village had breathed a relieved sigh. Jill had no secrets, nothing to hide, but it was a delight to use the post office and know that the entire village wouldn't be told she'd posted a present for her niece's birthday or collected a form to buy more Premium Bonds.

She walked past the post office and the church to the Weaver's Retreat. Judging by the cars parked there, Ian was doing a good trade. She carried on. The air was lighter now and everywhere smelled clean and fresh after the downpour.

She was heading for home, but then decided to call on Louise. It would be refreshing to forget Carol Blakely's murder for an hour or so. She walked up the path, rang the doorbell and had the shock of her life when Grace answered the door.

'What on earth are you doing here? Is everything all right? Louise?'

'You'd better come in,' Grace said, answering none of her questions.

Heart in her mouth, Jill followed her into Louise's familiar lounge. Except this evening, nothing was familiar about it. For one thing, Max was standing in the middle of the room. The expression on his face made her stomach clench.

Louise had been sitting on the sofa, head in her hands, but, when she saw Jill, she rushed forward, threw her arms around her and howled. It was the sound a wounded animal might make. A sound that would stay with Jill always.

Jill instinctively held her close as she howled.

A couple of months ago, she'd visited when Louise and Nikki had been in the midst of a blazing row. Nikki's language had been foul and Louise had yelled at her, 'Drugs? You don't know you can control it. You can't! You'll end up dead!' The memory made her want to scream. Surely Louise's words hadn't come true . . .

It was a full five minutes before her friend stopped sobbing. In all that time, no one had said or done anything. Max had stood by the window with an awful, unreadable expression on his face. Grace had simply stood and watched Louise, now and again putting a soothing hand on her shoulder and giving it a squeeze.

'My little girl,' Louise wailed. 'They've taken my little girl, Jill.'

Jill looked at Max, needing answers to a dozen questions, but all she received was an almost imperceptible shake of his head. It was enough to tell her that Louise's little girl was dead.

'You need Charlie,' Jill said, tears smarting in her eyes. 'Let me call him.'

But Louise wouldn't release her hold. The woman could barely stand and Jill was taking most of her weight.

'Grace, call Charlie,' Jill said quietly. 'His number will be in Louise's book by the phone.'

Jill still had no idea what had happened. She only knew that they needed Charlie.

Fortunately, his number was easily found and, although Grace didn't go into details, the fact that a policewoman was asking for him must have motivated him into action because he was there in under fifteen minutes.

There was more howling as Louise told him that her little girl was dead. Charlie held her close, making soothing sounds to try and calm her.

Jill still needed answers.

'Was there an accident?' she asked Grace quietly. 'An overdose?'

'No.'

Grace, trained to deal with these cases, if one could ever be trained for such a situation, soon had Charlie and Louise sitting down. She spoke quietly and calmly to them.

Jill wanted a word with Max, but what words were there?

'I have to go,' he said quietly. 'Grace will stay. What will you ...'

She didn't want him to go. In a sudden moment of panic she thought that, if he went, she wouldn't be able to deal with it. But, of course, he had to go. Just as she had to deal with it.

'I'll stay with Louise for a while. Just until I know she can cope. Although with Charlie here ...' The truth was, she didn't know what to do. Shock was setting in. Her teeth were beginning to chatter. 'Can I call at your place – later?'

'Of course. But get a taxi. Don't drive.'

'I'll be OK.'

175

'For Christ's sake, Jill, get a bloody taxi!' Each word was an angry snap.

'OK.'

'I'm sorry,' he said, and Jill wasn't sure what he was apologizing for, the fact that he'd snapped at her or the fact that Nikki was dead.

It was odd. He was like a stranger to her, and yet there was something familiar about that hard-edged expression. She'd seen it before. It looked for all the world like anger, and perhaps he was angry, but it ran a lot deeper than that.

'Right, I'll see you later,' she said, and she had to turn away before she burst into tears.

Jill and Grace stayed until midnight, until Charlie and Louise made it clear they would rather be alone, until there was nothing more that could be said or done.

'I'll call round tomorrow,' Jill said, giving Louise a hug and fighting back tears. 'You've got my mobile number. Call me, any time, if you need me.'

The world outside was at complete variance with the four walls that had seen such scenes of grief. It was a beautiful night. The sky was clear and thousands of stars were visible.

'As the boss has done his usual trick of abandoning me, I'd better call a taxi,' Grace said, taking her phone from her pocket. 'I don't suppose you know the number offhand?'

Jill shook her head. 'Walk back to my place, and I'll give you a lift home.'

Max could say what he liked, but she had no intention of getting a taxi out to his place. It would involve making polite conversation with a stranger, and she couldn't face that.

'No, you're all right,' Grace said, tapping in the number for directory inquiries.

'Really, it's no trouble. I'm going to Max's so it'll be on my way.'

She still didn't know why she was going to his place. All she knew was that she couldn't bear to spend the night in an empty house.

'Oh, OK. Thanks.'

Apart from the sound of Grace's voice, calm and unmoved as she filled Jill in on the details of Nikki's fate, Kelton Bridge was silent as they walked back to Jill's cottage. Lights were on in Finlay Roberts's cottage, but that wasn't unusual. He often had lights on until one o'clock in the morning.

As they walked up Jill's drive, the security light clicked on, bathing them in a welcome orange glow.

It took Jill less than five minutes to put food out for the cats, grab her key to Max's house, and lock up the cottage.

Dropping Grace off didn't take her out of her way and it was good to have company as she drove. Listening to Grace grumbling about the weather stopped her going to pieces.

'I'll probably see you tomorrow then,' Grace said, getting out of the car.

'Yes, I expect so. Goodnight, Grace.'

'See you.'

Jill drove on to Max's house through streets that were eerily quiet. Even Harrington town centre was almost empty.

Lights were on at Max's, but there was no sign of his car on the drive. The front door was unlocked.

'Oh, Jill,' Kate greeted her. 'I'm so sorry, love. How's Louise?'

Again, Jill found herself biting her lip to stop herself bursting into tears.

'It's difficult to tell. Charlie's with her so she'll be OK, but, oh, it's hell. Nikki was everything to her.'

They chatted for an hour and then Kate, who usually stayed the night if Max was out late, decided it was time to head to her own flat.

Jill sat in the lounge with just a table lamp to light the room. At least she wasn't alone. Holly, the faithful collie, was keeping her company – waiting for Max, more like – and the boys were fast asleep upstairs.

When two o'clock came, she knew she had to lie down. She locked up, left the light on in the lounge and went upstairs to the bedroom she had once shared with Max. It was exactly the same. Nothing had changed.

She knew sleep would be a long time coming, but it was a relief to lie down . . .

Although she didn't know what had woken her, the room, once in darkness, now had the benefit of light from a street lamp outside. The curtains had been pulled back. And Max was there. He was sitting in the chair by the window, staring out, with a glass in one hand and a bottle of whisky in the other.

The memories rushed at her – Max's drinking, their fighting, the nightmares she'd had when Rodney Hill hanged himself. On countless occasions, she'd woken in the middle of the night to see Max staring out into the darkness, a bottle in one hand and a glass in the other, and that dark, hateful expression on his face.

Watching him now, she finally fathomed that expression. He *was* angry. Not with her, or with anyone in particular, but with himself. He was one of those old-fashioned types who was born to protect. Now, he felt he'd failed to protect Nikki and Louise. Just as he'd once felt he'd been unable to protect Jill from those nightmares.

'It's not your fault, Max.'

The sound of her voice startled him and he swung round to face her.

'Of course it's my fault. Who else's is it, for God's sake? If I'd done my job properly, Nikki would be fast asleep in her bed.'

'No.'

'Yes.' He drained his glass and immediately refilled it.

'Can I have one?' she asked.

'What? Yes. Sorry.' He walked over to her, handed her the full glass, sat on the bed beside her and took a swig from the bottle.

'Drinking yourself into oblivion won't help, Max.'

'Oh, Christ! Don't let's start on that again!'

That's exactly how it used to start, she realized. She'd make a comment about his drinking, he'd fire off an angry retort and they'd soon be hurling abuse at each other.

He was right; the last thing they needed was to go down that route again. They'd done that too many times in the past.

She grabbed a pillow and used it as a back rest. The whisky was neat, but she couldn't be bothered to fetch water. Besides, she needed a stiff drink.

'It really isn't your fault, Max,' she said again. 'You can't be a one-man vigilante. You can't weed out people who might, just might, be capable of murder. It's your job to see that justice is done and –'

'Justice? God, that's a laugh. I'll get the lowlife responsible for this if it's the last thing I do, but justice? How long will he get? Hm?'

She knew how he felt. Louise would have to spend the rest of her life without her little girl and the perpetrator would spend a few years in prison. Max was right; justice wouldn't be done. It couldn't be done.

'So much for my hunches,' he muttered. 'While I've been wasting time fixating on Roberts, the real killer has destroyed a family.'

The whisky was burning Jill's throat, but it was warming. Maybe if she drank enough, the horrors of the night would recede. She doubted it. She knew from experience that she would feel ill long before that happened.

'Come and lie down,' she said.

He did, but with great reluctance. Jill lay down beside him, rested her head on his shoulder and felt his anger in every tense muscle . . .

The next thing she knew, Max was leaning over her to kiss her forehead. He'd showered and changed.

'I have to go,' he said, adding a grim, 'I've got an autopsy to attend.'

The horrors rushed back at her, and she sat up quickly and held him briefly.

'I'll be in about –'

'No. Stay here.'

'No, I don't want to. I'll call on Louise first to see if she's all right, or as all right as she's likely to be, and then I'll be in.'

'I'll be there at some point, but talk to her, Jill. I want to know the name, address and phone number of everyone – and I mean everyone – that Nikki's been in contact with since she returned to Kelton.'

'I'll talk to her, but I doubt Louise knows. Nikki didn't discuss her friends. She spent hours on her mobile phone or in internet chat rooms.'

'If it were up to me, I'd ban the bloody internet. It causes nothing but sodding problems.' He squeezed her hand and his voice was gentler as he said, 'I'm so sorry.'

'We're all sorry, Max, but it's not our fault. Not yours and not mine.'

He wasn't going to argue, and a couple of minutes later she heard him drive off.

Chapter Twenty-Six

Jill's arrival at Louise's house coincided with the departure of Dr Thorpe. She had a few words with him, and then went inside.

Charlie was in the kitchen, finishing his breakfast. It looked to Jill as if he'd had a full English. She hadn't been able to face a thing.

'He's given her some sedatives,' he explained between mouthfuls. 'She's not good,' he added in a whisper, 'but at least the doctor's persuaded her to go to bed. I expect she'll sleep now.'

'Let's hope so.'

When he'd finished his breakfast and put the plate in the dishwasher, he moved restlessly from one corner of the room to another. As he did so, he picked up items of Nikki's – a magazine that had been on top of the microwave, a bottle of black nail varnish, a long, black scarf – and put them in a pile.

'I'll get rid of these while Louise is out of the way,' he said, speaking in a whisper.

Jill suspected that Louise wouldn't want anything belonging to Nikki getting rid of, but it wasn't her place to argue.

She watched him pacing around. He was a good-looking man and, even in times of stress it seemed, impeccably dressed. This morning, he was wearing immaculate cream-coloured trousers and a crisp, blue shirt. His dark hair was thinning, and Jill guessed it bothered him. It had never struck her before but she had the feeling that he might be vain about his looks.

She remembered Louise telling her he'd been married before, and even had a couple of children – sons, she recalled – somewhere.

'As terrible and as shocking as this is, Charlie,' she began, feeling awkward, 'I have to work with the police. We need to catch the maniac who did this.'

'Of course.'

'I don't suppose you've spoken to Nikki lately,' she said, and he pulled a face at that.

'I tried, as you probably know, but she didn't want to know. She'd rather die than speak to me.'

Jill cringed inwardly at the choice of phrase.

'I'm wondering if she met someone new recently,' she said. 'Louise said she was spending a lot of time on the internet. It can be a dangerous place for the reckless.'

'She was certainly that.'

Reckless, yes. She was a young woman who made some foolish choices but, no matter how low she had slipped, she hadn't deserved this.

'Do you think Louise would mind if I had a look in her room?' she asked him. 'I expect the police will take her computer away to see if there are clues on it, but I'd like a look.'

'I'll ask her when she gets up,' he said.

Jill guessed he was merely trying to protect Louise from unpleasantness, but that was impossible. 'It's OK, I'll pop my head round and ask her.'

'No need to disturb her,' he said. 'I'm sure she won't mind. I'll show you where it is.' He seemed reluctant to let her see Nikki's room, probably because it was too unbearable to think that she would never walk into it again. 'Mind you,' he added as they walked up the stairs, 'I doubt you'll find anything on her computer other than her moaning to her mates about the evil Charlie trying to wheedle his way into her mum's life.'

Louise, the woman he loved, was suffering the worst pain imaginable so Jill supposed that gave him the right to sound hostile. Max was furious with the world and taking it out on everyone, so why shouldn't Charlie?

He pushed open the door to Nikki's bedroom and stood back to let her enter. Jill had assumed he would leave her alone, but no. He was like a shadow as she moved around the room.

The bed was neatly made, Louise's work no doubt. On the dressing table was a child's jewellery box given to her, Jill supposed, by her mother or her grandmother. It was clearly cherished and, sitting on top of several cheap bangles and beads in every colour, was the ankle bracelet Jill had bought her.

Next to the box was a photo of Nikki dressed in black and looking like something from a second-rate horror film. It was in a frame that had the legend *World's Best Daughter* on it.

Considering Nikki had only been in Kelton Bridge for a few months, and considering that she'd only wanted a room for a 'few days', there were a lot of CDs and DVDs. Despite turning up with only the clothes she'd stood in and a small backpack, the wardrobe was crammed full, too.

'Probably all stolen,' Louise had worried.

Jill pulled open a drawer that was stuffed with scraps of paper, magazines, an empty crisp packet, pens, jewellery –

'I wonder if she kept a diary,' she mused.

'That went out with the ark,' Charlie scoffed. 'Young folk are barely literate these days.'

'Nikki was an intelligent girl,' Jill said, reminding herself to use the past tense.

She walked over to the window and gazed out at a view that was the same as the one from her cottage. Apart from half a dozen white clouds, the sky was clear after yesterday's downpour. The Pennines were bathed in sunshine.

Charlie was behind her, six inches from her right shoulder. It was almost as if he was checking to make sure she didn't steal something.

You don't know him.

Nikki had been right, Jill didn't know the man. At the moment, he was making her uneasy, but how did she expect him to behave? How were any of them expected to get through this with any semblance of normality?

Louise had fallen in love with him so he must have something going for him.

Jill turned away from the window and looked around the room.

'She was very close to her grandmother, wasn't she?' she murmured as her gaze rested on a photo of a woman who was an older version of Louise.

'She was close to anyone who gave in to her demands.'

He was wrong there. Louise had given in to her, but the two hadn't been close for years . . .

'I'll have a quick look at her computer.'

Nikki's laptop was sitting amid a pile of clutter on a small desk in the corner of the room. Louise had bought it a month ago and, as might be expected, it was one of the best models available. In Jill's opinion, it was far too good to be used only for games, internet chat rooms and the like, but Louise had hoped Nikki might use it for job applications or looking at training courses.

She switched it on, immediately received the message that the battery was almost flat, and, with Charlie's help, hunted through a pile of clutter for the mains cable.

Charlie plugged it in for her and she switched it on.

The laptop's screen had a picture of a devil bedecked in black cloak and boasting huge red horns. Jill went straight to the email program. It was impossible to download any waiting emails without knowing Nikki's password, but someone on the force would manage that.

There were a dozen messages that had been sent on Sunday and Jill read through those.

One message, to her friend, Rhianna, said: 'It was gr8. Jills ok 4 a shrink. We LOL. An escape from PC.'

OK for a shrink. Coming from Nikki to her friend, that was praise indeed. What was LOL? Jill never had been able to grasp text-speak and, if anyone used it on her mobile, she replied asking them to put it in English. Did LOL translate as laughed out loud? Perhaps. And what was PC? Jill doubted it was anything to do with political correctness.

'Any idea what PC is, Charlie?' she asked.

He shook his head. 'It's all gobbledegook to me, I'm afraid.'

'Yes, me, too.'

The other messages were of no obvious interest. They were short notes to various friends. One simply said she was 'bored, bored, bored'. Another was arranging to meet someone called Jodie next week. That meeting would never take place.

Jill looked through the history on the web browser but there was nothing obvious there, either, and it was impossible to connect to the internet until they had her password.

'Nothing there then,' Charlie said.

'No.'

Unless she was mistaken, he was relieved that she hadn't stumbled across something. What could that be? Something bad that Louise didn't know about?

'What were you expecting us to find?' she asked lightly.

'Me? Nothing.' He made a show of looking at his watch and being amazed at the time. 'Look, I've got to shoot off. Do you think Louise –'

'I'll stay with her,' Jill offered immediately. 'You'll have the business to manage.'

'I ought to show my face. Are you sure you don't mind?'

'Of course not. You go. Hopefully, she'll sleep for a bit and then I'll try and get her to eat something. What time will you be back if she asks?'

'Don't worry, I'll be back this evening. About nineish, I expect.'

Nine? That was almost twelve hours away.

You don't know him. Nikki's words seemed to echo around this room. How right the girl had been. Jill had imagined he would stay by Louise's side every minute of every hour. Some people, however, simply couldn't handle

185

other people's grief. With no idea of what to say, time dragged on hopelessly.

'I'll be here until you get back,' she said, adding, 'She'll be OK, Charlie. Try not to worry too much. She's strong. She will get over this.' At least, Jill hoped she would.

'Yes. Yes, I know she will.' He gave her an awkward smile. 'I'll see you later then, Jill.'

She stood at Nikki's bedroom window to watch him drive away. He hadn't even popped his head round Louise's bedroom door to see if she was sleeping. As he drove off, he didn't so much as glance at the house.

Last night, Jill had thanked God that Charlie was there for Louise. Now, she wasn't sure that he was going to be as much help as she'd anticipated.

And what had he expected her to find?

Curious, she began a thorough search. She checked every pocket, every drawer, every book – nothing. She even checked under the bed.

At a little after one o'clock, when Jill was tidying up in the kitchen, Louise came downstairs. She looked awful, worse even than Jill had expected and she'd tried to prepare herself for the worst. Louise's face was grey and her eyes were like black holes.

Jill went forward and held her close for a few minutes. 'Sit down, love.'

'Where's Charlie?'

'He'll be back. He thought he'd nip out while you were having a rest.'

'Ah, yes. He'll have work to do. Life has to go on, I suppose.'

'He said it was work,' Jill agreed, 'but I'm sure he's struggling, too, Lou. Anyway, I'll keep you company until he gets back.'

'Thanks.'

Normally, Louise would have told her not to bother, but she wasn't fit to argue with anyone.

'Have you managed to get some sleep?' Jill asked.

'Not really. The pills the doctor gave me knocked me out

for a while, but that's all.' She bit on her bottom lip. 'I'll be all right, though.'

Jill hoped so.

Right now, Louise was numb with shock and all the pills in the world wouldn't lessen that. When it finally gave way to reality, Jill had no idea how she would get through the days.

Soon, reporters would be gathering outside the house. Everyone in Kelton Bridge would be calling to see if there was anything they could do. The phone would be ringing constantly. Nikki's smiling face would be splashed across the newspapers and on television screens.

'I'll do some lunch,' Jill suggested.

Unlike Jill's cupboards, Louise's were well stocked. A lot of the food, she guessed, was bought specially for Nikki, but at least Louise didn't have to think about shopping for a week or so.

Louise was toying with the first spoonful of soup when she said, 'Charlie's a good man, isn't he?'

The question, or rather the needy tone, took Jill by surprise. But Charlie wasn't there. Just when Louise needed him most, he'd gone to tend to his business. The used-car market needed him.

'He certainly is,' Jill said briskly, determined to reassure her friend. 'Wild horses wouldn't have dragged him away if you hadn't been sleeping so soundly.'

Louise eventually ate her soup, but didn't touch the bread roll.

Soon afterwards, Max and Grace arrived with an officer Jill didn't recognize. The man in question was soon looking around Nikki's room while Max and Grace questioned Louise.

Max sat next to Louise on the sofa and held her hand as he asked questions. Grace made notes, speaking only occasionally.

'Tell me about yesterday morning,' Max said gently.

'We had breakfast together,' Louise said softly. 'That's rare because Nikki often stayed in bed all day. She'd decided to take up running, though. There's this lad she fancies – fancied,' she corrected herself, 'and he's a bit of a fitness freak. You know what she's like. So she was up with the larks and going for a run. She had a yoghurt for breakfast, then left. She said she was going to run along the valley, from here to Rawtenstall and back. What's that? Twelve miles?'

'About that,' Max agreed.

'I didn't expect to see her the rest of the day,' Louise went on. 'I guessed she'd meet up with friends and come home in the evening. Except . . .'

She never did come home.

'This lad she fancied,' Max asked, 'what do you know about him?'

'Nothing. I'm not sure she ever spoke to him – just saw him and asked about him, if you know what I mean. Oh, wait, it was something like Julian. Yes, I'm sure that's it. I have a feeling he worked in the record shop in Harrington.'

'OK.' Max patted her hand. 'What about other friends? Can you give us the names of her friends?'

'I never knew her friends,' Louise said wistfully. 'To be honest, I didn't want to know them. Only the other day, I was telling Jill how awful they were. Aggressive types.'

Louise spent a good fifteen minutes telling them of Nikki's antics, but she didn't know any of the girl's friends. She was more than willing to talk about Nikki, sometimes in the present tense as if the girl might walk in the room at any minute, and sometimes in the past tense as if she'd been dead for years.

When Max and Grace were about to leave, Louise put her hand on Max's sleeve.

'Max, will it have been quick?'

He gave her shoulder a reassuring squeeze. 'She wouldn't have known anything about it.'

Jill could tell he was lying.

'I know it won't bring her back, Louise,' he went on, 'but

we will catch the bastard who did this. I promise you that. And although you won't think so now, it will help. It will give you some sort of closure.'

'But you can't bring her back,' Louise said, eyes staring off into the distance.

'I'm sorry.'

While Grace spoke to Louise, telling her once again that she must get in touch if she needed anything, anything at all, Jill had a quick word with Max.

'Where's Charlie?' he asked.

'Gone to work. He said he'd be back around nineish so I'll stay till then.'

He nodded. 'And then?'

She didn't know. She supposed she should go home to her cottage and her cats.

'Come back to our place,' he said, making the decision for her. 'You can feed the cats on your way over.'

'OK.' The relief was immense. She simply couldn't face going home to brood alone in her cottage. 'See you later then.'

He put a finger to her forehead and then he and Grace were heading out of the door.

They were midway down the path when the phone started to ring and, for the next hour, it didn't stop. It was either reporters or Kelton Bridge residents who had heard the news. Jill began fielding calls, but it was going to be a full-time job.

'Leave the answer machine to deal with it,' she said in the end. 'People can leave a message and you can call them back if you want to speak to them.'

'Yes, that would be best. And Charlie will call my mobile.'

Jill hoped so. Louise needed to know that he was there for her.

There was no word from him, however, and it wasn't until nine thirty that they heard his car pull up outside.

Louise went straight into his arms.

'I didn't like to call in case you were sleeping,' he told her. 'And stuff kept coming up at the office.'

Jill wondered if he really had been to the office.

'I'll call in tomorrow morning, Louise,' she said as she was leaving.

Maybe then, Charlie would be the rock Louise needed.

Chapter Twenty-Seven

The following morning, there was no sign of Charlie at Louise's house. Connie was there, however, and was bossing her sister. She was being brisk which was possibly what Louise needed and, despite the fact that her eyes were red and swollen from crying, she was determined to drag her sister back from the brink.

She was a smaller edition of Louise, but a stronger character, Jill guessed.

'Go! Now!' she was instructing Louise firmly. 'I'm not speaking to you until you've had a shower and washed your hair. Turning into a bag lady won't help matters. Go on, shoo!'

With a helpless shrug in Jill's direction, Louise, who had little choice, went off to have a shower.

Three bouquets of flowers sat in the kitchen sink waiting to be arranged. Connie looked in a cupboard, grabbed a vase and put one lot of flowers in it.

'These are nice, I suppose,' she said, 'but the bloody phone hasn't stopped ringing since I arrived.'

'Ignore it,' Jill suggested. 'If it's anyone Louise wants to speak to, they can leave a message.'

Connie's hands stilled on the flowers. 'She keeps telling me that everyone has been marvellous. Someone hasn't though, have they? Who could have done this, Jill?'

'God knows.'

'I know Nikki was difficult, a pain in the arse really, and I know she was hell-bent on self-destruction, but she didn't deserve to die.'

'No.'

'As for Charlie,' Connie snorted, 'you'd have thought he could have hung around a bit, couldn't you?'

'Where is he? At his office?'

'So he says.'

'I expect it's difficult for him,' Jill said.

'Difficult for *him*? Pah! It's a damn sight more difficult for Lou.' Connie lowered her voice to a whisper. 'Between you, me and the gatepost, I hope he never comes back. He's a complete waste of space.'

'Ah, you're not a fan then. I don't really know him so I can't comment.'

'You haven't missed anything. What Lou sees in him, I can't imagine. He's the biggest flirt on the planet, and always flirting with young girls. He makes me sick.'

'Young girls? How do you mean?'

'He's what? Forty? And he thinks he's God gift to the female of the species. Every time he's out, he's chatting up girls young enough to be his daughters. I suppose he's good-looking, in a way, but even so. Sorry, Jill, but he makes me sick.'

Jill was amazed. All she'd heard from Louise was how kind, thoughtful and considerate he was. Louise wasn't an expert on men, though. In fact, she was a walking disaster where relationships were concerned.

'Nikki didn't like him, did she?' she said.

'She couldn't stand him. Pervy Charlie, she used to call him. Mind, the feeling was mutual. Because she didn't fawn all over him, he accused her of being a stuck-up cow. He didn't like it at all.'

Pervy Charlie? PC? That must have been what Nikki had meant in her email. She had escaped Pervy Charlie for the day . . .

Louise looked better when she came downstairs. She was wearing clean blue jeans and a pale lemon shirt, and her hair was still wet from her shower.

Jill stayed for a few more minutes then, reassured that

Connie was the best medicine Louise could have, she left the sisters to cope as best they could with the day.

She managed to avoid the gaggle of reporters that had gathered, and drove into Harrington. Now she came to think about it, she realized she didn't even know Charlie's surname. All she knew was that he owned a used car business. That and the fact that, apart from Louise, no one seemed to like him . . .

She went straight to Max's office. He was reading through the autopsy report and, when he looked up, she was shocked to see how weary he looked.

'How's Louise?' he asked.

'Being bossed around by Connie. She'll be OK.'

She supposed it was no wonder he looked shattered. Last night, she'd gone to bed – his bed – and had fallen asleep in minutes. When she'd woken in the early hours of the morning, he'd been sitting in the seat by the bedroom window, staring out, lost in his own thoughts. She'd lain there quietly for a few moments, wondering what she could say, and the next thing she knew, the shower had been running and, minutes later, Max had left the house.

'What does that tell us?' she asked, nodding at the report. 'Anything new?'

'Not really. It has her as being killed between ten and twelve o'clock,' he said, 'but I think it's closer to twelve. She was seen in Waterfoot at a few minutes to ten and then nothing. I suppose if someone she knew came along in a car –'

'Like Charlie?'

'Charlie?'

'Connie hates him,' she explained, 'almost as much as Nikki did. Nikki used to refer to him as Pervy Charlie, apparently. According to Connie, he was always chatting up girls young enough to be his daughters. She also said he didn't like the way Nikki refused to fawn all over him, as she put it.'

'Pervy Charlie? That sounds like Nikki-speak. It doesn't make him a killer, though.'

'No, but it does put a question mark over him. We know nothing about him, Max. Where was he when Nikki was killed?'

'Selling used cars.'

'Can anyone vouch for that?'

'Yes. One of his salesmen. Apparently, one was off sick, so there was just Charlie and his sidekick, a chap called Alan.'

Which put him in the clear. Not that she'd suspected the man of murder. Not really. He and Nikki may have been at loggerheads but it had to be said that Nikki was difficult.

'Why Nikki?' she murmured.

'Why Carol Blakely?' he returned, and she sighed.

They didn't know. What they did know was that Phil Meredith would go berserk if she didn't come up with some sort of profile . . .

She spent the rest of the day in her office going through everything they had on Carol's and Nikki's murders. The connection to Edward Marshall's victims couldn't be ignored, so she went through those, too.

The photographs were grim and depressing, yet she spread them out across her desk.

Grace came in to ask after Louise, and that was her only interruption. For the rest of the time, Jill stared at the photos hoping for inspiration.

There was nothing. To be more accurate, there was nothing she could put her finger on. Something was bothering her, but she wasn't sure what it was. Finally, when photos and reports were beginning to blur into one, she decided to call it a day. She stopped at Max's office on her way out to see if he'd come up with anything.

'Zilch,' he said grimly.

Fletch burst through the door, breathless, and hitching up trousers that were constantly falling down. On first meeting him, Jill had thought he must have lost weight. Now she knew he was simply incapable of buying clothes that fitted.

194

'Charlie Denning, guv,' he said. 'It seems he lied about being at his dealership.'

'Go on,' Max urged him.

'His sidekick, Alan Graham, has just phoned us. Apparently, they've had a bust-up. Graham's told him where to stuff his job and walked out. It seems like he's out for a spot of revenge, too, because he now claims that Denning asked him to tell us he was at the showroom all day.'

'So where was he?'

'Graham has no idea, but he says he didn't see him at all.'

'Right. Let's go and have a word with him.'

Fletch looked at his watch. It was getting on for seven o'clock.

'OK,' Max said, 'you go home, Fletch. I'll go and have a word with him.' He looked at Jill. 'Do you want to come along for a chat with Pervy Charlie?'

'Oh, I'd love to!'

Chapter Twenty-Eight

As Max drove them out to Victoria Street, he silently questioned the wisdom of having Jill with him. This case was too personal now. She might not have known Nikki well, but Louise was her friend and she was suffering on her behalf. At a guess, he'd say she was suffering more than she was letting on, too.

'Has anything interesting about Terry Yates come to light?' she asked him.

He shouldn't have been surprised by the question. She might be feeling wretched, but her mind would still be on the job.

'Not really. He and his wife – ex-wife – used to live in Kelton Bridge. Did you know that?'

'No.'

'Yes, before they split up. Then they sold up, divided the proceeds and bought places in Harrington.'

'Whereabouts in Kelton?' she asked curiously.

'Haver Road. Newish houses, aren't they?'

'They were built about fifteen years ago. It's only a small development, about fifteen homes, I think. Big houses, though. Four or five bedrooms, en-suites, double garages.'

'No wonder Yates is bitter.'

'Hm. I'll ask around.'

Max drove on to the forecourt at Denning's used car lot where the man himself was showing a couple the benefits of a Vauxhall Vectra. He was all smiles, like something from a toothpaste ad, but Max saw the smile slip when he recognized his visitors.

'Dodgy Motors R Us,' Max murmured.

'They look OK,' Jill pointed out. 'All fairly new.'

'He looks the type who'd rip off his own grandmother.'

Smiling, Jill shook her head at that. 'You can't know that just because he sells used cars.'

'True.'

Max supposed Charlie was a good-looking bloke in a smooth salesman sort of way. But come the winter, Max would bet his life he'd be wearing the regulation used car salesman's uniform of sheepskin jacket.

They got out of the car and had a walk round the forecourt.

'I'll be with you in a couple of minutes,' Charlie called out to them.

'No rush,' Max assured him.

Max reckoned he could do this job. Done properly – legally – it must be a doddle. No stress, regular hours and enough money to live on.

The couple went away to 'think about' the Vectra and Charlie, still smiling, crossed the forecourt to them.

'Hello, there, what can I do for you?' His smile faltered, but only slightly. 'Is Louise OK?'

'Haven't you seen her?' Jill asked.

'Sadly not. I'm having a right time of it, I can tell you. I've got Gerry off sick – some sort of gastro-flu, he reckons – and now Alan has walked out on me. Just like that. Can you believe it? At a time like this, too. Mind you, he'd only been here three weeks and he's no great loss. He couldn't sell ice to Eskimos.'

'Few people could,' Max put in, and Charlie, not having a clue what was meant by that, just smiled and agreed.

'So what can I do for you?' he asked.

'We'd like a word, if you don't mind. Can we go inside?' Max asked.

'Of course.'

He led the way into the smart but small showroom. Inside were two cars, both Fords, a modern desk and three chairs, a computer and a coffee machine.

'Can I get you a coffee?' he asked pleasantly.

'Please,' Jill said, and Max nodded. Why not? Machine coffee was better than no coffee.

'It might improve my temper,' he said.

'Oh?'

'I'm in a bad mood,' Max explained as Charlie put coins in the machine and waited for sludge to fall into three plastic cups. 'In fact, I'm totally pissed off. It gets me like that when people lie to me.'

Charlie didn't take the hint. 'I'm sorry to hear that.'

They sat on two chairs on one side of the desk, and he took the one opposite. Three plastic cups of pale brown coffee were between them.

'When I asked you where you were on Monday,' Max began, 'you thought you'd been here all day. Even Alan, your assistant, thought you had. I don't suppose your memory's improved since I last asked you, has it?'

'What?' He gave a hearty laugh. 'I'm not a suspect, am I?'

'We have to eliminate those who were close to Nikki,' Max told him. 'So? Has your memory improved?'

He had the grace to look shamefaced as he glanced at Jill and then back at Max.

'OK, I wasn't here,' he said. 'It's a bit, um, delicate.'

'We're used to delicate,' Jill told him, and Max could hear her barely controlled anger. 'A good friend of mine has lost her daughter. It doesn't get much more delicate than that.'

'No, no of course.' Charlie, duly contrite, took a breath. 'The thing was, I was with a woman.'

'Who?' Max asked.

'That's just it, I don't know. As I said, it's a bit delicate. I mean, with Jill being a friend of Louise. It's just – well, to tell you the truth, the sex with Louise hasn't been great. She's a lovely woman, but well – so, I –'

'You had sex with someone else.' Jill finished for him.

'Yes.'

'Does this woman have a name?' she asked. 'Or did you just pick her up off the street?'

He stared back at Jill with no hint of embarrassment. No hint of anything.

'Yes. I picked her up off the street,' he said. 'That's why I don't know her name. She told me it was Roxanne, but they all say that, don't they?'

'Do they?' Jill asked. 'I really wouldn't know.'

'What did she look like?' Max asked.

'Like they all do,' he replied, and Max knew a longing to hit him.

'Come on,' Jill goaded him. 'Some are short, some are tall. Some are old, some not even fourteen. Some are red-heads, and some are blonde.'

'Blonde, I think,' he said uncomfortably. 'Young. Not that young, though,' he added hastily.

'You're an experienced man with the ladies, right?' Jill pressed on.

'Well, I like to –'

'And the sex with Louise wasn't great,' she went on, cutting him off. 'Now, I don't imagine for a minute that you're a come in thirty seconds flat sort of bloke. You must have been banging away at her for – what? – an hour?'

'Maybe,' he said, clearly surprised to find Jill talking of such matters so easily.

'Long enough to see what she looked like then,' Jill said. 'So try again!'

'Blonde,' he said. 'Yes, definitely blonde. About twenty. Maybe a couple of years older.'

'Why didn't Nikki like you?' Jill asked, changing the subject.

'Oh, you know what kids are. She was jealous. Jealous of her mum. She hadn't got a boyfriend and her mum had.'

'Fancy you, did she?'

'Probably. Look, I never asked her.'

'Fancy her, did you?'

'Of course not. She was Louise's daughter, for God's sake.'

'I've heard you like them young.'

'Who told you that?' he demanded, but Jill merely shrugged it off.

'Is it true?'

'Of course not.'

'So why,' Jill asked patiently, 'would someone say you enjoyed flirting with young girls if it wasn't true? It seems an odd thing to invent, don't you think?'

The sudden smile had Max really longing to hit him. He shuddered to think how Jill was feeling. This was the man she had assumed would help her friend cope with the death of her daughter. Now, if Jill had her way, he'd never see Louise again.

An involuntary shudder ran down Max's spine. Every time he thought of Louise, he couldn't begin to imagine how she was going to cope. If he lost Ben or Harry, he simply didn't know what he would do. He couldn't bear to think about it . . .

'I bet I know who's said that,' Charlie said, still grinning. 'The lovely Connie.'

'Why would she say that?' Jill asked him. 'Oh, don't tell me. She's jealous, right? She's jealous because you're going out with her sister instead of her.'

'Well, yeah –'

'You're – how did someone put it? – God's gift to the female of the species, and we're all angry, twisted and jealous because you're not shagging us. Well, get real, Charlie. None of us are jealous. Nikki wasn't, Connie wasn't, I'm not – we're just grateful we haven't fallen for your crap.'

He flushed at that.

'Nikki called you Pervy Charlie,' she pushed on. 'Why?'

'Who knows how her mind worked?'

'Pervy? Some kind of pervert, are you, Charlie? You like them young, don't you? Nikki's age or younger? Why's that, eh? It makes me think you're crap at sex –'

Max decided it was high time he took over.

'This woman you were with,' he put in quickly, 'where exactly did you see her?'

'Harrington,' he answered.

'Come on, Charlie,' he said. 'Getting anything from you is like getting blood from a stone. Be a bit more precise, will you?'

'Castle Street,' he said, looking sulky now. 'She was hanging around there looking for business. There's often a couple of them there, no matter what time of day.'

'You were in your car, right?'

'No, I was walking.'

'So where did you go?'

'To her place,' he answered.

'Which was where?' Max was rapidly running out of patience.

'I don't rightly know,' Charlie said thoughtfully. 'We walked up a couple of streets and up a flight of steps to her flat. It was quite a decent place. Considering.'

'Considering what?' Jill demanded. 'That she was a whore?'

'Well, yeah.'

'Did you know Carol Blakely?' Max asked him.

'Nope. Oh, I know she ran the florist's – I read about it in the paper. Murdered, like Nikki, wasn't she?'

'Ten out of ten, Charlie.' Max emptied his plastic cup. 'What about Ralph Atkins? Did you know him?'

'I did, actually,' Charlie said. 'I sold him his car,' he added proudly. .

'Did he pay for it?' Max asked.

'Of course. Why?'

'Oh, I just wondered if you'd felt obliged to go and torch his house.'

The look of shock on Charlie's face more or less convinced Max that he was innocent. More or less.

'Tomorrow,' he said, standing up, 'I want you to come to the station and look through some photographs. I need to know how to contact the young lady you were with.'

'Eh? I can't do that. I have a business to run.'

'And I have a murder to investigate,' Max retorted. 'Ten o'clock. And don't be late!'

As they walked out of the showroom, a couple pulled up in an old Ford. Charlie strode across the forecourt to greet them.

Max pulled out on to the road, ignoring Charlie's cheerful wave.

'Bastard!' Jill muttered. 'The total bastard. God, I thought that Charlie was the best thing to happen to Louise. The man's a –'

'Total bastard,' Max finished for her. 'I agree, but did you believe his story?'

'I don't know. Did you?'

'Probably.'

She sighed. 'Yes, I think I did, too.'

It was after seven thirty and, at this time, Harrington's one-way system was fairly easy to negotiate.

'Are you coming back to our place tonight?' he asked her.

She didn't even hesitate. 'If it's OK, yes.'

It was more than OK. He only wished she was there because she wanted to be with them and not because she couldn't bear the idea of going home to an empty cottage and dwelling on the events of the last few days.

'In that case,' he said, 'we may as well leave your car at headquarters.'

'I need to go home and check on the cats.'

'That's OK. I'll drive us home via Kelton Bridge.' Without waiting for further argument, he took the Kelton turning.

'Do you want to call on Louise while we're here?' he asked as they neared the village

'We should, shouldn't we?'

'Yes.'

'But don't mention Charlie,' she said quietly.

'I wasn't going to.'

Chapter Twenty-Nine

The following evening, Max was ready to head home. Indeed, if he'd left ten minutes earlier, he wouldn't have witnessed the kerfuffle as PCs Major and Buckingham brought in half a dozen youths.

Max would have left them to it. He could do without listening to lads who were no older than fifteen hurling abuse at everyone and everything. But he recognized one of the boys.

'Darren? What are you doing here?'

Darren's young face, suffused with the red of anger, swung round to face him. 'I didn't do nothing,' he vowed furiously. 'I shouldn't be here!'

'If you didn't do nothing,' Max pointed out, 'you must have done something.' But it was lost on Darren.

'It's on camera,' PC Major, an enthusiastic young recruit, told Darren. 'You were hurling bricks at –'

'It weren't me!' Darren insisted.

It was mayhem, with everyone shouting at once, but eventually, Max gleaned the gist of it. The gang of lads had allegedly set fire to an old chair in the middle of the road, called out the fire crew and then proceeded to bombard crew and appliance with bricks, stones, chunks of wood and anything else they could lay their hands on. When PCs Major and Buckingham had arrived on the scene, they'd started throwing stuff at them.

'Darren,' Max said, 'the fire engines have cameras on board. Whatever you did will be caught on film so there's no point lying.'

'It's not a lie,' he insisted. 'I might have chucked a couple of bricks, but they were at Robbie Taylor, not the firemen. I wouldn't have done that cos I'd seen the fireman before.'

Max could barely hear himself think as PCs Major and Buckingham tried to get names from their young criminals. One was claiming to be David Beckham while another insisted he was the Mayor of Bacup. In Max's view, the whole thing was a waste of time, paper and manpower. Putting this lot through the youth courts would solve nothing. They had no respect for anything and would have benefited far more from a good old-fashioned clip round the ear.

'Right, Darren, come with me and give me your story,' he said, grabbing Darren by the shoulder and marching him to his office where he stood half a chance of being able to hear himself think.

'I didn't do nothing,' Darren insisted again.

'So you said.' Max pushed open the door to his office and shoved Darren inside. 'Right, tell me again what happened. And tell me the truth, eh? It'll save us both a lot of time.'

Darren gazed around at his surroundings. It was a smart office and the lad was duly impressed.

'Come on then, Darren. Out with it.'

Darren swung the swivel chair round on its stand.

'Have a seat,' Max offered, nodding at his executive chair.

'Cool.' Darren sat and swivelled himself round a few times – very much like Max had when the chair had first been delivered.

'Come on,' Max prompted and Darren, still now, sighed.

'Someone had chucked an old chair out and Robbie Taylor and the rest of 'em dragged it into the road and set fire to it. One of 'em, don't know who it were, phoned the fire brigade.'

'And decided it would be fun to hurl stones at firemen?'

Darren shrugged. 'Spose. It were just a laugh.'

'Not a very good one, was it? You wouldn't find it funny if someone threw bricks at you, would you?'

Darren shrugged again.

'So these bricks you threw –'

'I didn't throw 'em at the firemen,' Darren insisted again. 'I chucked 'em at Robbie Taylor.'

'And that's all right?'

'I was trying to stop him chucking stuff. I knows that fireman, you see. Well, I don't know him, but I seen him before. There were a swan tangled up in some wire down at New Line and he got it free. There were a bloke from the RSPCA turned up, too. I thought he were a nice bloke so I didn't want Robbie chucking stuff at him.'

'I see. You like swans, do you?'

'Yeah. I like all birds an' all animals.' His grubby face softened.

Max imagined a house overrun with cats, dogs, hamsters, rabbits and God knows what else.

'I had a puppy once,' Darren said wistfully, 'but it went off.'

'Went off?'

'Yeah. It were a stray I found. I only had it three days. It peed on the carpet and me mam went mad. Then Dave, me stepdad, kicked hell out of it and it ran off. I couldn't find it again.'

Max despaired. In ten years' time, when Darren was twenty-four and a hardened criminal, because that seemed to be his destiny, Max would be able to deal with him. But now, as a kid – God, he despaired. What hope was there for him? Dave Walsh would kick out at anything, dogs or stepsons included.

'So pets aren't allowed?'

'No.'

'You've got plenty of time on your hands,' Max pointed out. 'Why don't you visit the rescue centre? I'm sure they'd be glad of another pair of hands. Dogs always need walking and feeding.'

Darren looked at him as if he'd suggested flying to Mars and back. For Darren, life trudged along with one day the same as the next. There was no point thinking about tomorrow because it would be as grim as today. He had no dreams, no ambitions – everything had been knocked out of him by life with a mother and stepfather who didn't give a toss.

'You've got a bike, haven't you?' Max told him. 'Weren't you getting a new one?'

'Yeah.'

'Then you could be there in no time.'

'Who'd I see?' he asked, unsure.

Max thought for a moment. 'Leave it with me,' he said at last. 'Come and see me on Monday. OK?'

'Do you reckon as they'd want me?'

'I'll ask.'

Max might have promised the lad the sun, the moon and the stars.

'Aw, thanks, mister.'

'Max.'

'Max.' Darren was grinning now.

'Come on,' Max said, 'let's go and sort out this business. You're in trouble, Darren.'

'Can't you tell 'em it weren't me?'

'We'll see . . .'

As Darren stood up, an iPod fell from his pocket. Max bent to pick it up.

The lad had nothing – no love, no guidance, no decent shoes. So how the hell did he come to have an iPod?

'Very nice,' Max murmured, turning it over in his hands. 'Very expensive, too.'

'Found it,' Darren muttered, his face scarlet again.

'Darren!'

'Did, too,' the lad protested. 'There were a big box of 'em in our shed.'

'Did they belong to your stepdad?'

'Dunno.'

Max didn't know either, but he had a damn good idea. He'd bet his life that this iPod had been taken from a certain computer and electrical shop in Kelton Bridge. And he'd bet that Dave Walsh's shed also contained several

MP3 players and an assortment of DVD players, as well as stuff pinched from private residences.

'Right, Darren, listen carefully. I'll get you out of here and then you'll go straight home, right?'

Darren nodded.

'And you won't say a word to anyone – not your mother or your stepfather – about being here, right?'

Darren nodded again, eyes like saucers.

'As for this . . .' Max held out the iPod. 'This stays here.'

'OK.' Darren shuffled his feet. 'Will you still ask the kennels if I can go?'

The loss of the iPod was as nothing in comparison.

'I will,' Max promised.

But first, he'd get a search warrant organized.

Chapter Thirty

'Jill, my darling girl!'

Jill, a bag of shopping in one hand and keys in the other, locked her car with the remote. 'Hi, Finlay. How are you?'

'All the better for seeing you. You're a stranger to me.'

'Just busy.'

There was no point telling him she'd been staying at Max's. Thinking about it, though, he'd probably noticed her absence. Despite his happy-go-lucky exterior, she suspected he didn't miss a lot.

'Too busy for a drink? I'm about to stroll down to the pub.'

She was all set to decline the invitation, but it was another pleasant evening and she had nothing planned. 'Yes, I'd like that. Give me two minutes, will you?'

'As long as you like!'

He took her shopping bag from her, allowing her to open the front door of her cottage, then followed her inside.

All three cats gave her a royal welcome. They always did when she'd been out for a few hours, especially when their food bowl was empty. She fed them, grabbed a sweater and checked her purse for cash.

'We'll all rest a lot easier now those thieves have been caught,' he said as she locked her door.

'Until the next lot come along,' she agreed.

But he was right. The village could relax again. Thanks to their finding Darren in possession of an iPod last week, Dave Walsh was now in custody.

That was often how crimes were solved. They could have the best officers and the best technology in the world yet, very often, all it needed was a piece of luck. Officers had spent hours trying to figure out how the burglar had known when people were going to be away. Dave Walsh hadn't done a day's work in his life. Consequently, he had the time to watch and listen. It was that simple. If he'd stuck to private houses instead of growing greedy and breaking into the local computer shop, he might have had a few more months of freedom.

'So tell me, darling girl, will you miss me when I'm gone?'

The question took her completely by surprise. 'You're leaving?'

'Of course. I only rented the cottage for three months. I'll be gone on Sunday.'

She'd known it was a short-term let. It was the fact that those three months had passed so quickly that took her by surprise. 'Where are you going?'

'Who knows? I'll do what I usually do and go where the whim takes me.'

'What a lovely way to live.'

He laughed at that. 'You'd hate it. You're too settled here.'

She *was* settled. The locals might not agree, but Jill felt as if she belonged in Kelton Bridge.

'It has its drawbacks, too,' he added, grinning. 'As a traveller, you're always first on a list of suspects.'

She smiled, as was expected, but his nomadic lifestyle hadn't put him on the list of suspects. His association with the murder victim had done that. As had the file found in his kitchen. And the fact that he'd bought red ribbon. Not *the* red ribbon admittedly, but red ribbon.

'Your time in Kelton has been nothing if not eventful,' she said.

'And I've enjoyed every minute of it.'

She didn't doubt that. For a while, he'd been the centre of attention and he'd revelled in it.

'Will you be glad to leave?'

'Three months in the same place is about my limit.' Which didn't answer her question.

He pushed open the door of the Weaver's Retreat and the noise hit them. Early evening, there was usually a good crowd in. This evening, the locals were making fun of Barry who, once again, had backed the outsiders and lost a hefty sum. Barry was lucky; Jill hadn't even had a chance to look at the runners.

On A Whim. She was sure he was running tomorrow. In the morning, she might put a few pounds on him.

Finlay was popular with the locals, yet they were wary of him and kept him at a distance. They remained suspicious of newcomers for a long time, as she'd found out. If you gained their trust, however, you were soon accepted as part of the community.

She watched him as he bought their drinks and it struck her that he considered himself above other people. He was all charm, yet beneath that there was an aloofness, a cockiness. Just as he'd played with Max during the long hours he spent in the interview room, he played with the locals. He was big on mind games.

He must enjoy his work. What better way of playing with people's minds than doing tarot readings? He could tell clients what they wanted to hear. Or he could tell them what they didn't want to hear which, more likely than not, would have them returning for a second reading and a third.

'How's that policeman of yours?' he asked as he put her drink on the table and sat beside her.

'Max? He's fine.'

Right now, she was terribly proud of him. True to his word, he'd taken Darren to the kennels on Monday night and Darren had hardly left the place since. He was in his own idea of heaven – feeding the dogs and taking them for walks.

On Wednesday night, Ben, who must have forgotten he was banned from the place, visited and, the next thing, Darren was sitting down to dinner at Max's place.

It was exactly what Darren needed to help him stick to the straight and narrow . . .

'He's too busy catching burglars to catch killers, I suppose,' Finlay broke into her thoughts.

'That wasn't his case, but sometimes you get a stroke of luck.' She didn't want to answer his questions; she would rather he answered hers. 'How's your business going, Finlay?'

'Very well,' he answered with satisfaction.

'You'll have to do a reading for me,' she said lightly.

'Any time, sweetheart. What is it you're wanting to know from the cards?'

She wanted to know who had killed Nikki and Carol Blakely. And she wanted to know about the man she was currently sitting with. She didn't like him. It was the first time she had admitted that. He was charming enough, but she was aware of depths to his personality that disturbed her. She didn't trust him. At one point, she had been as convinced as Max that he was guilty of Carol Blakely's murder.

She brushed the thought aside. He wasn't guilty. Luckily for him, the real killer had struck while he'd been detained.

'I'd like to know if I'll going to Spain for my holiday,' she answered his question. 'I'd like to know which horses are going to win tomorrow, and I would really love to know which lottery numbers will come up.'

'Wouldn't we all.' The idea made him laugh.

'And the cards can't tell me?'

''Fraid not.' He took a large swallow from his pint of beer. 'They can tell you whether it's the right time for you to go on holiday, just as they can suggest the right time to back horses or buy a lottery ticket. They can suggest the path you should take on the road to happiness.'

Jill wanted more than suggestions; she wanted answers.

Over a week had passed since Nikki's body had been found and, despite having questioned literally thousands of people, they had no strong suspects.

Pervy Charlie's mysterious prostitute had been found. She was known by the police and considered to be reasonably honest and she had vouched for Charlie.

Thankfully, the relationship between Charlie and Louise was cooling. That was due mainly to the fact that Louise had no interest in anything. She was grieving for her daughter and nothing else registered with her. Despite that, she was showing a strength of character that surprised Jill. She would get over this. Perhaps spending so many years not knowing if Nikki was alive or dead made it easier.

'I want him caught,' she'd said to Jill. 'I know it won't bring Nikki back, but it will at least prevent any other mother having to go through this.'

They'd staged a reconstruction, but, although many people had seen Nikki that fateful morning, no one had seen her meet up with anyone or get into a car . . .

The pub's door burst open and half a dozen laughing and slightly inebriated women came inside. A birthday celebration, Jill guessed, or a hen night. They were laughing as they thrust money at the girl entrusted with the night's drinks fund.

She became aware of one woman watching her and was surprised to recognize Ruth Asimacopoulos.

'Excuse me, Finlay.'

She walked up to the bar. 'Hello, Ruth, I didn't recognize you for a minute. How are you?'

'Hello, Jill. Of course, this is your local, isn't it?' She gestured to her companions. 'We're celebrating Mel's birthday. Twenty-one today!'

'I hope you have a good night.'

'It's already feeling like a long one,' Ruth confided. 'I'm old enough to be their mother. Mel lives next door to me so I offered to be taxi driver for the evening,' she added as way of explanation.

'Then I don't envy you.'

'You're more than welcome to join us,' Ruth offered. 'The more the merrier.'

Jill was touched by the invitation. 'Thanks, Ruth, that's really kind, but I'd better not.'

The others were trying to attract Ruth's attention. 'Have a good evening,' Jill said, leaving her.

'I'm sure I know her,' Finlay said, nodding at Ruth as Jill retook her seat. 'Does she live in the village?'

'No. She worked with Carol Blakely.'

'Ah, yes, in the shop. I knew I'd seen her before.'

He turned away, and gave Jill his full attention. 'Another drink, darling girl?'

'Please.'

While he went to the bar to get their drinks, Jill was aware of Ruth glancing her way now and again. It made her uncomfortable. If Ruth had recognized Finlay, it would upset her to see the man who had once dated her employer buying drinks for another woman.

A cloud of depression settled on her. For the police and the press, a murder was over as soon as the killer was caught. For those close to the victim, it was never over.

Chapter Thirty-One

Sunday was hot. They had been promised the hottest day of the year, and Jill thought they must have it. Even the cats were inside. Jill was sitting in the garden, taking advantage of the shade of her old lilac tree, but even there it wasn't particularly comfortable. She refused to move, though. When the sun shone, she felt obliged to make the most of it.

She was trying to read a magazine, but the latest celebrity gossip didn't interest her and she had no wish to lose half a stone in a fortnight. It was too hot to do anything more energetic, though. When the sun had lost some of its intensity, she would tidy up the garden. Until then, she was doing nothing.

'Coo-ee!'

'Round here!' Jill called out, chuckling at the sound of Ella's voice.

Ella came into the garden and, as ever, was managing to look cool. How she did that, Jill had no idea.

'I've brought those raffle tickets,' Ella explained, sitting on the bench beside Jill. 'What a scorcher. I like the heat as much as the next person, but this is a bit overpowering. Still, no point complaining. It'll be no time at all before the roads are blocked by snow and we're all complaining about frozen pipes.'

Jill laughed at that. 'Oh, don't. It's only August and I refuse to think about winter already. Mind you, it is hot. Fancy a drink?'

'I'd love one.'

'White wine?'

'Sounds perfect. But don't let me have more than one glass. The last time I left here, I got home and slept the day away.'

Jill went to the kitchen and took a bottle of chilled wine from the fridge. She filled two of the biggest wine glasses she possessed, returned the bottle to the fridge, and carried the drinks outside.

'Thanks.' Ella took the glass from her. 'I called at Louise's house on my way here,' she added, 'but I couldn't get her to hear. I hope she's all right.'

'She's away for the weekend at her sister's,' Jill said.

'That's good.' Ella nodded approvingly. 'Her sister's good for her. High-handed,' she added with a smile, 'but that's probably what she needs.' The smile faded. 'It'll be so difficult for her. I can't begin to imagine how she'll cope. But people do. Somehow.'

'They do,' Jill agreed, 'and she's coping a lot better than I thought. I just hope it lasts.'

'So sad for the village, too,' Ella murmured. 'I know Nikki left, and I know most locals didn't have a good word for her, but she was still considered one of their own.'

How right she was. The villagers stuck together and it had sent the whole community into shock. There was a sense of hopelessness about the village. People wanted to do something, but there was nothing they could do. Nothing would bring Nikki back.

'Terry and Beverley Yates,' Jill said. 'Do you know them, Ella?'

'Yes. They lived up Haver Road for a couple of years. The house on the end that the Williamses have now.'

Jill knew the house she meant, and Dorothy and Pete Williams.

'What were they like?' she asked.

'OK, I suppose. Terry was all right, but I can't say I really took to Beverley.'

'Really?'

215

Jill didn't know either of the Yateses well, but it was Terry *she* hadn't taken to. She'd found Beverley to be friendly enough.

'Mm. My Tom broke his leg, daft fool, and it was Terry who drove me to visit him. Nice chap, Terry. Couldn't do enough to help. Lovely children they had, too. Twins, you know.'

'Adam and Cherie.' Jill nodded.

'Why do you ask?'

'Terry Yates once had a bit of a fling with Carol Blakely,' Jill explained.

'Ah.' Ella considered that for a moment. 'Don't take this as gospel, Jill, it's just the impression I got, but I think a lot of men would have looked elsewhere if they'd been married to Beverley. The children were everything to her. In fact, she was quite possessive about them. Terry must have felt excluded. When a wife has no interest in him, and when he's not allowed near his children – yes, I think a lot of men would stray.'

Ella was shrewd and perceptive, and Jill respected her judgement. She recalled Beverley Yates's voice on her ex-husband's answer machine. It had been the voice of a woman keeping her children away from their father. Was that because the children didn't want to see the father who'd abandoned them? Or was it because she was naturally possessive of them?

'You're looking tired,' Ella noted.

'I need a holiday.' Jill smiled ruefully. 'I've only just started full-time work again and already I'm thinking of holidays.'

'Not long till Spain,' Ella pointed out.

'If we go. And it's looking more and more unlikely.'

Bees were buzzing around the tall foxgloves and that was the only sound until a car came along the road and pulled on to her drive.

'I'd better see who that is,' Jill murmured.

Before she'd reached the cottage though, Max was already walking round the side, a cigarette in his hand.

'God, it's hot!' He threw his cigarette butt on to the border. 'Hello, Ella. How's life with you?'

'It's good, thanks, Max. You?'

'Not bad.' As the bench was occupied, he grabbed the plastic seat and sat on that. He looked at their glasses. 'I'll get my own, shall I?'

Jill handed him their glasses. 'Bring us a refill, Max.'

'No,' Ella protested. 'I'll be getting along, Jill.'

'Don't go on my account,' Max said. 'I can only stop long enough to drink a glass of wine.'

'A small one then,' Ella said, settling herself down again. Max was soon back.

'Have you been working?' Ella asked him curiously.

'Some would call it working, Ella. Others would call it wasting time. I'm inclined to fall into the latter camp.'

'Oh, dear.'

In other words, there had been no breakthrough, nothing new. Jill saw her holiday slipping further and further away.

She needed it, too. Kelton Bridge was too sombre at the moment, and she wanted to escape . . .

Everywhere smelled hot and parched, but at least the bees were enjoying themselves. A blackbird stabbed at the ground with his beak, but soon gave up. The earth was as hard as stone.

They spoke of the weather, and places in Spain that Ella had visited, and then they discussed the rubbish being shown on TV and the state of the country . . .

'Jill? Are you there?'

The familiar voice silenced the three of them and they all turned to see Finlay Roberts striding across her lawn, half hidden by the huge bouquet of flowers in his arms.

'Hello, Finlay.'

'My darling girl!' He thrust the flowers at her. 'A small thank-you for being such a lovely neighbour.'

'For me? Gosh, um, thank you. They're beautiful, Finlay. Thanks.'

'Gorgeous,' Ella agreed.

'I'm leaving now,' he said, 'so goodbye Kelton Bridge and goodbye all of you.'

He reached for Ella's hand. 'It's been a privilege to know you,' he said, bending to kiss her hand.

Then he tried to shake Max's hand, but Max was having none of it.

'No hard feelings, I trust,' Finlay said, smiling broadly.

'I wouldn't go that far,' Max muttered.

'Where are you going?' Ella wanted to know.

'No idea,' he answered easily.

Jill found that difficult to believe. He must know where he was heading, or at least where he would be sleeping that evening.

'It'll be wherever the car takes me,' he added.

'Will you be back?' Ella asked.

'Who knows?'

'Haven't you consulted the cards?' she asked him, and Jill had to chuckle at that.

'Have a safe journey,' she said, 'wherever you end up.'

'Thank you. Right, goodbye and good luck to you all!'

Jill, Ella and Max were silent as they watched his retreating back. They remained silent until long after his car was out of earshot.

'An interesting fellow,' Ella mused, breaking that silence. 'I can't say I cared for him much, though.'

'You and me both, Ella,' Max agreed. 'And why do I feel as if he's escaped the net?'

Jill had no answer to that, but she felt exactly the same.

'I'll go and put these in water,' she said. 'They really are beautiful, aren't they?'

There was no card with them, and they were wrapped in cellophane with a wide yellow ribbon. She wondered if they'd come from Carol Blakely's shop.

They *were* beautiful but, as she put them in her favourite container, a simple white jug, they didn't give the pleasure they should. Perhaps she was being fanciful, but they seemed to be mocking her.

When she returned to the garden, Max and Ella were still discussing Finlay Roberts.

'An intelligent chap, mind,' Ella was saying. 'Certainly believed himself to be a cut above the rest of us.'

'A game player,' Jill said, agreeing with everything Ella had said. 'He loved to play games. He was supposed to be giving me a tarot reading, but he never got round to it.'

'What?' Ella's expression seriously questioned Jill's sanity.

'I don't believe in any of that rubbish,' Jill assured her, 'but I was curious to see what he told me.'

'A dangerous game,' Ella warned.

'Oh well, he's gone now. I wonder who my next neighbour will be.'

'According to Olive, it's a young family. A mother and two children if I remember rightly. The father has just taken up a job abroad and, while he sorts out accommodation over there, they're going to rent the cottage. Dubai, I think she said. Not that you can take much notice of Olive, old gossip that she is.'

'Tsk. She speaks so highly of you, Ella,' Jill put in, and they both laughed. Ella and Olive had been at loggerheads for years.

Max left them soon afterwards, but it was good to sit and chew things over with Ella. The heat wasn't quite as oppressive now, but it was still too hot to do anything other than be totally idle. Jill only wished her mind didn't keep straying to Finlay Roberts. Like Max, she had the feeling she'd just seen a guilty man walk. Yet that was impossible. When Nikki was murdered, he had been safely under lock and key.

Her mind kept returning to the murder victims' photographs. From the start, something had been bugging her about those. But what?

'I really do need to be off now,' Ella said, getting to her feet. 'Thanks for the wine and the good company.'

'Thank *you*. I think I'll sit here a little longer . . .'

She couldn't settle, though. Her mind was too busy.

In the end, she went inside and switched on her computer. But it was the victims' photos that bothered her, and she didn't have copies of those on her machine.

The photos of Edward Marshall's victims were identical. Every detail was the same. Carol's were different. So, in some way that she couldn't pinpoint, were Nikki's.

Oh, no!

What had her mum said? *Why is it that two people can use exactly the same ingredients, the same utensils, do exactly the same things and end up with different results?*

Edward Marshall's victims had been laid out with a sense of theatre. At the time, she'd thought he'd set them up like that for their cameras. Now, she knew it was for his own camera.

Carol Blakely's killer had done just the same as Marshall. He'd cut her throat with a short, sharp knife, he'd wrapped her naked body in a shroud, he'd removed her wedding ring and threaded it through the red ribbon tied around her waist, and he'd put coins on her closed eyes. Yet there was a stillness there, a touch of respect.

Nikki's killer had done the same, too. He'd cut her throat with a short, sharp knife, he'd wrapped her naked body in a shroud, he'd removed her grandmother's wedding ring and threaded it through the red ribbon tied around her waist, and he'd put coins on her closed eyes. There was no stillness about Nikki in death, however. It had been a hasty job.

Carol's killer had acted calmly. Nikki's killer had worked in a sense of panic.

Max wasn't going to like this, and Phil Meredith was going to like it even less, but Jill was beginning to think that Carol and Nikki had been killed by two different people . . .

She was still debating the wisdom of telling Max her idea at eleven o'clock that night. Hang it, she may as well mention it. If she didn't, she wouldn't settle. She grabbed her phone and hit the button for his number. He answered on the third ring.

'You're not going to like this,' she warned him.

'Now what?' He sounded wary already.

'I think there's a very strong possibility,' she said carefully, 'that we're looking for two killers.'

'What? Don't talk bloody stupid, Jill!' There was a pause as he considered it and dismissed it. 'No. The murders are identical. We're pretty sure that the ribbon was cut from the same length. That sheet – shroud, whatever you call the bloody thing – it's the same.'

She'd known he wouldn't like it.

'You did say that Nikki put up a fight,' she reminded him. 'Carol didn't.'

'That's the only difference,' he said. 'Nikki's throat wasn't cut as cleanly, and the killer, judging by the cuts on Nikki's arms, had a struggle on his hands, but the same weapon was used. Nikki's murder was bodged –'

'Or done by someone less capable.'

'No, Jill, it's the same man. It has to be. It's the same knife.'

'So? Two people in this together could use the same weapon.'

'No. It's complete crap.'

Perhaps he was right; perhaps it was complete crap. Murder wasn't the same as making a cheesecake. Besides, Jill could make six cheesecakes and every one would look different. All the same, the thought refused to be banished. The more she thought of those photos, the more convinced she was.

They were looking for two killers.

Chapter Thirty-Two

Late on Tuesday afternoon, Max walked into his office and saw that some thoughtful soul had left the evening paper for him. The press were having a field day with this case, and he wasn't sure he wanted to read it. However, he glanced at the front page and was relieved to see they didn't have anything new.

Sadly, he didn't either.

He'd read thousands of witness statements over and over until his eyes could barely focus. He'd been through every report. Nothing leapt out at him.

There were dozens of officers working on this case, dozens of *good* officers, and he knew they'd find something sooner or later. He only hoped it was sooner rather than later. At the moment, he was living in dread of hearing that another body had been found . . .

Thinking of good officers, he left his office and went in search of Fletch.

Grace was on the phone and managed to mouth, 'He's out, guv.'

While waiting for her to end the call, he glanced through the paperwork that was piling up. His own desk was the same. What had happened to the great dream of computers giving them a paper-free world?

Jill was walking through the room and she came over. 'Anything new?'

'Not that I know of,' he replied.

'You want me, guv?' Grace asked when she'd finished her call.

'Just wondered how it was going?'

'You'd be better not asking,' she replied easily. 'That was a waste of time,' she said, nodding at her phone. 'I can tell you where Finlay Roberts's father is, but that's pretty academic now.'

'Totally,' Max agreed.

'Where is he?' Jill asked curiously.

'Blackpool.'

What did it matter where he was? Max wondered. No way was Finlay Roberts involved in this. They might *want* him to be guilty, but he wasn't. He'd been in this very building when Nikki had been murdered.

'What's he doing?' Jill asked.

'Drinking, probably,' Grace replied with a grin. 'He was an alcoholic. Supposedly a reformed character now, though.'

'It doesn't matter what he's doing,' Max reminded them both. He knew Jill; whatever case they worked on, she had a habit of going off on a tangent. They couldn't afford to waste time now.

'Aren't you curious?' Jill asked him.

'Nope. I'm only curious as to who killed Carol and Nikki.'

'Yes, but –'

'No, Jill.'

'Finlay has no real alibi for when Carol was murdered,' Jill pointed out, 'and if –'

'We're not looking for two men,' Max and Grace said together.

'We might be,' Jill argued, and Max recognized that stubborn set of her chin. 'Aiden said he could only be ninety-nine per cent certain the murders were committed by the same man. As he said, the same knife was used, but Carol was tall and Nikki was tiny –'

'OK,' Max said, rapidly losing patience. 'Let's imagine that we have two killers and Finlay Roberts is one of them. Why in hell's name would we want to talk to the father he hasn't seen since the year bloody dot?'

223

'You won't know that until you talk to him,' Jill replied.

'Crap!' Max nodded at Grace. 'Keep me informed.'

'Will do, guv.'

Max went back to his office but, try as he might, he couldn't rid his mind of Finlay Roberts. And wasn't that what had got them into this mess? Fixating on Roberts?

With a sigh, he phoned the Grim Reaper.

'Aiden,' he greeted him. 'Carol Blakely and Nikki Craven. How possible is it that they were killed by two different people?'

'I've told you, Max, I don't think it *is* possible. I wouldn't stake my life on it, or my house for that matter, but I'm as sure as I can be. As I told you, if the victims had been of a more similar height, I wouldn't have hesitated in saying no. Carol Blakely was – what? it's in my report – five feet eleven?'

'Yes. And Nikki was five feet exactly. That's eleven inches.'

'Hm.' Aiden was thoughtful. 'In my opinion, Max, they were killed by the same man.' He hesitated. 'There is a very tiny chance – millions to one – that they weren't, but that's all.'

Millions to one.

The photos of the victims were the same. They were laid out in exactly the same position. The weapon used, a five to six inch knife, was the same. The ribbon tied around their waists was cut from the same length. The sheets their bodies had been wrapped in were the same. Everything was the same . . .

Sod it. It was time he finished for the day.

On his way out of the building, he stopped at Jill's office, but she wasn't there. He'd been hoping to have a drink with her before going home.

He walked back to Grace's desk. 'Do you know if Jill's left?'

'She has, guv, yeah.'

'Oh, right. Well, it wasn't important.' He turned to walk away.

'She said something about wanting some sea air,' Grace murmured, her attention on the forms in front of her.

'What? Oh, for God's sake. I might have bloody known!'

Chapter Thirty-Three

Thanks to her satellite navigation system, Jill found Sean Roberts's address easily. She'd phoned ahead to ask if he could spare a few minutes and he had insisted on giving her a convoluted set of directions.

'Turn left by the post office then you'll see that the road curves to the right.'

'It's OK, Mr Roberts, I'll find it,' she'd promised.

'I'm sure you will. Now, when the road curves, you'll see a small newsagent's. Indicate left there. The left turn will come on you real fast so watch out for it. Then, go right up to the top of the bank, past the junk shop with lots of clutter on the pavement, and past the off-licence. Right up to the top. Then you'll see a left turn . . .'

Totally confused, Jill had let him give her directions, thanked him, and found her own way.

His flat was in a pleasant-looking block at the very end of the road. There was no real view, but a stiff breeze was blowing and the air was salty and fresh. She walked up the front path, went into a small hallway, and rang the bell for Mr Roberts's flat.

'You'll be the police then?' a distorted voice answered.

'Yes,' she replied. Technically it was true.

The lock clicked and she pushed open the door. There was a lift – with a large handwritten *Out of Order* sign stuck on it. Great. She walked up the three flights of stairs and was breathless when she reached his door. Thankfully, he had it open for her.

'The lift's still not working then,' he grumbled.

'No,' she said, gasping for breath.

'So what's he done now then?' he asked, having done with social niceties.

There was no resemblance whatsoever between father and son. The man looking at her now was older than Jill had expected. He was a ruddy-faced, portly man with thinning hair. However, just like his son, he chose to dress very casually. His big toe poked through a hole in a grubby brown slipper and the shirt he was wearing didn't look as if it was familiar with the inside of a washing machine. The other similarity was an expression on his face that said he intended to enjoy every minute of this. Why?

'We're not sure he's done anything,' Jill said. 'May I come in?'

'Aye. Yes, come in.'

Unlike the son who had few possessions, the father's home was crammed with a lifetime's collection of knick-knacks. In the small sitting room, there were photographs by the dozen, a collection of porcelain springer spaniels, books, several piles of mail, an old radio, an old television that didn't look as if it had been switched on in a decade . . .

'When did you last see your son?' she asked when she was seated opposite him on an old, hard sofa.

'About a year ago,' he answered, taking her completely by surprise.

Damn it. She'd believed he hadn't seen him since Finlay was six. Why the hell hadn't someone checked that out?

'Why do you want to know?' he asked.

'I'm helping with a murder investigation in Harrington,' she explained, 'and your son's name has cropped up. We'd like to eliminate him from our inquiries.'

'You reckon he's killed someone?' The old man chuckled at that. 'It wouldn't surprise me.'

'Why do you say that?'

'Cos he's half-mad. Takes after his mother.'

'Really?'

'Yes. She's mad, too.'

'You and Finlay weren't close, were you?' Jill asked. Or had they got that wrong, too?

'No. He blamed me for a lot of things. For walking out on him, his mother and his sister, among other things. He knew nothing about the situation, of course. How could he? He was barely out of nappies. But he wasn't the forgiving type.' He shrugged. 'It's no skin off my nose. As I've told him many times, he's big enough and ugly enough to take care of himself.'

'Why did you see him a year ago?'

'Beats me. He was in Lancashire, he said, and he decided to call on me. Said it was time we buried the hatchet and all that. I told him, as far as I'm concerned, there was no hatchet needed burying. He wanted to buy me a drink but I was on the wagon. Still am,' he added with a touch of pride.

'Before that,' Jill said, 'when did you see him?'

'Oh, years ago. That's why I was surprised he found me. The last time will have been when all the trouble kicked off.'

'Trouble?' Jill asked, frowning.

'You don't know about that? You haven't heard about Lorna?'

'No.'

'Ah, now here's a tale.' Mr Roberts relaxed back in his chair and lit a cigarette. 'Let me see, he would have been about sixteen when he met young Lorna. Perhaps even seventeen. Puppy love it was, nothing more and nothing less, but he wouldn't have it. As far as he was concerned, it was the real thing. Nothing would sway him from that. Talk about love's young dream.' He chuckled. 'She was his soulmate, he reckoned, and he would rather die than be parted from her. Gets all that emotional nonsense from his mother, too. Well, we had to put a stop to it. At least, his mother did. That's why she got in touch with me. I was summoned to sort it out. Lorna, you see, was my daughter. By my second wife.'

'He fell in love with his half-sister?'

Jill recalled the framed black and white photograph that had boasted pride of place next to Finlay Roberts's bed. Could it have shown a young Finlay and Lorna?

'Love? Pah!' the old man scoffed. 'He said it was love, but if she hadn't been his sister, it would have fizzled out. Young love?' He laughed at the very notion. 'It was illicit. Exciting, you know what I mean?'

Jill did.

'When you saw him last year,' she asked, 'did he talk of Lorna?'

'No. I bet he can't even remember her name. He'll have grown out of it, just like I said he would.'

He hadn't. Jill would bet her life on that.

'What about Lorna?' she asked. 'When did you last see her?'

'Not since the trouble kicked off,' he answered. 'As you can guess, I'm not the world's best father. Not that it was entirely my fault,' he added quickly. 'Her mother was a flighty piece and left me for someone else. She took young Lorna with her and that's the last I heard of them till I was ordered to split the pair of 'em up.'

'How did they meet? Finlay and Lorna?'

'Typical of Karen, it was,' he explained. 'Having run off with someone else, she grew bored and tried to find me. Instead, she found my first wife – Finlay's mum. It must have been a sort of Ex-Wives Club,' he chuckled, 'because damn me if they didn't become friends. Karen stayed with Petra, Finlay's mum, for nigh on six months.' He shook his head at the absurdity of life. 'Young Finlay and Lorna were thrown together, I suppose you'd say. The stupid thing was, neither kid was told they were brother and sister. No one thought twice about them spending so much time together until they were found in bed together. That's when all hell broke loose.'

He was like his son in that Finlay would have found the situation highly amusing, too. So long as his own emotions hadn't been involved.

'And how did you split the pair of them up?'

'Young Lorna had enough sense to leave Finlay,' he explained. 'She just took off and, as far as I know, no one's heard from her since. She knew it couldn't be and she accepted it.'

Was that why Finlay moved around the country, Jill wondered? Could it be that he was still looking for her?

'Do the initials TMD mean anything to you?' Jill asked him, and he shook his head in bewilderment.

'Should they?'

'I don't know,' she admitted. 'So you've no idea where Lorna is now?'

'None at all,' he said in a couldn't-care-less way. 'As I said, after the trouble kicked off, she went away. I've no idea if she's alive or dead.'

'Where was Finlay's mother living when he and Lorna met?'

'Somerset. She took quite a liking to the place.'

'You say your son was in Lancashire a year ago?' Jill reminded him. 'What for, did he say?'

'He didn't say. But that's him all over. Itchy feet. He never has been able to settle in one place.' He laughed softly. 'I expect he blames that on me, too.'

He looked at her, and Jill saw the resemblance then. His unwavering stare was the same as Finlay's.

'I know you want to, how do you put it, eliminate him from your inquiries, but that usually means he's suspected of something bad. Do you really reckon he's killed someone?'

'Two women have been murdered,' Jill explained, 'but, no, he's not a suspect. As I said, we simply need to eliminate as many people as possible from our inquiries. When he visited you a year ago, how long did he stay in Lancashire?'

'I've no idea. I got the impression he was just passing through, but he didn't say and I didn't ask.'

'Has he been in touch during the last three months?' Jill asked.

'No. Why?'

'I just wondered. As he's been in Lancashire, I thought he might have.'

'He's been in Lancashire again? Well, well, well. He must be getting a liking for the place.'

She asked him a few more questions, but there was nothing more he could tell her.

'Thank you for your time,' Jill said as she was leaving. 'I appreciate it.'

'Can you eliminate him from your inquiries?'

'Oh, yes, I think so,' Jill said, smiling.

Her mind was racing as she got back to her car and drove off.

The traffic was busy for some reason, and it took her an age to get back on to the motorway. Her phone was showing three missed calls from Max, but he hadn't left a message. There was no need; he'd only be wanting to know why the hell she'd raced off to Blackpool without telling him. He'd want to remind her that Carol and Nikki were killed by the same bloke. He could remind her all he liked but, despite what everyone thought, and despite what the pathologist said, she reckoned they were looking for two men.

Finlay Roberts was still in love with Lorna. That photo by the side of his bed proved that. He was a traveller, and he liked to travel light. He wasn't a possessions sort of bloke. Yet he must have been carrying that photo all over the country with him for years. Oh yes, he was still in love with her. There was no doubt about that.

Perhaps now she might get Max's attention . . .

Hands free or not, she didn't like talking on her car phone. Half the time it was impossible to hear what was being said and concentrate on the road at the same time.

As soon as she got home, however, she fed the cats, made herself a good strong coffee and tried his number.

'How was the sea air?' he asked drily, and she smiled.

'Exhilarating!'

'And? Out with it then, I can tell you've got something interesting to tell me.'

231

She told him all about her meeting with Mr Roberts senior.

'So,' she said, 'there are two things of interest really. Firstly, Finlay saw his father twelve months ago. He was in Harrington or Kelton – well, Lancashire at any rate – a year ago, Max.'

'Around the time those videos went missing?'

'He couldn't be specific,' she admitted, 'but it's possible.'

'Mm.' Max wasn't convinced, she could tell. 'What else?'

'Well, the fact that he's still in love with Lorna.'

There was a pause.

'So? What does that have to do with anything?'

'It means,' she informed him, 'that he lied about trying to get Carol into bed. He was chatting her up, we know that because Ruth and Carol were at the florist's to witness it all, but it wasn't with the intention of getting her into his bed. He had an ulterior motive.'

'Not necessarily,' Max scoffed. 'I very much doubt he's lived like a monk since Lorna took off.'

'I still think he had an ulterior motive.'

'Like killing her?' Max asked sarcastically.

'Maybe.'

'OK, so what about Nikki? Where the hell does she fit in?'

'I don't know,' Jill admitted.

'Christ, Jill, you're dreaming up something from the twilight zone here. So we'll assume that, a year ago, he came across – stole them, found them, bought them – those videos. He then kills Carol the same way to make us think Eddie is still alive. Then, with that job done, he either sells the videos or throws them away and, lo and behold, someone else finds them or buys them and he too decides to kill someone by the same MO to make us think Eddie is still alive.'

'Put like that, it's crap,' she agreed, growing exasperated. 'But it won't have been like that.'

'How the hell will it have been then?'

The truth was, she had no idea. Finlay Roberts was a

loner. He wouldn't enter into something as serious as murder with someone else. If he wanted a job doing, he would have to do it himself.

'Max, I'm telling you what I know. As you constantly remind me, I'm not a detective. If you want my opinion, he's still a suspect for Carol Blakely's murder.'

Chapter Thirty-Four

The following morning, Max received a phone call from Yvonne Hitchins, Vince Blakely's former employee and current lover. She sounded very nervous.

'Can you meet me somewhere?' she asked quickly.

'Of course. Where?'

'Somewhere no one will see us.'

It was tempting to suggest the Sea of Tranquillity. Max's face was on TV every day at the moment so, wherever they went, he would be recognized.

'Can't you come here?' he asked.

'No. Someone would see me.'

'OK, then, how about –'

'There's a viewing spot on the Burnley to Bacup road,' she cut him off. 'A lay-by. It overlooks the wind farm. Meet me there at two o'clock.'

Before Max had a chance to respond, the line went dead.

What on earth did the stunning but dim Yvonne want with him? Presumably, she had something to say about Vince Blakely, but what? And why was she so scared?

'Do you want me to come along, guv?' Grace asked.

'No, I can handle Yvonne, thanks.'

'Must be your lucky day.' She grinned at him. 'What will you do if she cries rape?'

He shook his head, unsmiling. 'She's too scared to cry rape . . .'

Max was at the lay-by at ten minutes to two and there was no sign of her. He got out of his car and leaned against the bonnet to enjoy the view. The sun was shining and the air was pleasantly warm rather than oppressively hot.

At two fifteen, a car pulled up alongside his. Yvonne Hitchins killed the engine, put on a pair of sunglasses, and got out.

She was wearing amazingly tight jeans, and a light-weight cotton top with a hood that she pulled over her head. Oh, yes, she was scared.

She stood next to him, hands in her jeans pockets. Max wouldn't have thought there was room for her hands.

'You OK?' he asked her, and she nodded, although she looked far from OK.

'What happens,' she asked, coming straight to the point, 'to people who lie to police?'

'It all depends,' he said. 'Why? Have you lied?'

She was a long time answering, and she wasn't looking at him. Her gaze was locked on some distant spot. 'You know you asked where Vince was on the night of that fire? When the architect was killed?'

'Yes.'

'Vince told me to say I was with him all night.'

'Ah.'

'I wasn't,' she said shakily, still not looking at him. 'But I didn't think it would matter. He said you suspected him of killing his wife . . . but he was in Scotland then, wasn't he?'

'He was.'

Max had been over it a dozen times and there was no way Blakely could have driven or flown down from Scotland to kill his wife and then raced back there. No way. Max had even been shown photographs that Blakely's friend and fellow golfer had taken, and Blakely had been smiling for the camera.

He could have paid someone else to get rid of his wife, but they could find no evidence of that.

'So he couldn't have done it, could he?' she persisted.

'It seems not,' Max agreed. 'So the night of the fire, where do you think he was?'

'He says he was at home alone.'

'Don't you believe him?'

'I don't know what to believe any more.' She hunted in her bag for a cigarette and lit it with hands that were shaking. 'I suppose he's a suspect in the other girl's murder?'

'What makes you say that?'

'It's obvious, isn't it?' She took a deep drag on her cigarette. 'People he knew – OK, he says he didn't know the architect who died in the fire, but that sounds doubtful. People he knew are getting killed.'

'He knew Nikki Craven?' Max's heart skipped a couple of beats before racing off at a dangerous pace. 'Are you sure?'

'Knew of her,' she said, not quite so confident now.

'How did he know her?' And why the hell had his name never cropped up in the investigation?

'She was drunk in Harrington one night and smashed his car's lights in.' Yvonne was frowning at him, mistrustful, as if he was trying to catch her out. 'That was about a month ago. I was with him at the time. We'd been to the club. Reno's, you know?'

'Yes. Tell me exactly what happened, Yvonne.'

'We were only going out for a bite to eat that night,' she explained, 'so Vince drove. Then we decided to go to Reno's. As he was driving we didn't intend to stay long, but then he said we'd get a taxi and he'd come back for the car in the morning. Anyway, we came out of the club and there were half a dozen young louts hanging around the car park. Vince saw that the headlight on his car had been smashed and he shouted at these louts, wanting to know who'd done it. They were all young blokes, except one, and it was this girl who came forward. "I did," she told him, and she was laughing. She gave him her name and address as if it was a joke. I suppose she knew that Vince couldn't do anything about it. Especially with her friends hanging around. There was a lot of abuse thrown, but Vince knew he couldn't prove anything. He drove us home,' she admitted. 'He'd had too much to drink, but he was furious and he wasn't going to leave his car there. There was no knowing what they might have done to it.'

'Did he report it?' Max asked.

'No. There was no point. As he said, that Nikki Craven would have denied saying anything. A couple of days later,' she went on, reaching for another cigarette, 'the window at his office was smashed. He swore it was her, this Nikki Craven. I told him it could have been anyone, but he was convinced it was her. He was livid.'

'Did he report that?'

'No, but he was really angry.'

'Where was he, Yvonne, when Nikki was murdered?'

'I don't know,' she said, taking a long drag on her cigarette.

'I see. So if he claims he was with you, it's a lie. Right?'

'He won't do that.' She ground out her cigarette. 'I haven't seen him lately. It's all over between us.'

'Oh?'

'Yeah. He was round at my place one night and we were having a bad evening. It was the day of the fire at the architect's house. You lot had been to ask if I was with him that night and, because he'd told me to, I said yes. So I asked him what would happen to me if you found out I'd lied, and he lost his temper. He hit me. I thought he'd broken my jaw. He hadn't,' she said quickly, 'but I told him to get out. I haven't seen or heard from him since.'

'Had he hit you before?'

'No. He's always had a bit of a short fuse, but no, he'd never gone that far. He apologized immediately,' she said, 'but I wanted out. I'm glad now I chucked him out. People round him keep friggin' dying.'

That's why she was so scared. She thought she might be next on the list.

'Thanks for that, Yvonne. I appreciate it.'

'What will happen to me now?'

'Nothing.' But she was terrified. 'I'm sure you're quite safe,' he went on, 'but we can send someone round to your house to check on your security and give you some advice.

OK? And if he tries to contact you, let me know.' He handed her a card with his number on it. 'This will reach me day or night. OK?'

She stared at the number, and looked slightly reassured. 'OK. Thanks.'

'Day or night,' he repeated.

'Thanks.' She ground out her cigarette. 'I'd better be going.'

'Keep in touch, Yvonne.'

She nodded, and then unlocked her car and slid inside. A few seconds later, she was driving off.

Max lit a cigarette and stared at the view, his thoughts racing. What had he learned? That Vince Blakely had a temper and wasn't above hitting a woman. That he had no alibi for the night Ralph Atkins – a fellow architect – was burned alive in his house. That he knew, or had at least come into contact with, Nikki.

That was their first real link. So far, he was the only person they'd come across who knew, or knew of, all three victims.

Max flicked his cigarette butt away and returned to his car.

Suppose Vince Blakely had wanted his wife killed. He'd hire someone, then take off to Scotland and make sure he was photographed at the hotel to give himself the best of alibis.

Who would he hire?

Nikki had come into contact with some highly unsavoury characters. If she'd discovered the truth, Blakely would have wanted her dead, too.

Max fired the engine and headed back towards Harrington.

He'd been back at headquarters long enough for a bollocking from his superior when Fletch sought him out.

'Here's a coincidence, guv. Ralph Atkins – his wife –'

'Late wife,' Max corrected him.

'Yes. Well, you'll never guess what her parents did for a living.'

238

'Then save me the trouble, Fletch. I'm not in the mood for guessing games.'

'Her dad,' Fletch said triumphantly, 'was a trapeze artist. Not only that, he was a trapeze artist with The Experience. The same circus as Finlay Roberts grew up with. She must have known Roberts. Must have. Which means Ralph Atkins must have known him, too.'

'Eureka! That's it, Fletch. Roberts and Blakely were in on it together. Right, I want Blakely in for questioning. If we put enough pressure on him, he'll crack. That smug bastard Roberts won't, but Blakely will. Meanwhile, find Roberts. Sod it, he could be anywhere by now, but find him!'

Chapter Thirty-Five

The following evening, after a particularly fruitless and frustrating day, Jill was locking up her cottage and setting off for a good long walk in the hope that it might relax her. It was cooler than of late, and perfect for a stroll.

She was halfway along her lane, about a hundred yards from her cottage, when Max drove along. He slowed to a stop and the window went down.

'Where are you going?'

'For a walk, but it doesn't matter.' She held up the bag she was carrying. 'I was going down to New Line to chuck stale bread at the ducks.'

'Good idea. We'll come with you.'

It was then that she noticed Holly was lying on the back seat.

'Unless you want to be on your own?' he added.

'Not particularly, but I warn you now, I'm not the best company in the world. You would not believe the day I've had.'

He smiled at that. 'If it's been any worse than mine, I'll buy you dinner at the pub.'

He drove on to her cottage, left his car on the drive and walked back to join her. He'd taken off his tie, and the jacket to his suit was nowhere to be seen, but he wasn't dressed for walking.

Holly was trotting by his side as she always did. The dog idolized him.

'Right,' he said, reaching into his trouser pocket for cigarettes and lighter, 'tell me about your day.'

'You know I was in court today?'

'Yes.' She could see the smile tugging at his lips.

'And I bet you know the rest of it,' she muttered. 'It took me ages to prepare for that. Ages. Today, I've been kicking my heels at the court. All bloody day. Then, at the very last minute, the little sod changed his plea.'

'So I heard.'

'That shouldn't be allowed. All that taxpayers' money wasted. The little shit should be banged up for that alone.'

'He should,' Max agreed.

'As if I don't have anything better to do with my time,' she grumbled.

'Indeed,' he agreed. 'You could have spent the day at the bookies.'

'Fortunately, I did manage to nip out and place a bet at lunchtime.'

'Ah. So you can afford to buy me dinner?'

'Nope, sorry.' She smiled at that. 'They're still running.'

They left the road and walked down to the disused railway line. Holly ran a few yards ahead occasionally, but she didn't stray far from Max's side.

'What was so bad about your day?' she asked.

'Everything. I wish I hadn't bothered getting out of bed this morning. The highlight was a one-hour-twenty-minute bollocking from Meredith. One hour and twenty minutes!'

'Blimey, that must be a record.' She grinned at that. 'What happened to your usual escape plan?'

'He was having none of it. I was just about to fall to the ground clutching my chest when he had to take an important call. You'll be delighted to hear that, thanks to all the speed cameras, the number of road accidents in the area is down. The TV company wanted to know if he'd like to comment on that.'

'It's nothing to do with the cameras. The roads are so congested you're lucky to get out of second gear.'

'You won't convince Meredith of that.'

'So what was this particular bollocking about?' she asked.

'The usual. My lack of delegation skills. My complete ignorance of the correct procedure. If I did things by the book, apparently, I'd have our killer – or killers – banged up by now. What else was there? Oh yes, overtime payments are sky high. The press are making us look like morons. There was plenty more, but I think those were the salient points.'

They reached the small reservoir and, as was usual, the assortment of ducks and geese came to inspect them. As far as the geese were concerned, visitors had to be carrying bread. Holly ignored them until Jill threw the first chunk of bread into the water. Then she leapt in, retrieved it, shook herself dry and ate it.

Spluttering with laughter, Jill threw another piece, only to have it brought back and eaten by Holly.

'What's the point of that? I may as well give her the bagful. Don't you feed her?'

'She's like me. She's had nothing since breakfast.' Max grabbed her collar. 'Lie down, you stupid animal.'

One word from her master and Holly forgave the insult. Grudgingly, she watched as each piece of bread landed in the water and was gobbled up by greedy ducks.

There were a couple of fishermen on the other side of the reservoir but, otherwise, it was deserted. It was a blissfully peaceful spot. Jill leaned on the wooden rails and gazed into the water. Occasionally, she spotted fish swimming around.

'So what's new?' she asked Max. 'You must have something by now.'

'You're beginning to sound like Meredith,' Max said with a grimace. 'And no, nothing's new. I've got nothing at all. Nothing that would stand up in court at any rate.'

'There's something we're missing,' Jill said.

'Vince Blakely is sticking to his story and protesting his innocence. He admits to making threats to Nikki when she and her mates damaged his car, and he was as mad as hell when his office window was smashed, but he claimed he knew he couldn't make anything of it because they would deny all knowledge.'

'That sounds feasible.'

'And he still maintains he never knew Ralph Atkins. He has, however, admitted to asking Yvonne to lie for him the night the fire was started. He insists he was merely trying to save our time and his.'

'I can't see Blakely as guilty of murder,' she murmured.

'I can. We're talking about an estate amounting to millions of pounds, Jill. That's one hell of a lot of money.'

He had a point. That would be a huge incentive.

'Have you found Finlay yet?' she asked.

'Yes and no. We've found the house where he's supposed to be staying.'

'Where's that?'

'Preston.'

'Preston? You're kidding me. So he's gone – what? – thirty miles away?'

'Supposedly. The trouble is, he's not there. We're having the place watched, but there's no sign of him. He's vanished into thin air.'

What the devil was he doing in Preston? He'd said he was going where the whim took him. Why move thirty miles away?

'What about his father?' she asked. 'Did you talk to him about Katherine Atkins?'

'Yeah. He claims to remember her well. He's sure Finlay would remember her, too. But whether they were in touch . . .' Max shrugged. 'Who knows? At the time those videos were – what shall we say? – found – she was terminally ill, though.'

Without conscious decision, they strolled around the perimeter of the reservoir.

'Anything on the person who leaked the story to the press?' Jill asked.

'DC Johnny Simpson's on the case,' Max told her. 'This week, the paper's received two phone calls, both taped, and both from a man claiming to be Edward Marshall.'

'Two?'

'It's bollocks,' Max dismissed that. 'One was made from a phone box in Nottingham. The other from a phone box in Stoke.'

'How do you know it's bollocks?' Jill demanded. 'What if we're on the wrong track completely? What if, after all this, Marshall is still alive?'

'He isn't.'

'How do you know?' Jill demanded, exasperated and starting to panic.

'Come on, Jill, you said yourself that he didn't kill Carol.'

'Yes, but what if –'

'You're not wrong,' he said firmly. 'Marshall's dead, Jill. I don't know who is making those phone calls, but it's not Marshall.'

'It's our killer though, isn't it?'

'I imagine so, yes. There's CCTV near the phone in Stoke. It's not as near as we'd like, but Johnny's going to have a look at that and see if he recognizes anyone. We know the time of the call. Ergo, we'll know – assuming we get a good enough picture – who made it.'

Jill was suddenly besieged by doubt. She'd made a mistake before, and that mistake had been responsible, in part, for Rodney Hill committing suicide. If she'd made another mistake –

'Marshall's dead,' Max said quietly as if he could read her thoughts.

But what if he wasn't? What if they were making no progress in this case because they weren't focusing on Marshall?

'If it were Marshall,' Max said, 'he'd speak loudly and clearly. What we've got is a tape recording.'

He was right. If it were Marshall, he wouldn't bother with a recording. Would he?

'Come on,' Max said, taking her hand, 'let's walk back to the pub and get something to eat. I'm starving.'

'Yes, me too.'

'You're always starving . . .'

Jill had thought a walk would relax her, but now she was more tense than ever. She couldn't rid herself of the idea that Marshall might still be alive. If he was, then she'd made the biggest mistake of her life. She had possibly made a mistake that had cost Nikki her life. She'd told Max he couldn't blame himself for Nikki's death. She'd said it wasn't his fault and it wasn't hers. But what if it was? What if the blame could be placed firmly at her feet? She'd been so certain they were looking for a copycat . . .

'Are you OK with eating outside?' Max asked. 'It'll save having to leave Holly tied up outside.'

'Yes, fine.'

Several other people had had the same idea, and most of the tables on the lawns were taken. Jill wasn't surprised. It was good to make the most of the late evening warmth.

She was soon eating chicken and chips and her mood lifted. It had been a tiring day, one way and another, and she was determined to put it from her mind for an hour or so.

'By the way,' Max said, 'I've told them you'll be in to pay the bill in a minute.'

'What? My day was far worse than yours. You only had Meredith to contend with, and you should be used to him by now.'

'Huh. The bloke will be the death of me.'

'My horses didn't win,' she reminded him.

'And that's my fault?'

'I suppose not. But I know you've paid the bill. Thanks,' she added belatedly. 'It's good.' The white wine was equally good.

When they'd eaten, and were walking back to her cottage to collect Max's car, Jill was feeling nicely relaxed. Perhaps that was due to the way Max's arm was resting on her shoulder . . .

'Perhaps,' she said thoughtfully, 'we ought to have another chat with Ruth. She was as close to Carol as anyone could be. If we have a good long chat with her, perhaps she'll think of something. Something she's thought too

245

unimportant to mention. Carol must have said something about Finlay. Ruth would have asked how her date went. Maybe Carol introduced him to her husband even. Or perhaps she said something about Vince. Or Ralph Atkins. And what about Terry Yates? Ruth must have noticed him hanging about outside the shop. She must have.'

'Why not? We've got nothing else. OK, we'll see her tomorrow. In the afternoon because I'm in Manchester all morning.'

'Really? Meredith sending you down there so you can learn how it's done?'

'Don't even joke about it. He did ask if I fancied seeing myself in uniform on crowd control at Turf Moor next season.'

Jill grinned at that.

'It's so long since I've had a chance to watch a game, I said I'd be delighted . . .'

Tomorrow afternoon suited Jill because she had things to do, too. Every time she thought of it, the sheer recklessness had her taking several calming breaths, but she'd made up her mind. Well, more or less. She was going to see Andy Collins in the morning and ask him to bid on her behalf at the auction for Kelton Manor.

Being in Spain at the time of the auction, assuming they got to Spain, would be a godsend. That way, with Andy bidding on her behalf, she wouldn't be tempted to go over her budget.

Chapter Thirty-Six

DC Simpson had watched this particular piece of film at least thirty times. No matter what they tried, it was impossible to get a half-decent view of the person who walked into that phone booth in Stoke-on-Trent to call the paper. For all Johnny knew, it could be a chimpanzee.

The camera had been positioned to capture the shops and pubs that formed a small square in the town. Unfortunately, the phone booth was in the top right-hand corner. This was their best clue yet, almost their only clue, and it was proving useless.

It was lunchtime and he was hungry.

He left the building and crossed the road to the Green Man for a quick sandwich and a drink. What he really fancied was a long cold pint of lager, but he ordered a Coke. At the moment, he and Trentham were getting on OK and he didn't want to jeopardize their relationship.

The pub was quiet. Come six o'clock, it would be packed. Trade was always good on Fridays.

The Coke didn't do much for him, but the sandwich – hot roast pork with stuffing and chips – was delicious. When he'd finished, he walked outside for a smoke. Three others were standing out there, but he didn't recognize them and no one bothered with the usual moan about smokers being forced outside.

As he walked back to headquarters, he wondered what else he could do to find this hoax caller. If it was a hoax.

Johnny wasn't convinced. They'd all look pretty stupid if it really was Edward Marshall making those calls.

He also wondered if the film was waiting for him.

He'd watched CCTV footage they'd got from Nottingham. Sadly, the phone booth in question was a hundred yards from the nearest camera and the closest they got was a nearby road junction. He'd watched people walking along the pavement, but nothing had struck him as odd. No one looked as if they were walking to a phone booth – although how anyone would manage that, he had no idea – and, as far as he could see, no one walked back along the same route.

And then he'd seen it. A small sign pointed in the direction of the railway station. The phone booth in Stoke-on-Trent had been a short walk from the station, too.

Johnny was convinced that their man was travelling by train. That would be why the calls had been made from all corners of the country. He'd checked the timetables and those calls had been made within fifteen minutes of a train arriving from Manchester. Anyone travelling from Harrington by train would go via Manchester ...

He was feeling better after his food, and better still when he saw that the CCTV footage was set up for him.

He sat before the screen.

Manchester railway stations were always busy and Johnny stared in dismay at the milling crowd. Some strolled, some dashed for trains and others looked as if they had been dropped in a foreign country.

Minutes ticked by. Hours passed and then Johnny thought he recognized someone. He hit the button to freeze the frame.

'Oh, my –'

Johnny hadn't expected this.

Wait until he dropped this little bombshell on Trentham.

Johnny still couldn't tell Trentham if the voice on the recording belonged to Marshall or not, but he could tell him who was making the calls and playing the tape.

No wonder it had taken so long for him to spot the culprit. He'd looked closely at every man captured on the screen, but he'd paid scant attention to the women. In fact, if this particular woman hadn't glanced straight up at the camera, he would have missed her, too.

Chapter Thirty-Seven

When they arrived at Forget-me-nots just after three that afternoon, Cass was there, as was a young girl Jill didn't recognize, but there was no sign of Ruth.

'This is Barbara,' Cass explained, introducing the other girl. 'She's come from the Burnley shop to help me out. Ruth weren't feeling well, so she spent most of the morning in bed. It's probably this forty-eight-hour thing that's going around.'

'Oh dear. Let's hope she's better soon.'

'She rang in not five minutes ago and said she was feeling much better. She were talking of coming in, but I told her not to be so daft. Me and Barbara can cope. Besides,' she added, grinning, 'I don't want her passing on her germs to me.'

'Wise move.' Jill had to smile at the girl's honesty.

'Pop over and see her,' Cass suggested. 'I'm sure she'll be glad of it. She were complaining of cabin fever when she rang.'

Jill hadn't been to Ruth's home. Max or Grace had spoken to her there, but Jill didn't even know where she lived.

'It's only in Dale Street,' Cass told her. 'Number fourteen.' She looked at Max. 'You know where it is, don't you?'

He assured her he did.

'We'll take her some flowers to cheer her up,' Jill suggested, then she realized the stupidity of that. 'Maybe not,' she added. 'That must be like taking coals to Newcastle.'

Cass laughed at that. 'She loves flowers. Chrysanthemums are her favourites. Here, I'll get some. They can be from all of us.'

A few minutes later, they crossed the road, with Jill carrying an armful of yellow and white chrysanthemums, and walked the few hundred yards to Dale Street. Number fourteen was a large terraced property with bay windows. A long-haired grey cat sat in the window watching their approach.

Max rang the bell and Jill saw, through the double-glazed panel, a multicoloured shape moving.

Ruth opened the door. She was wearing a skirt and blouse in dramatic black and reds.

'Hello, Jill. Oh, and Max. Come in. Are they for me? They're beautiful. Thanks, but you really shouldn't have. I feel such a fraud now.'

'They're nothing,' Jill assured her, 'and they're from Cass and Barbara, as well as us. How are you feeling?'

They followed her along the hallway, where a huge display of flowers sat on a well-polished table, and into that front room where the cat gazed at them from her spot on the window sill. There were two vases of flowers in this room, too.

'I'm feeling fine now,' Ruth told them. 'I was as sick as a dog this morning. Really, I felt like death. Now, I feel fine. Well, a bit battered and bruised, but other than that, you'd never know there had been anything wrong. Here, let me put these in water.'

While Ruth went to the kitchen to deal with her flowers, Jill went to the window and introduced herself to the cat.

'What's her name?' she called out.

'Smoky!'

'You're very beautiful, Smoky,' she murmured, stroking the cat. 'Well aware of it, too,' she added with a chuckle.

The cat allowed herself to be stroked for a few moments then, with a toss of her head, leapt down from the window sill and went in search of her mistress.

While Max inspected a shelf filled with books, Jill looked around a room that was beautifully decorated and very comfortable. The flowers taking pride of place on the table, a huge display of red chrysanthemums, were stunning. There was a small card by the side of the vase. Inside, it read: *Truly, Madly, Deeply.*

The sentiment took Jill by surprise, yet it shouldn't have. Ruth was a very attractive woman and it was obvious there would be a man in her life. Ruth had never mentioned anyone, but why should she?

'Beautiful flowers,' she said, when Ruth returned.

'Aren't they?' Ruth smiled. 'You'd think I'd be sick to death of the sight of them after a day's work, but I love them. I couldn't imagine a house without flowers.'

'Me neither,' Jill agreed, 'but I usually cut mine from the garden.'

They chatted about Smoky, about Ruth's house, about the shop, and then, seeing that Max was beginning to fidget, Jill came to the point of their visit.

'We're after some help, Ruth,' she began. 'We want you to think back to any conversations you had with Carol, and give us the names, no matter how insignificant they seem, of people she mentioned.'

'There's no one I haven't already told you about.'

'You remember when she saw Finlay Roberts? Do you know if she introduced him to Vince?'

'Vince Blakely? I can't think why she would. No, I'm sure she didn't. Why do you ask?'

Jill wasn't sure how to answer that.

'We're fairly certain he met Vince Blakely,' Max put in.

'I wouldn't know about that. I wouldn't have thought so, but I wouldn't really know.'

'She had two dates with Finlay Roberts,' Jill pushed on. 'What did she say about them, Ruth? Can you remember? Where did she go? Who did she see? Did she enjoy her time with him?'

'Well . . .' Ruth thought for long moments. 'I can't really remember. It was all insignificant, you see. I don't remember her saying anything about it. They were strangers, you know, and it was only a bit of fun.'

Ruth was their main chance of finding out about Carol, yet she couldn't seem to help them.

'When Vince phoned you to tell you about Carol,' Jill asked, changing tack, 'how did he sound?'

'Businesslike.' Ruth didn't hesitate with that one. 'Cold and businesslike. All he was concerned about was making sure I opened the shop that day.' She put her cup on the table. 'At the time, it didn't strike me. I was too shocked, I suppose. But I've thought about it since and I can't believe anyone could sound so cold at such a time.' She looked straight at Max. 'You don't think he killed her, do you?'

'Do you think he's capable of murder, Ruth?' Max asked.

She thought for a moment. 'Yes. Yes, I do. It's a dreadful thought, but yes, I do.'

Jill didn't. No matter how many trails led them back to Vince Blakely, she didn't see him as capable of murder. He was too image conscious, too aware of what he thought of as his position. A precise man, he wouldn't like death in any form. It would be too messy for him. Jill didn't like the man particularly, but she admired his views. He was doing his bit to save the planet and was trying to make the public aware of conservation housing. No, she couldn't see him as a killer.

Then again, as Max was constantly reminding her, there was one hell of a lot of money at stake.

'What about Terry Yates?' Jill asked her.

'The name meant nothing to me until your people asked about him.' Ruth thought for a moment. 'I knew there had been someone in her life. I suspected she'd had an affair. Funny, but I never asked her about it because I thought she was ashamed of it somehow. Also, I thought it was over before I started working for her.'

'It was over soon afterwards,' Jill agreed.

'At the time,' Ruth went on, 'I was just an employee. It was only when Carol's sisters died that we became friends.'

253

That was reasonable enough. Not very helpful, but reasonable.

'We believe Yates often followed Carol,' Max put in. He handed her a photo, a bad one, of Terry Yates. 'Are you sure you don't recognize him?'

Ruth studied the photo then handed it back. 'Sorry.'

She got up, walked into the hall, and came back carrying a sheet of paper.

'I did find this, though,' she explained. 'After you'd asked me about this Yates chap, I looked through our old orders. You see, I thought afterwards that perhaps I had heard the name, after all. A woman, name of Beverley Yates, placed a couple of orders. I don't know if that helps. And her I would recognize. For a few months, she came in the shop regularly. Always paid by credit card.'

That would be Beverley Yates. She'd visit the shop hoping for a glimpse of Carol. She would have dreaded seeing her, too.

Beverley Yates was a very disturbed woman. The more Jill heard about her, the more concerned she became . . .

They spent another half-hour with Ruth, but she couldn't really help.

'We'll leave you to recuperate,' Max said at last. 'We've already stayed longer than we intended. I hope you're soon feeling back to normal, Ruth.'

'I'll be back at work tomorrow,' she assured them. 'And thanks again for the flowers. I really appreciate them . . .'

Jill was almost at the front door when she stopped so suddenly that Max cannoned into the back of her and Ruth narrowly missed colliding with Max.

Oh, my –

'Sorry,' Jill said, surprised that her voice was not only functioning normally, it was also managing to make her sound calm, 'but I've just thought of something else I meant to ask you. Do you mind if we keep you a couple more minutes, Ruth?'

'No, of course not.'

Jill exchanged a brief glance with Max that was supposed to say 'trust me', but from the expression on his face, she guessed she'd merely exasperated him.

They went back to the sitting room, but no one sat this time.

'It's about Finlay Roberts,' Jill said, wondering where to begin, and wishing she hadn't said anything. She should have left and discussed this with Max. He was the detective, not her.

'Oh?' Ruth said.

Did she sound wary?

'You know he lived next door to me?' Jill said, and Ruth shrugged.

'I knew he lived in Kelton Bridge so, as it's a small place, I gathered you and he must be near neighbours. And I saw you together in the pub that night.'

'Yes. Did you ever meet his father?' Jill asked.

'His –? Me?' Ruth gave a shaky laugh. 'Why would I do that? As you know, I only saw the man a couple of times –'

'His father said you knew Finlay well at one point,' Jill said casually. 'This would have been when you were both children.'

'What?' Ruth threw a wild look in Max's direction. 'I'd never seen Finlay Roberts until he walked into the shop that day.'

'And that happened during the fortnight that Cass should have been on holiday,' Jill murmured. 'Her backing out at the last minute spoiled your plans, didn't it? It was Cass who remembered seeing Finlay with Carol, not you.'

'I really don't know –'

'If it hadn't been for Cass, we would never have known about Finlay's relationship with Carol.'

'But only because it was – meaningless, I'd forgotten all about it.'

'No, Ruth. You knew Finlay. You knew him *very* well. You were in love with him.'

255

Ruth laughed at that, a wild sound that immediately had Max alert. Jill could sense him as he stood by her side, ready to – well, she didn't know what he was ready for, she was just glad he was ready.

'I'd never met the man until he came into the shop,' Ruth said firmly. 'I've no idea what you're talking about, but you've got the wrong woman.'

'No,' Jill said softly. 'You're Lorna.'

'Lorna? Are you mad?'

'I spoke to his father, you see. Spoke to your father, too. Well, it's one and the same, isn't it? You and Finlay – you share the same father. But no one told you, did they? No one told you that you were brother and sister until it was too late. By that time, you were in love. Truly, madly, deeply in love.' She walked, nervously, to the centre of the room and picked up the small card next to the flowers. 'Truly, madly, deeply,' she murmured. 'Why did he send you those, Ruth? Because you were both so close to getting away with murder and inheriting a fortune?'

'I don't have to listen to this. I've no idea what you're talking about, but I think it's time you left.'

'As soon as you knew you shared the same father, you tried to put Finlay out of your life, didn't you? What did you do? Change your name by deed poll when you left him? You went right away, didn't you? You went abroad. You even married a Greek. That didn't work though, did it? Your choice. After all, your husband – Andreas, did you say his name was? – cared enough to come to England to make you change your mind about a divorce. He loved you, didn't he? Probably wanted children, too. That couldn't happen though, could it? Any children you had would have to be Finlay's. And that was impossible. Yes, you tried to put Finlay out of your mind, but he haunted your every thought.

'You carried on as best you could, keeping contact to a minimum. You worked for Carol and became her best friend. Why not? You're a lovely woman, and she desperately needed a friend after the accident that claimed the lives of her sisters. Then, one day, she told you how much she was worth. Not only that, she told you that you'd inherit the lot. Hey presto. A solution. You and Finlay could be together. You could go right away, to somewhere no one knew you. You could live as man and wife. With millions in the bank, you could live anywhere. No longer would you have to fight the attraction.'

'You're mad!' Ruth cried. 'Mad, mad, mad! I won't listen to this. I won't.'

'Then tell us your version of events,' Max suggested.

'How can I? I've never heard of Finlay Roberts. I never knew – I swear I never knew that Carol intended to leave me her money. Even if she had, it wouldn't have mattered because I had no idea she was worth so much. It's the truth, I swear it.'

Never in a million years.

'Finlay would have come across the video tapes. He knew Ralph Atkins's wife, didn't he? I don't know how, but he got hold of those videos. Ah – Finlay used to buy and sell stuff, didn't he? Ralph Atkins intended to sell those videos. So Finlay bought the videos from him. Oh, yes, the idea of copying the murders would have fascinated Finlay. He enjoys playing games. That's why he was threading red ribbon through Carol's hair. More games.'

Jill paused for breath. Her heart was racing, but she had no doubts, none at all. With every second it all became much clearer.

'It was Finlay getting those tapes that put the idea of murder into your heads, wasn't it? That's when the whole thing started and you realized you could be together. He killed Carol while you were safely on holiday in Spain. He was bright enough to know that, if Cass remembered him flirting with Carol in the shop, the finger would be pointed at him. But hey, that didn't matter. If he was taken in for questioning, you could get him off the hook. You killed Nikki while he was under lock and key, didn't you? You chose Nikki because she had a link to Vince Blakely. You'd heard him or Carol talking about the girl who damaged his car, the girl who had the audacity to tell him her name and dare him to call 999. You tried to make us think that he was behind it all. And you chose her because she was small – far easier for a woman to kill.'

'No!' The word came with all the force of a bullet.

'Ruth Asimacopoulos –'

Max got no further. A tall, rangy dark mass hurled itself at him.

Finlay Roberts!

Jill felt something hot and sticky splash on to her face. Blood. It was pouring out of Max's arm as he tried to over-power Finlay Roberts.

Ruth was screaming. 'Finlay, no! Enough!'

Jill lifted that heavy vase and brought it down on Roberts's head. It dazed him, and he staggered sufficiently for Max to get him on the ground and pin him down.

Jill tore off her shirt and tied it tight around Max's arm. She hated the sight of blood, always had.

Just as she was groping for her phone, Max's rang and Jill grabbed it from his shirt pocket.

'Never mind that,' she cut off DC Simpson, 'get an ambulance for Max and some back-up. Fourteen Dale Street. Quick!'

DC Simpson didn't stop to ask questions. Before he cut the connection, Jill heard him shouting, 'Officer down!'

Ruth had stopped screaming.

'I'll get you a shirt, Jill,' she said, and her voice was chill-ingly calm now.

Jill didn't care that she was only wearing a bra and jeans. All that mattered was trying to lessen the amount of blood that Max was losing.

Ruth returned with a long-sleeved black shirt. She draped it gently around Jill's shoulders. 'I'm so sorry,' she whispered, and she gave Jill's shoulder a brief squeeze.

Then, quite still, she gazed at Finlay. 'It's all over, my love,' she whispered.

Too late, Jill saw the gun in her hand. 'Ruth, no!'

The noise was deafening.

Jill glimpsed the hole in Finlay's head, and quickly looked away.

'Oh, Christ!' Max lunged at Ruth, but he was a second too late.

Ruth put the barrel of the gun inside her mouth and pulled the trigger.

Chapter Thirty-Eight

The sun was relentless, and Jill knew she ought to seek out some shade. On the other hand, with a Lancashire winter ahead of her, she wanted to make the most of every ray the Spanish sun could offer.

She was lying on her stomach with her eyes closed. As she wriggled her toes, hot sand wedged between them. This was the life. No work, no chores, no mail, no phone, nothing to think about other than summoning enough energy to wander back to the bar. Bliss.

OK, so no phone was a slight exaggeration she thought as it rang out, but she wasn't answering it unless she wanted to.

Shielding her eyes from the sun, she groped in her bag and saw from the display that it was Louise. This was one call she did want to take.

'Louise, hi.'

'Did I wake you?' Louise asked, concerned.

'No. I might sound half asleep, but that's only because it's far too hot on the beach and I'm too lazy to move.'

'Oh, poor you. Really, my heart bleeds for you,' Louise said, and Jill laughed.

'Sorry. So how are you, Lou?'

'I'm good,' she answered immediately. 'I have bad days and good days, you know, but, on the whole, I'm OK. Anyway, I thought I'd let you know that I've decided to stay in Kelton Bridge. You were right; running away won't solve anything. In any case, as much as I love Connie, she'd

260

drive me mad if I lived on her doorstep. She's wonderful, but only in small doses.'

'Yes, I can understand that.'

Jill couldn't have loved her own sister more, but life with Prue in close proximity would be sheer hell.

'Oh, and I'm going out to dinner this evening.'

'What? Who with?'

'Only Jon,' Louise told her, 'and, really, it's to discuss the fund I'm setting up in Nikki's name, but, well, I thought you'd be interested.'

'Jon?' she teased. 'I suppose that's Dr Thorpe to the rest of us.'

'Ha!'

'I don't suppose you could discuss such things in his office? No, of course you couldn't. Oh, Lou, I'm only joking. I couldn't be more thrilled. He's so good for you.'

'He is. I couldn't have coped without him.'

Since visiting Louise the morning after Nikki's body was found, Jon Thorpe had called on her every day. Sometimes twice a day. Jill had suspected he had more than a professional interest in his patient.

'So how about you?' Louise asked. 'How's Max?'

'He's gone wind surfing with the boys,' Jill told her. 'Mad fool. Still, it's his neck.'

'And how are the, um, accommodation arrangements working out?'

Jill spluttered with laughter. 'Just fine. And stop fishing for information. I'll tell all when I get home.'

Tears from nowhere filled her eyes, and she had to blink them back. Louise was going to be fine and the relief was immense.

Jill ended the call and, although it was tempting to remain slothlike, she knew she had to get out of the sun. With great reluctance, she gathered up her few belongings and strolled along to the nearby beach bar. There were postcards to be written and she could deal with those while she enjoyed a long, cold drink in the shade.

She was midway through a gloating note to her sister when Max strode up the beach and dropped on to the chair opposite her.

'I'm knackered,' he said. 'God knows where they get their energy. Thankfully, they've just gone out on the boat so we've got some peace and quiet.' He eyed her critically. 'You're looking very . . .'

'Burnt?' she suggested.

'Well, yes, but that wasn't the word I was groping for. Relaxed. Happy.'

'I am.' She nodded with satisfaction. 'Louise just phoned me. She's going out to dinner with Jon this evening.'

'Jon?'

'Dr Thorpe.'

'Is she indeed? I told you he'd got his eye on her.'

'You did. That was very observant of you, Max.'

The waiter came over, recognized Max and, as usual, tried out his English. 'A big beer, yes?'

'Very big, yes,' Max replied. 'Jill?'

'No, thanks. I'm OK for the moment.'

'Do you think Louise will get over this?' he asked when they were alone again.

'Yes, I do. As much as anyone ever does, at any rate.'

He nodded at that. 'And how about you?'

'Me?'

He moved his chair closer to her so that he wasn't squinting. 'You liked Ruth, didn't you?'

'I did, yes.' For as long as she lived, Jill would never forget the way Ruth had turned that gun on herself . . .

Max's drink was put down on the table, and he nodded his thanks to the waiter.

'It was good work, Jill.'

'No,' she said quietly. 'You know as well as I do that instead of blundering on like that, we should have left the house and discussed it together. That way, two lives might have been saved.'

'Two people would have been banged up for life,' Max

corrected her. 'And neither of them would have wanted that,' he added.

Jill knew he had a point.

'If the initial letters on the card with those flowers hadn't been so large, I wouldn't have associated the *Truly, Madly, Deeply* message with the TMD on the photo in Roberts's bedroom,' she mused. 'It all made sense then. I knew that the only person Finlay Roberts would trust when it came to something as serious as murder was his much-loved half-sister. Ruth stood to cop the lot, yet we never gave her a second thought, did we?'

'Because she was in Spain when Carol was murdered.'

'I cocked up big style,' Jill said. 'I shouldn't have faced her like that. But I liked her. I even thought of her as a friend. I certainly didn't consider her dangerous.'

'A plan might have come in useful,' he agreed.

'But how the hell was I to know Roberts was there? I mean, in the building. God, that gave me the shock of my life.'

'It didn't do much for me, either. Still, it's over now.'

It was certainly over for Ruth and Finlay.

When Jill thought back to that day, the thing that stuck in her mind most was the way Ruth had draped that shirt so tenderly across her bare shoulders.

Max's phone rang and, just as Jill was cursing the things and thinking they should be banned on holiday, her own rang.

She saw from the display that Andy Collins was calling her and her heart skipped a quick beat. What had seemed like a good idea now resembled madness.

She hesitated briefly, but Max was busy talking on his phone, so she answered it.

'Hi, Andy.'

'How's Spain?' he asked her.

'Hot and sunny. Just what the doctor ordered.' But she didn't want to discuss the weather. She wanted to know if she owned Kelton Manor. 'Well?'

'Sorry, Jill. It made far more than we expected. One point four million, in fact.'

'One point four million?'

Her shocked outburst had Max looking at her, an unreadable expression on his face.

'Oh, well, never mind, Andy. It was a stupid idea.'

'An American businessman's bought it,' he told her. 'Sorry.'

'Don't be. Actually, I'm quite relieved . . .'

She was, too. It had been a crazy idea.

She ended her call at the same moment that Max ended his.

'One point four million, eh?' he murmured.

'Kelton Manor,' she explained. 'I'd asked Andy to let me know how the auction went.'

'Really.' That unfathomable expression was still there. 'You weren't bidding for it, were you?'

'Me? Good heavens, no.'

It was fortunate that the hours spent in the sun meant the wave of colour that invaded her face wasn't noticeable.

'Apparently, an American's bought it,' he said.

She looked at him, frowning. 'How did you know that?'

'I asked someone to let me know, too.'

'You weren't bidding for it, were you?' she asked in amazement. 'Good God, you were, weren't you? Would you believe that? Between us, we've made that American pay a fortune for it.'

'Ah, so you *were* bidding.'

'I might have been,' she admitted. 'I heard it wasn't expected to fetch much. The reserve was only five hundred grand.'

'I know.'

'But why the devil would you want to live in Kelton? You hate villages.'

'Ah,' he said with amusement, 'I might hate them, but there's something in that particular village that I'm desperate to get my hands on.'

She laughed at that. 'You're full of crap.'

She watched him take a long drink from his glass, absently rubbing the scar on his arm as he did so.

'So,' he said idly, gazing around at the tables, 'how much do you reckon this place is worth? I reckon we could easily afford it. We could have Shergar fixing the drinks –'

'Lord Lucan in charge of the cellar –'

'Elvis knocking up the burgers –'

'Phil Meredith cleaning the tables –'

'Now you're talking.' Max grinned at that. 'Yes, I like that idea.'

They lapsed into silence and sat back to enjoy their surroundings. Max soon ordered them more drinks and the minutes ticked by in a companionable silence.

At long last, they were easy together, Jill thought. Three years had passed since they split up and, somehow, they'd weathered the ups and downs. Now, finally, they were at ease.

'What are you thinking?' he asked curiously.

'Max, if I wanted you to know what I was thinking, I'd be talking to you.'

'Hm.'

The silence lasted a few more minutes.

'I suppose a quick shag's out of the question?' he asked at last, and Jill felt a smile tugging at her lips.

'Why not? I've got a couple of minutes to kill. It must be your lucky day, detective.'